King Harald's Heist

A Canine Cozy

by Richard Audry

The Second King Harald Mystery

Published by Conger Road Press
Minneapolis, Minnesota

ISBN: 978-0-9850196-5-5

Cover art © 2015 Steve Thomas
Cover photo © 2013 D. R. Martin

Visit drmartinbooks.com
Contact the author at drmartin120@gmail.com

In memory of Fiver

Chapter One

He was sleepy. So sleepy.

He could barely keep his eyes open, sprawled there beneath the little maple.

He should try to stay alert. What if there were intruders?

The air was warm and a breeze wafted seductively, like a gentle massage. He drifted off into a little dream of eating a piece of steak right off the boss's grill. It tasted so good that he almost gulped it down in a single bite.

The buzzing of a fly briefly summoned him up out of his reverie. But the sirens of slumber beckoned him again, this time to a meadow where the boss was about to toss a stick and...

BANG!

King Harald woke with such a start that he nearly levitated off the turf. He barked out three quick, low-pitched, angry woofs, twirling around as he did.

But once the big ginger mutt got his four feet planted

solidly beneath him and regained his composure, he could see there were no interlopers anywhere. Just a couple of chickadees hopping across the lawn and a few orange leaves drifting down one by one. There *was* something very interesting, though. Something Harald had never seen before.

The screen door on the back of the house had blown wide open. It banged again on the side of the house when the wind caught it a second time, and Harald backed up a step or two, just to be safe. After a few more seconds the gust waned to a gentle zephyr, but the door remained ajar.

It so happened that this was not the boss's backyard, where Harald usually spent the afternoon hours. This backyard was next door, and the boss sometimes left him here with the old lady who lived in the house. Harald liked her. She was very generous with dog biscuits.

This was a new situation, however. That door was never left open. And an open door, in Harald's opinion, was an invitation to go in.

He ambled over to the back stoop, climbed up on it, and looked inside. The old lady was nowhere to be seen.

Harald stepped quietly into the back entrance. No sense in making a fuss. He looked to his left, where three steps led up to a closed door. Right in front of him were stairs going down into a darkened place, with no door. It was an easy choice.

Harald trotted quickly down the steps, nearly losing control, and came into a broad room that was paneled in knotty pine. It was dim down there, but the small glass block windows up on the walls let in enough of the sun outside to illuminate the space. Scattered about were several pieces of stuffed furniture, which didn't interest Harald. He was well past the age when noshing on a sofa was something he enjoyed.

He sniffed around a bit, then surveyed his new discovery. Ringing the room on the top of the walls were dozens of baseball caps—not that Harald knew a baseball cap from a button. And there appeared to be two deer heads hanging on the far wall, their big black shiny eyes peering at him. He glanced uneasily in their direction again and again, but they didn't blink.

Twisting around, Harald noticed that part of a wall was almost entirely yellow—the only color he could see, apart from blue and gray. He went over for a closer look and ascertained that it was actually hundreds of yellow vertical things jammed together. He stuck his snout up against them and sniffed deeply. They smelled good. He tilted his head sideways, to see if he could pull one out for closer examination. But they were packed in too tightly.

On a lower shelf, though, one of the things was protruding a couple of inches.

Harald grabbed the item with his teeth, and pulled it out. He gnawed on it and then understood that it was made of paper. Harald liked paper. As a puppy, he had spent lots of time being made to sit on paper. It was also very good for chewing.

Harald took his prize up the stairs and out into the sunlit backyard. He returned to the environs of the shady maple tree, but not before shaking the yellow paper thing vigorously. He chewed on it for a few minutes.

That's when Harald heard the boss's truck pull into the driveway next door. He knew the sound well.

I'm here, Boss, he woofed. *Come and get me.*

Chapter Two

Andy Skyberg eased his blue Silverado into the driveway at a quarter past five.

He had planned all week to spend that Saturday afternoon working on the first serious commission he had gotten since he returned to New Bergen—a big canvas of a sprawling cabin on a piney, rocky lake up north. The palatial getaway belonged to the CEO and chairman of Lovely Lena Macaroni Corporation. Bud Storbakken counted as just about the biggest wheel in Beaver Tail County business circles, and the commission represented a nice piece of change for Andy. It was a feather in his painter's beret, for sure.

But just before he and Harald walked out the door later that morning, the phone on Andy's hip had trilled. It was his twin sister Kirsten, owner of Ansel's Café. It seemed that J. J. Lindquist had come down with a stomach bug. Could Andy fill in at the front of the house from noon to five?

Andy had a pretty darned good idea what J. J. had

actually come down with.

The waitress and sometime hostess had told him the day before that she and two of her best pals had plans for an evening on the town in Hobartville. Their mission—and they had already decided to accept it—was to determine which bar mixed the best margarita in the county seat. J. J. figured they might have to sample a half-dozen spots before they picked the winner. So as Andy seated diners all day, J. J. was undoubtedly nursing a bruiser hangover and mainlining black coffee.

Of course, Andy had done the same thing a time or two, back in the day. But he was glad he had matured to the point where getting hammered at regular intervals didn't seem like a good idea. Sure, he would love to have his twenty-five-year-old body back again, with knees that never ached and a middle that never thickened. But not that twenty-five-year-old brain. At that age, it was making some pretty stupid decisions.

Andy just hoped that J. J. would have the good sense to back away from the sauce. He wanted her to get from twenty-five to forty in one healthy piece.

When his shift was over, Andy had no time to put his feet up. He needed to run home, grab Harald out of his neighbor's backyard, and clean up and change clothes, so he could get over to Aunt Bev's by six-thirty. Pulling up in his driveway, he hopped out of the pickup and headed up the sidewalk toward his back door. As soon as he did, he heard a woof from next door.

"Be right with you, Harald," he hollered, giving his

dog a wave.

First order of business was to check the mail. Two ads, a solicitation from the animal rescue shelter where he had found Harald, and three bills. Andy added the bills to a stack on the dining room table and went to find a plastic bag.

He walked back out to the alley, around his garage, and up to Elsie Bjorklund's gate. It was a matter of honor to Andy that every one of Harald's droppings got promptly picked up and dealt with. Elsie was always happy to dog-sit for Andy, even on short notice, like today. All she asked in return was for Andy to do a few handyman chores around the house. But he would have been mortified if she had ever stepped in any doggie doo-doo.

As Andy shut the gate behind him, the big canine came bounding up, tail wagging fiercely. Andy leaned over and tousled Harald's bristly head.

"How you doin' there, old scout? Had a fun day?"

Harald woofed once, apparently in the affirmative.

"Glad to hear it. Me, not so much."

Andy scanned the grass for the brown items he had to gather. It seemed that Harald hadn't been particularly productive, scatologically speaking. Andy checked a couple of objects that turned out to be woodchips Elsie had scattered under her lilac bushes. He was just about finished when he noticed something strewn about under the maple tree. It looked like papers crumpled on the ground.

He might as well grab those, too, and save Elsie the trouble. As he bent over to pick them up, Andy saw what they were. Pieces of a torn-up, masticated *National Geographic*. The cover was somewhat intact and he could read the list of story titles: "*Calypso* Explores for Underwater Oil" by Captain Jacques-Yves Cousteau. And "Skunks Want Peace—or Else!" Andy glanced at the issue date. August 1955.

He turned and glared at his dog. "Harald, what have you gotten into?"

Perhaps sensing that his prize was about to be confiscated, Harald picked up the damp, demolished magazine and growled quietly in an unconvincing manner.

"How the heck did you get inside, you…"

Then Andy's eyes lit upon the screen door, hanging open at the back of Elsie's house. Fixing that door closer had been on his job list for weeks. It looked like the wind had caught the door and busted it for good.

Harald had obviously made a sortie into Elsie's basement, where she kept her semi-legendary collection of *National Geographics*.

Andy regarded his dog again. "You know, Harald, I'm gonna have to replace this magazine. And the money's coming out of your dog biscuit budget."

Harald looked ashamed of himself.

"Anders? What's going on?"

There in the gaping back door stood Elsie Bjorklund, in white slacks topped with a lavender T-shirt. Just barely an eighty-something, Elsie was petite and attractive, with a pixie face that must have made her quite the catch in her younger days. Andy knew that she had her wavy white hair fixed twice a week at Laurel's Spa and Salon down on Perch Street. But at the moment, she looked a bit disheveled.

Feeling like a guilty schoolboy, Andy walked over to her. Harald followed, the ruined *National Geographic* still clenched in his jaws.

"I'm really sorry, Elsie. It looks like the wind banged open your screen door and Harald invited himself in. Down to your basement, to be precise." Andy sighed. "He grabbed one of your *National Geographics* and decimated it. But don't worry—I'll replace it. I'm sure I can snag a copy on eBay."

Elsie seemed a bit bewildered. She came down the steps, then blinked up at Andy.

Which she had to do, since he towered over her at about six-four. Andy looked back at her through gunmetal blue eyes, the right peeper being a bit lazy.

"I didn't hear the door bang," Elsie said. "I took out my hearing aid because I wanted to have a nap. Guess I slept a lot longer than I intended to."

"I'll get the door fixed tomorrow, Elsie. First thing in the morning."

"Yes, dear, that would be a good idea. But how in the world did Harald get at my *National Geographics*? They're packed in pretty tight."

She stooped over. Harald didn't protest as she plucked the munched-upon, slightly slimy magazine from his mouth. Elsie straightened up and began to examine the remains, holding the corner of the thing daintily between her thumb and her index finger.

As she did, a piece of green paper fluttered out of it and onto the grass near her.

She quickly snatched it up and slid it back into the magazine. But not before Andy had a chance to see what it was.

A U. S. bank note. With the words "One Thousand Dollars" on the bottom edge of it. And the picture of a dead president. It looked very old.

"Elsie, what's a thousand-dollar bill doing in your *National Geographic*?"

She laughed nervously, avoiding eye contact. "Oh, I mislaid it years ago. Forgot where I put it. How lucky that Harald found the thing. Well, I gotta run, Anders," she said hurriedly. "See you tomorrow."

And with that, she darted back up the steps and firmly closed both doors behind her.

Chapter Three

"I kid you not, Frank. It was a thousand-dollar bill."

Andy was sitting on the plush sofa in the ranch house that his Aunt Bev and Uncle Frank owned on the far side of Elbow Lake. In his hand he gripped a jumbo gin martini on the rocks, with a huge queen olive. The happy yipping of Aunt Bev's cockapoo, Crackers, and the exuberant woofing of Harald echoed from out in the backyard. Quite the odd couple, those two, but fine friends nonetheless.

Andy wasn't exactly thrilled to be dining with his aunt and uncle. It was a Saturday night, after all. He would have preferred to be up in Hobartville with some foxy lady, sampling those margaritas that had taken down J. J. the night before.

But since his former squeeze Cass Conlin had decamped to D.C. a couple months ago for a job with the FBI, Andy's social life had hit rock bottom. Desirable females did not, so to speak, lie thick upon the ground in New Bergen or greater Beaver Tail County.

So, lacking a better offer, he had accepted Aunt Bev's invite to a pot roast dinner, with her killer Bavarian cream pie for dessert. She had mentioned something about an idea she wanted to run by him. For martinis and pot roast, Andy would listen. He just hoped he would be clear-headed enough to not get sucked into whatever wacky notion she was pitching.

"So Elsie's got some cash stashed away, huh? Maybe she's looking for a boy toy to help her spend it." Uncle Frank took a slow sip of his own jumbo martini. "You play up to her, she might buy you that new set of Michelins for the Silverado." He winked at Andy.

Aunt Bev entered the living room, carrying a tray of rye crackers, cream cheese, and smoked oysters. When she put it down on the coffee table, Andy noticed that she needed a top-up on her henna hair job. Some gray roots were showing.

"Now you stop that, Frank Engebretson," she said as she plopped down on the sofa next to Andy. "That's not even funny. Elsie Bjorklund is one of the most solid, decent members of this community. Why, if it weren't for her and that sister of hers, I don't think Elbow Lake Lutheran Church could have pulled off our big turkey supper last winter. Those two gals took on the job of roasting four big birds, and the meat was so tender, you could cut it with a fork."

Andy knew Elsie's sister Emma almost as well as

he knew Elsie. When he moved into his little bungalow on Willow Street, he had discovered that he lived
right between the two sisters. They were both good
neighbors, though Elsie was a bit more sociable.

"Well, I just hope Elsie isn't getting absent-
minded," he said. "I mean, how can you forget a
thousand-dollar bill?" He took a sip of his drink. "Hey,
Frank, killer martooni. What kind of gin you use?"

"Boodles. Bev said she wanted nothing but the best
for her favorite nephew."

Uh-oh, Andy thought. Boodles was pricey stuff.
Uncle Frank, who was known to make every nickel
scream, usually served the cheapest store-brand gin he
could find. If Aunt Bev had asked her husband to get
Boodles, she must be pulling out all the stops. What
kind of nutty plan was she concocting?

The aroma of pot roast suffused the house, and
Andy couldn't wait to dig in. But it was fun to sit
there, getting pleasantly buzzed on the Boodles and
shooting the breeze with the aunt and uncle. They had
been like second parents to him. Those summer weeks
spent at the lake cabins they rented were among
Andy's favorite memories of childhood.

Uncle Frank withdrew the olive sticker from his
drink and gobbled up the salty green treat. "So how are
things going with Kirsten's new project? I'm not seeing any signs of action down there at Trudi's old
location."

The new business, a combination deli and gallery,

was to go up where Trudi Bock's Karma Kubbyhole store had been, before it burned to the ground. Kirsten had purchased the Esbensen Insurance Agency Building next door as well, providing a bigger footprint for the new structure.

And she had drafted Andy as the manager of The Nordic—the new deli and art gallery's official name. This was the best opportunity that had come his way in years, and he was going to make the most of it.

"We're meeting with the architect and his project manager on Wednesday, for a final consultation before we get things rolling," he answered.

"I had lunch with your folks on Thursday," Aunt Bev said. "Your dad's really looking forward to a whole bunch of sidewalk supervising."

Andy's parents were back in town, staying in Kirsten's guesthouse. They spent most of the year traveling the country with their Airstream. But Andy's mom always wanted to be back in New Bergen in the fall, when the leaves were turning and the air was just starting to chill. And his dad was a big booster of the high school football team. Even though Andy hadn't been that good a defensive tackle, the old man remained proud of him for all the knocks he had taken out on the gridiron.

Aunt Bev spread a cracker with cream cheese, topped it with a smoked oyster, and handed it to Andy. "We were all wondering," she said, in that direct manner of hers, "whether you've found someone to replace

Cass."

Ah, that's it, Andy thought. *She wants to set me up with someone.*

"Nope, I'm playing the field," he replied. In fact, he hadn't had a single date since his breakup with the deputy sheriff. He steeled himself for a pitch about some nice woman who Aunt Bev knew would be just perfect for him. But the buzzer on the oven went off and Aunt Bev scurried back to the kitchen.

Andy and his uncle padded into the dining room, the walls of which were festooned with a number of Aunt Bev's early rosemaling efforts. The swirling colors around him, combined with Uncle Frank's generous pour of Boodles gin, almost made Andy dizzy.

Dinner was delicious. The pot roast came out perfectly done, and it was accompanied by warm French bread and a surprisingly tasty salad of mixed greens, picked right from Uncle Frank's garden. After he had finished his last bite of Bavarian cream pie a half hour later, Andy pushed back his chair and turned to his aunt.

"Okay, Aunt Bev. Time to talk turkey. You wanted a jaw-wag about something."

Aunt Bev looked at her husband, who suddenly shifted his gaze to the ceiling. She poured Andy a cup of coffee, then rested her clasped hands on the table. "Well, Anders, you know that Mayor Bergholt is planning to vacate his office early."

Though he wasn't much interested in politics,

Andy had heard about Sherman Bergholt's decision to resign the post that he had held for nearly twenty years. He had easily won reelection each new term—mainly because no one else wanted the job.

"Yeah, I heard Sherm's wife took an early retirement from the school district," Andy said. "And she doesn't want to spend another winter in New Bergen. Heard they bought a condo down in Sarasota."

"That's right. Sherm tried to get the city council to let him telecommute, but the city charter says the mayor has to perform his duties in person."

"Well, all I can say is, good luck with finding a replacement," Andy snorted. "I can't imagine anyone in their right mind would want that gig."

Aunt Bev scowled disapprovingly. "I've always said that a job is what you make of it. I don't want to sound critical, but I think Sherm could have conducted himself in a more professional manner. He was good with the gimmicks and publicity, but there's a lot more that a mayor could do for the town."

Andy was suddenly flabbergasted. "So, are *you* thinking about running for mayor, Aunt Bev?"

She laughed as if she couldn't imagine such a thing. "Oh, heavens no, Anders. I think of myself as more of a worker bee than a queen bee."

Uncle Frank shut his eyes and made a little shake of his head.

"But I've always thought that Ronnie has just the right kind of personality for a political career."

Myron Engebretson was Bev and Frank's oldest son and a senior manager at Lovely Lena's. Andy liked his cousin and thought he was as rock-solid as they came.

"Ronnie for mayor?" Andy thought about it and slowly nodded his head. "Great idea, Aunt Bev. I'm all in. What do you want me to do? Put up some lawn signs? Go door knocking?"

"That's a bit premature, Anders. The city council has to call a special election, but they don't want to hold it until May. So they'll appoint an interim mayor to fill in until then."

"And I'll bet Ronnie would be their top choice." Andy liked the idea. It would be cool to have a mayor in the family.

Aunt Bev glanced over at her husband, who appeared to be examining the wood grain in the table.

"Well, there's a little bit of a problem," she explained. "You know Ronnie's down in Nebraska, helping set up Lovely Lena's new gluten-free pasta plant."

"Yeah," Andy replied. "So I heard. How's that going?"

Uncle Frank seemed relieved to finally be able to join the conversation. "Just great, Andy. It's gonna be a big money spinner. The gluten-free biz is goin' nuts."

"The thing is," Aunt Bev said, "Ronnie won't be back in New Bergen permanently until March. He could still run. But if the council puts in an interim mayor, that person will have a clear edge in the election. Incumbents always have the advantage, you know. It'd be a lot easier for Ronnie to win if the temporary mayor doesn't run."

Andy shrugged. "Guess so. But what can I do to help?"

Aunt Bev leaned toward him, as if she were about to share the most wonderful news ever. "Anders, we want *you* to keep the mayor's chair warm until Ronnie gets home. We want *you* to appear before the city council and convince them that you're the best man to temporarily fill the mayor's shoes."

Andy tried to say something, but the sound that came out of his mouth more resembled a squeak. He cleared his throat and spoke hoarsely.

"You want me to...?"

And then he erupted into a fit of rib-cracking coughs.

Uncle Frank pushed a glass of water toward him. As he chugged a few healthy gulps, Andy felt himself once again being swept into the vortex of another of Aunt Bev's cockeyed schemes.

Chapter Four

From his perch behind the lectern at the front of Ansel's Café, Andy glanced around the dining room to see how soon a table might open. Folks were waiting in line for the restaurant's popular brunch, and he needed to seat a party of three.

Sunday was the day of the week when Ansel's saw the most local customers. Lots of church-goers turned up, along with the less religious who ambled in with newspapers under their arms. But there were also out-of-towners who had overnighted at motels and B&Bs in the area. They came in droves for the eggs Benedict, huevos rancheros, and heavenly rum-raisin waffles with genuine Beaver Tail County maple syrup.

Ansel's proprietor, Kirsten Skyberg, made her way through the tables, asking diners how they liked the fare. Andy's twin sister was a tall, willowy blond, with striking blue, almond-shaped eyes that never missed a thing. Kirsten knew all, saw all.

"Wanna hear Aunt Bev's latest brainstorm?" Andy

asked when she arrived at the lectern.

Kirsten eyed him. "Will I regret it?"

Andy smiled. "Maybe."

His sister had been the target of their Aunt Bev's lobbying in the past. Most recently, Aunt Bev had wanted to embellish Ansel's pristine white walls and genuine Ansel Adams photos with flowery Norwegian folk paintings. Andy couldn't wait to see Kirsten's reaction to their aunt's political plans.

"Okay." Kirsten sighed. "I'll bite. What is she up to now?"

"She wants me to go after the interim mayor job."

Andy figured *that* would get an eye roll and a good laugh. So it shocked him when Kirsten looked intrigued.

"Hmm," the wealthy restaurateur said. "Not a bad idea. Let's talk about it later." She started to leave, but turned to face Andy again. "Oh, by the way, I'm throwing a little dinner party for Mom and Dad and a couple of their RVing friends next Saturday. Can you come?"

Andy nodded and then watched her head back toward the kitchen. "Well, that was weird," he muttered under his breath.

Why in the world would Kirsten think that Aunt Bev's scheme was "not a bad idea"? Andy Skyberg as mayor of New Bergen sure sounded like a bad idea to him. What was his sister thinking?

Andy wasn't even certain what the mayor of New Bergen did. Mayor Bergholt's photo was usually in the newspaper every few weeks, officiating somewhere or other. From the looks of it, the job required a lot of time—something Andy didn't have a lot of.

He was so deep in thought that he didn't notice J. J. standing in front of him, holding a brown paper bag. The Queen of Margaritas still looked as if she had a bit of a hangover.

"Hey, Andy, here's the takeout for Jill Robeson at Uncle Sam's," she said. "Would you mind running it down there? I'll cover for you."

"Sounds good. I could use a leg stretch anyway."

"Then off you go."

Andy took the bag, but didn't move from his spot. "I had dinner last night with my Aunt Bev."

"That's nice," J. J. replied, looking a little quizzical. "Bev's a sweetie."

Andy stood there a few more seconds. "She thinks I should go for the mayor's job, after Bergholt leaves."

J. J. seemed a bit surprised, but then she started nodding. "Great idea. You'd be an awesome mayor, Andy. You're smart, you're good looking, you're tall and distinguished."

Andy's ego swelled an inch or two. "Well, thanks."

"Yeah," J. J. smiled. "Imagine me telling my friends that I bus tables with the mayor of New Bergen. That'd be a real kick."

* * *

Uncle Sam's Mercantile was a block and a half down Skjegstad Street. Its owner, Jill Robeson, was an Ansel's regular and often had her lunches delivered.

The mid-September weather was lovely, partly cloudy and warmish. A bit of color showed on the boulevard trees. The sidewalks were already starting to fill up with antiquers of all kinds. Buyers, browsers, rubberneckers. Not too bad for post-Labor Day, Andy thought. He felt lucky to be there, taking it all in.

After his limo business down in the Cities had tanked and his wife Tracy had run off with a Pilates coach, Andy's future seemed bleak. He was too defeated to even think about starting another career. The big city had beaten him, and he needed refuge. Then the call came from Kirsten, offering him a job in her new café. He briefly hesitated, but pride goeth before a fall. Okey-dokey, he had said.

Coming back home to New Bergen two years ago had been chastening. But it was the only smart move possible. And now things were coming together for Anders Skyberg.

Working at Ansel's was exhausting, but *good* exhausting. Part of the deal with his sister included free rental of the empty office upstairs. Perfect for his painting studio. And with the plans for The Nordic taking shape, exciting new possibilities opened up for him—as a manager, a curator, and an artist. Kirsten had even said she would give him some equity in Ansel's LLC.

But for the first time in a couple of years, Andy was starting to yearn for the perks of big-city life that he had left behind. He was starting to think that maybe he needed someday to tackle the Cities one more time. It felt like unfinished business.

Before he knew it, he was standing in front of Uncle Sam's Mercantile, with replicas of ten different historical American flags flying up above. The store was packed to the rafters with vintage advertising, political posters, ancient toys, 78-speed records and gramophones, empty whiskey bottles, tons of military memorabilia, sports cards, Disney items, old tin toys, and thousands of books. It occurred to Andy that Jill might even have a copy of the August 1955 issue of *National Geographic,* to replace the one that Harald had tried to eat.

But when he entered the store, Andy was greeted with a scene more appropriate for an old issue of *True Crime*.

Jill Robeson was thrusting a rusty bayonet at a man standing in front of the counter. From the enraged look on her face, she might have been planning to demonstrate just how the weapon actually worked—with an eviscerating stab.

"You're lying, you rotten SOB!" Jill hissed as she poked the bayonet toward the man's chest. "You didn't lose it! You *sold* it. That letter came down from my great-great-grandfather. It was supposed to be passed on to the girls. *Your daughters*."

That's when Andy figured out who the guy was. Jill's ex-husband, Lance Robeson. He knew the two had gone through a very acrimonious divorce earlier that year, and it didn't look as if everything had been worked out yet. And what kind of letter could cause such an outburst on Jill's part?

"Calm down, Jillie," Lance said, surprisingly nonchalant. The guy had a honeyed voice, like a TV anchorman. "Isn't this a little early to be into the vodka?"

"I haven't had any vodka," the woman growled. "And stop calling me Jillie! You either bring me that document, or I swear I'll come to your house and gut you alive!" As if to demonstrate, she made an upward thrust with the bayonet.

Ouch, thought Andy. No one had even noticed him standing in the open door. Jill glared at Lance, while Jill's assistant had her eyes riveted on both of them.

"Do you understand, you miserable troglodyte? I will slit you open from your breastbone to your brain!"

Lance suddenly seemed aware of Andy standing behind him. He twisted around and regarded the restaurant delivery boy, then rolled his eyes, as if to say, *Do you believe this woman?*

Lance Robeson was a good-looking man in his late forties with a neatly-trimmed beard and trendy metal specs. Andy knew he was a professor of history at St. Magnus College. He was a media darling, too, appearing on TV shows down in the Cities whenever the stations needed an expert to explain some historical mystery, especially as it related to crime. He did have a certain charisma, Andy had to admit. But right now, it wasn't having much of an effect on his ex.

Lance put his hands up, palms toward Jill, as if surrendering. "I don't blame you for being mad, Jillie. If I can't find the letter, I will pay you fair value."

"That's not the effing point," Jill grumbled, finally lowering the weapon. "I better not find out you sold it to raise cash for another one of your harebrained business ideas."

The professor sighed, as if dealing with an obtuse child. "I'm getting a nice advance for the new book. If I can't find the letter, I'll pay you its value. Don't worry. And I'm sorry I lost the kids' legacy, okay? My bad."

He turned to leave, but looked back at her. "I'll pick up the girls on Saturday at 9 a.m. sharp. And could you *please* try to have them ready on time? *For a change.*"

The professor spun on his heel and brushed by Andy on his way out.

"Oh, Andy," Jill said, finally noticing him. "I'm sorry you had to see all that." She came out from behind the counter, still holding the bayonet. Andy took a step backward.

Jill looked down at the old weapon in her hand. "Oops," she said sheepishly, then twisted around. "Deb, could you put this thing back in the case, please. And grab me a twenty out of the till."

She handed the money to Andy and took the bag from him. He could tell that she'd told the truth about not quaffing any vodka. It was whiskey she'd been drinking—the scent was unmistakable.

"I wouldn't have gutted him, really," Jill reassured

him. "My daughters wouldn't have approved. They still like the guy, for some reason. But when he borrowed my Custer letter…"

That caught Andy's attention. "General Custer?"

"A letter signed by Custer commissioning a new colonel in his Civil War brigade. My great-great-grand-father. Anyway, it didn't even occur to me that Lance had the balls to sell it. But it looks like he did."

"Holy cow," Andy said. "That's gotta be pretty valuable."

"Yeah, it is. For insurance purposes the document's worth an awful lot. But that's not the point. It was supposed to go to my girls. It's part of their legacy. I normally don't tee off on Lance in public. But he hasn't responded to any of my e-mails or phone calls for weeks. So when he showed up here, I was primed to blow."

Andy chuckled nervously. "I heard you two had a nasty split."

"Most of Lance's splits are nasty," Jill said darkly. "His relationships usually start with a warm, rosy glow. The guy's a charmer. He had me fooled for a long time. But eventually push comes to shove and you get to see the real Lance. He's a greedy, duplicitous bastard. I can't tell you how many people he's used and then left in the dirt."

Wishing that Scotty would beam him up, Andy made a sympathetic noise and began to back toward the door. "Well, I gotta go. Hope you enjoy the smørbrød."

"And to top it off, he's a horndog. Lance will screw anyone he can. Whether you're a business partner or a research assistant or his wife, *he will screw you.*"

Andy realized she wasn't even talking to him anymore, not even aware of him.

"But someday soon, Lance Robeson," she snarled, "you're going to get what you deserve. *Someday soon.*"

Chapter Five

Andy drove up onto Thor Hofdahl's acreage just after lunch the following Tuesday. As sometimes happened when he visited, the Border collie Angus attempted to herd him and Harald toward the goat pen. But Thor was waiting for his friend, and shooed the hard-working dog away.

Thor and Sonny Hofdahl's place was typical of old farmhouses around the county. Two stories with a roomy attic, square of build, white wood clapboard that was peeling a bit. But with the success of Sonny's goat cheese business—her Montrachet, Colby, and Muenster were now in a dozen markets and co-ops in the Cities— the Hofdahl household was undergoing some upgrades. Starting with a new kitchen.

As Thor led Andy through the construction mess, he explained all about the birdseye maple cabinets, the granite counters, the commercial-grade appliances, the new All-Clad pots and pans, and the porcelain tile floor.

"No one deserves this more than Sonny," he said.

"She's the breadwinner now, and I'm the dead weight. But you know how much this puppy's gonna cost?"

Andy shook his head. Thor told him.

"Man oh man," Andy whistled. "That's a lot of cheese."

A few minutes later, both men were ensconced comfy and cozy in twin La-Z-Boys in Thor's basement man cave. A late season ballgame was playing up on the flat screen. "A bird game," as Thor put it. The Jays versus the Orioles, from Camden Yards in Baltimore. Harald had sprawled on the big braid rug in front of the television and seemed to be snoozing.

"So, do you know Lance Robeson?" Andy asked, sipping on a cold Biberschwanz Pilsner.

"Just casually," the septuagenarian answered, sucking on his own bottle. "I've been to some of his public lectures up at St. Magnus and talked to him afterwards. He specializes in American crime history. His presentation last year on serial killers in the Midwest was standing room only. You know—H. H. Holmes, Gein, Gacy, Dahmer. Edge-of-your-seat stuff, I'll tell you. Bone chilling."

Andy told Thor about the dramatic scene in Jill Robeson's store on Sunday afternoon.

"Yeah, well, I didn't say the good professor was a noble human being," Thor responded. "Had a few business relationships that went sour, from what I heard. Was sued a few times. Not always a nice guy. Struck me as pretty arrogant."

"From what Jill said, he's a bit of a lady's man."

"That, too. There was that scandal about three years ago. You were still down in the Cities. He had an affair with an instructor, who got pregnant. St. Magnus tried to cover it up, but the woman took the thing public."

"Why does St. Magnus put up with him? Don't professors get sacked for that sort of thing?"

Thor snorted. "For one thing, he's tenured. And heck, he's what keeps that history program going up there. He's an academic celeb—lots of publications and media appearances. Had a book on the bestseller lists a few years ago. He brings in donor dollars and grad students to the department. In that situation, a few personal peccadilloes are easily overlooked."

The two men watched the game some more before Andy spoke up again.

"Hey, Thor, I want to bounce an idea off you. It's kind of ridiculous."

"If it's kind of ridiculous, I'm prepared to ridicule it in short order. Shoot."

"My Aunt Bev—"

"Yup, one of New Bergen's most charming schemers," Thor interrupted.

"—had me over for dinner Saturday night. Boodles martinis. Pot roast. Her amazing Bavarian cream pie."

"Sounds yummy."

"Then she laid it on me."

"Proceed."

"She explained that my cousin Ronnie wanted a shot

at the mayor's seat, what with Mayor Bergholt quitting. The council's going to appoint an interim mayor pretty soon."

"Yeah, I heard that."

"But Ronnie can't go after it, because Lovely Lena has him down in Nebraska until March."

"Uh-huh."

"So Aunt Bev thinks I should take a crack at it. To keep the seat warm for Ronnie, she said. That way, there won't be an incumbent running for the job when they have the actual election next spring."

Thor looked surprised. "Never would have pegged you for a political animal."

"Ronnie's a super guy—real salt of the earth. I wouldn't mind him running the town. But you're right. I'm not a political animal. I don't have the ego. I don't have the interest. I don't have the thick skin. And I don't want the responsibility."

In the days since Aunt Bev's bombshell, Andy had been thinking about how often he just fell in place and did whatever people wanted of him. Was this the time when he finally put his foot down? When he finally said, "No way, José!"? The sad thing was, he couldn't even answer that question.

"Well, I don't think the mayor really has that much responsibility," Thor said. "It's more of a figurehead position. The city manager handles all the heavy lifting."

The two of them stopped to watch a pop fly soar harmlessly back into a Toronto outfielder's glove. Andy took another slug of beer.

Thor regarded him with that fatherly look he'd get once in a while. It reminded Andy that his best friend was older than Andy's own dad. Thor just seemed so young, so in tune with the way Andy thought.

"Maybe you don't want to make that commitment, Andy. But comes a time, every now and then, when a man's gotta take a deep breath and do what needs to be done. Heck, I served on the school board back in the '80s for two terms, and it didn't kill me. And this would be good timing for you. You've still got a halo from saving a life last summer. People love a hero."

Andy nodded in Harald's direction. "He's the hero. He saved my hide."

"That's as may be," Thor said. "But the council's not gonna appoint King Harald mayor, however heroic. I think you should give it a shot. It's only half a year, and they'll even pay you a few bucks."

"Yeah," Andy said, "maybe enough for that new set of Michelins."

"You see?" Thor grinned. "You're already thinking like a politician."

* * *

The next afternoon, Andy and his sister sat on one side of a long mahogany table in Kirsten's meeting room upstairs from Ansel's, right next door to Andy's studio space. Across the table from them was a thin, intense, fortyish man in a black Armani suit. Next to him sat a stunning blond in a perfectly tailored black pantsuit. The man in the Armani was Peter Kamu, the architect from the Cities who was a rising star around the world. The stunning blond was his project manager, Katrina Makkonen, an architect from Helsinki and an associate in Kamu's firm.

Pinned to a large bulletin board were dozens of inkjet prints depicting Peter's evolving design of Kirsten's new deli and art gallery. The two-story, Skjegstad Street façade would be sheathed in weathered wood of different tonalities, cut and placed to depict the prairie sky and the contours of the horizon and land beneath it. A mosaic of wood.

That landscape was broken by several tall windows with panes etched to portray the sinuous birch trees of northeastern Beaver Tail County. Kamu had designed a roof of two elegant gables with very broad eaves, covered in custom-designed copper tiles. The sides and back of the structure were of native stone and recycled brick, handsomely configured. The downstairs would house the deli, and the upstairs the gallery.

Andy looked forward to these meetings for two reasons. First, it excited the artist in him to see this project come together. Peter was insanely creative, considering the small scope of the building. The guy had some pretty impressive credentials, including a contemporary art museum in Switzerland and an opera house in Finland. Kirsten was going to get the coolest-looking deli in the world.

And then there was the fact that Trina, as she preferred to be called, was a complete and utter babe.

Trina smiled at Andy a lot. He liked that. In fact, it made him feel a little warm and giddy at times.

She had a dancer's figure, sleek and lithe. Shoulder-length, white-blond hair and bangs that framed her face. Andy had a hard time not staring at those lovely lips of hers, done in the color of a fine merlot. Today she had on a pair of oval earrings that matched the shade of her lipstick perfectly.

Andy figured Trina was way above his pay grade, but a guy could always hope.

Unfortunately, Andy's sister could read him like a book. She warned her "little" brother—born only twenty minutes after her—that Trina was strictly off-limits. Kirsten didn't want to muddy the relationship with her architect's firm through any romantic entanglements.

Kirsten Skyberg was not only one of the smartest people in New Bergen, but one of the richest. She had moved back from Silicon Valley several years ago with a substantial bundle, rumored to be in the tens of millions. No one knew how much, not even her parents or brother. She and her husband had returned to her hometown for the sake of their two kids, but her early retirement made her antsy. From her boredom grew Ansel's Café, named for the Ansel Adams photos lining the walls. She intended to make her new project a star attraction in Beaver Tail County.

"Peter," Kirsten said firmly, "you promised any overruns would not exceed ten percent of your initial figures. And now you're coming at me with twenty-two percent? And you can't possibly make do with any less?"

Peter Kamu had narrow features, masked by stylish red spectacles. He betrayed no hint of a sense of humor. Tenting his fingers, he tucked them under his fashionably stubbled chin, and peered at his client.

"I know that's a substantial overage, Kirsten," he concurred. "But certain key vendors have had huge rises in their costs since I made my first estimates. For example, the copper roof tiles are absolutely essential for this project. But the price of copper is rising rapidly."

Kirsten looked unimpressed.

"In addition, I discovered that some of the engineering is more complex than I anticipated." He took a paper from the folder he had in front of him, then handed it across the table to Kirsten. "These are the details of the new costs."

Andy watched to see how this scene would play out. His sister had an eagle eye for budgets and she didn't like being strung along. This could be a deal breaker. And what a shame it would be to lose such a fantastic design.

Kirsten scanned the sheet, then shook her head. "Let me look at my numbers and we'll see what we can do. But if we can't impact the twenty-two percent by very much, well…" She made an ominous scowl. "I'll need to rethink."

"Understood," Peter said, gathering up his papers.

"I'm out of the country for a couple of weeks, but Trina will be at the Medallion Suites in Hobartville. She will liaise between the two of us and will keep you informed of our progress on fixing our budget differences."

And that was the end of the meeting. Kirsten rushed off to supervise a big catering gig for that evening. Peter spoke a few words into Trina's ear, then walked out the door.

That left Andy and Trina standing at the table, regarding each other self-consciously. He sure hoped they could come to an agreement on those budget figures. Otherwise, it would not only mean the end of Peter's wonderful design, but also the last of Trina.

"Peter has a flight to Amsterdam tonight, then onto Warsaw," Trina explained, in her intoxicating Finnish accent. "Another opera house we are developing a proposal for. Then he is off to the Helstok corporate HQ project in Stockholm. He is very busy right now." She looked at Andy, as if to say: *Do you know how lucky you are to have Peter Kamu design your little delicatessen?*

"I hope your sister can find her way to accommodate the new costs," she continued. "Your building could be a showplace, a destination in its own right. It will most certainly win prizes. Big prizes. Your café and gallery will become known around the world, Anders. People will come into the Cities and say, 'We have to go see The Nordic. How do we get to New Bergen?'"

For Andy, it was a heady vision—people coming from all over to sample Kirsten's cuisine and view exhibits in the gallery. *The gallery that he would manage.* Andy had all sorts of ideas for shows. Some juried, some curated by guests, some curated by himself. And, of course, a few paintings on the walls would be his own creations.

"It'd be a shame if Kirsten couldn't do it," Andy agreed. "But she's the boss. It's her money, and it's gotta work business-wise, Trina. I mean, maybe some stuff like the custom copper roof tiles and etched windows could go."

The gorgeous blond looked horrified. "But things such as the tiles and the birch windows are integral to the concept, Anders. Their absence would degrade it thoroughly. You might as well hire some architect from Hobartville."

The dig against the county seat was kind of unfair. No one expected world-class from Hobartville. But Andy understood her point.

Trina came around the table and sat on the edge of it, near Andy. Quite unexpectedly, she took his left hand. His heart rate bumped up. Her hand felt like velvet.

"Anders, I know the decision is Kirsten's. But anything you could do to help her make the right one would be so appreciated."

Andy looked into those remarkable green eyes, which blinked beseechingly. Up close, those lips were even more glisteningly merlot-red.

"I'll do what I can," he stammered.

Chapter Six

Driving home from the meeting, Andy indulged in a little daydreaming, with Trina in a starring role.

Andy wasn't born yesterday. He knew her flirtations with him were due to his relationship with her boss's client—his sister. In the contest of wills, he would always side with Kirsten. But it didn't hurt to imagine what it would be like to spend some time in the company of Katrina Makkonen. She was a class act, someone whom he'd be proud to show off to his big-city friends.

After he parked the Silverado, Andy let Harald out of the house and went inside to check the mail. He took a few slurps of orange juice out of the carton and stepped back out. His plan was to head downtown and catch a few hours in the studio. Harald could come along and watch him paint.

But over the fence, he saw Elsie come out of the back door of her two-story colonial. She waved at Andy.

"Anders," she said, "could you come over for a minute? Emma and I have something we want you to do for us. I have pie and coffee waiting."

Andy sighed. First Aunt Bev, now Elsie. He sure must look like an easy mark for any female over the age of sixty. Still, he did owe Elsie for keeping an eye on Harald.

"Sure, Elsie, be right there."

Andy looked down at his dog, who gazed expectantly up at him. "Be back with you in a minute, big guy," he said, scratching the dog behind the ears.

He went out into the alley and around to Elsie's backyard. Before going into her house, he checked the new door closer that he had installed. It seemed to be working fine. The door shouldn't get caught by the wind again.

Elsie and her sister, Emma Nelson, were sitting at the table in the tidy little kitchen, which was surprisingly contemporary. Elsie had an induction stovetop with a convection oven that sat between counters topped in blue ceramic tile. A spotless, stainless steel fridge stood on the opposite wall. The rest of the house was equally modern, not at all like most of the old-lady houses Andy had visited. Elsie definitely stayed in tune with the times.

Emma lived on the other side of Andy. A year older than Elsie, she was a bit reserved, compared to her gregarious sister. Her pretty face was only slightly more wrinkled, but she moved a lot slower because of her arthritis.

"How you doin', Emma?" Andy asked.

She gave him a raise of the eyebrows. "Well, Anders, still on the right side of the sod."

From the fridge, Elsie pulled out what looked like a homemade pecan pie. She cut a piece for Andy and put it on a plate. Then she took out a pint of vanilla ice cream and added a scoop to the pie. She poured his coffee from a Thermos.

"Anders," she said, sitting down, "you do so much for us. Mowing the lawn, shoveling snow, little chores around the house."

Emma nodded in agreement.

"We hate to ask another favor of you," Elsie continued. "Especially something that's a bit out of the ordinary."

A bit out of the ordinary? Andy was curious to know what the sisters had in mind. "If I can help, I will. Why don't you tell me about it?"

Elsie made a dramatic sigh. "Well, Emma and I have a little problem."

"What is it?"

"It's really just a case of mistaken identity. But we need someone who's more persuasive than we are to help us clear it up."

More persuasive? "Okay, fill me in."

Elsie fidgeted with the saltshaker that was on the table. "There's a man who lives in the area and he's trying to blackmail us. Because he thinks we're somebody we're not."

Andy's jaw dropped. "Blackmail? That's serious

stuff, Elsie. Who does this guy think you are?"

"Somebody not very nice," Emma chimed in.

This was turning into a very strange conversation. "I don't understand," Andy said. "Someone thinks you two aren't very nice?"

"No, it's not that exactly." Elsie put her hand to her cheek. "He thinks we weren't very nice many years ago."

Andy felt as if he were playing twenty questions and getting nowhere.

"And what does he think you did years ago that wasn't nice?"

"Well, he thinks that we ran around with bank robbers and gangsters from Chicago." Elsie paused, waiting for Andy's reaction.

He considered the notion for a second or two, then started to laugh. "That's ridiculous. Someone's just gotta be pulling your legs."

"I know," Emma chuckled. "Elsie and me, with gangsters from Chicago? Isn't that unbelievable?"

"I didn't even visit Chicago until I was fifty," Elsie said, joining in the laughter. Then her expression turned serious. "But this man doesn't seem to be joking."

Elsie's worried look made Andy stop smiling. He didn't like the idea of some con man trying to shake down Elsie and Emma. That rankled him good.

"So, how much money does this…"

The a-word almost came out of his mouth, but he just managed to stop it.

"What kind of money does this guy want?"

"Oh," Elsie said, "he's not interested in money."

That brought Andy up short. "Then what's he after?"

"He wants to interview us." Emma frowned fiercely.

The wheels in Andy's head were spinning hard. He tried to figure out what kind of scam this joker could be pulling on his two neighbors.

"Well, I think you should call Sheriff Mandsager and report the guy," he said. "Extortion's a major crime, even if he's not after money."

Elsie looked petrified. "Oh no, we can't do that. If we do, that terrible man might tell people that Emma and I were those women who did those awful things."

"Even though it's a lie," Emma put in, "people might believe him. It could make our lives miserable."

That was true, Andy had to admit. Plenty of innocent people had their reputations ruined by crazy, untrue accusations.

"But I just don't understand how I can help," he said.

Elsie straightened herself up and looked him in the eye.

"We would like you to talk to him. And make him stop. *By any means necessary.*" Suddenly, her sweet old face displayed a fierce resolve Andy had never seen.

What in heck did that signify? Had Elsie just put out a contract on the guy's life? Naw, that was just screwy. Of course not. Andy had misunderstood.

He shrugged. "Okay. But why don't you have Earl or Dennis do it?"

Earl and Dennis Nelson were Emma's sons. They both had graduated from New Bergen High years before Andy had. Andy had gotten to know Earl pretty well, but not so much Dennis, a retired cop who lived and worked up in Herkimer County.

"Oh, we couldn't send them," Emma said, shaking her head. "They'd get too angry at the man. And we don't want that kind of trouble."

Andy understood. Neither Earl nor Dennis had much going in the way of diplomatic skills. "Okay, then, I'll go talk to the guy. But I can't promise anything."

"Oh, Anders," Elsie burbled, grabbing his hand across the table, "you are just an absolute dear!"

He shrugged again. "Now who is this guy?"

She beamed at him. "He's a professor at St. Magnus. His name is Lance Robeson."

* * *

Lance Robeson's house was located on a roomy, heavily wooded lot right next to Fred Barnes County Park, on the northern edge of town, only a five-minute drive from Andy's place. The structure was a handsome rambler with dark-stained cedar siding, broad eaves, and big picture windows. It may as well have been a cabin in the woods, it was so appealingly rustic. Andy sure would not mind owning a house like that some day.

He pulled up in front of the place first thing Friday morning, then hopped out of the Silverado, followed by Harald. When Andy had called Lance to ask if he could come by for a chat about Elsie and Emma, the professor said on one condition: bring Harald along. He was writing an article for *Cavalcade Weekly* magazine on animals that had been involved in criminal investigations and wanted to send his editor a photo of King Harald.

Man and dog hadn't even arrived at the door when it swung open, revealing the professor, clad in cargo pants and a green St. Magnus College sweatshirt.

"Welcome, Andy. Welcome, King Harald." Lance shook Andy's hand, then leaned over and patted Harald on the head.

Harald, having become quite accustomed to such acknowledgement from his adoring public, wagged his tail several times, then gave Lance's hand a lick.

The professor smiled. "Sure doesn't look like a crime fighter, does he?"

Andy couldn't disagree. "No, Harald's special talent took us all by surprise."

"Why don't you two come in?"

The front rooms looked as if a research library had gotten up on its hind legs and wandered out into the countryside. They were packed with books and journals and piles of manuscripts. Five file cabinets crowded the living room, and photos and clippings covered two bulletin boards. A computer with dual-jumbo LCD monitors shared a desktop with a laser printer.

"Care for an espresso, Andy?" the professor asked, gesturing for Andy and Harald to follow him.

A little pick-me-up sounded awfully good. "Sure, that'd be nice."

"It's a gorgeous morning. Let's sit outside."

They went through the dining room—the big teak table also piled high with papers and books—and through sliding doors onto a brick patio at the back of the house. Andy lowered himself into a weathered redwood Adirondack chair, and Harald plopped down next to him. Maples rimmed the backyard and patio. The red leaves were wafting down. Multi-colored impatiens and showy hostas had been planted in the dappled shade. It looked like Lance was fond of garden gnomes. There were several scattered among the greenery, their cheery little faces and pointy red hats popping up here and there.

Lance disappeared for a few moments and returned with two tiny cups of frothy, steaming black liquid. The aroma arrived first and it was heavenly.

Andy took a sip. "Delicious, thanks."

"No problem," Lance said, sitting in another Adirondack. "Listen, Andy, before we go any further, I just want to apologize for that scene at my ex's store. Jill tipples a bit too much, and she can get nasty when she does. I'm sorry that you had to see that."

And she's sorry that you evidently sold a General Custer letter that didn't belong to you, Andy thought.

"Well," he responded out loud, "sometimes exes don't get along. I haven't talked to mine since our final meeting at the attorney's office."

Harald made a *whooof* sound as he got to his feet and ambled over to nose around the garden.

"Jillie's gotten pretty hard-boiled," the professor continued. "She and I were married for fourteen years. As the girls got older, we were too damned busy to really notice that we weren't talking as much, weren't connecting as much, weren't agreeing as much. She was drinking more and more. And, my bad, I developed what you might call a bit of wanderlust."

Andy raised his eyebrows. "You mean lustful wandering?"

The professor grimaced. "Yeah, that's it exactly. Monogamy wasn't working for me."

Harald had returned from his amble, with what looked to be a present for Andy. In fact, it was one of Lance's garden gnomes, about eight or nine inches tall, gripped firmly in the dog's teeth.

As Andy took the eccentric offering, Lance started to chuckle.

Andy blinked at the colorful plastic guy, who was wearing a green tunic and pointed red cap.

But no pants whatsoever.

The little fellow was quite anatomically correct. And fully aroused.

Andy regarded the naughty gnome. "Bet you didn't buy this on Skjegstad Street," he deadpanned.

"Nope, I did not," Lance confirmed. "I found him and his friends online and just couldn't resist. I can get you the website, if you'd like."

Andy said thanks but no thanks; he preferred his garden gnomes a bit less spicy. He was no prude, but he couldn't imagine folks from these parts leaving out pornographic statuettes where anyone could see them.

This guy wasn't like any professor Andy remembered from back in his college days. There was something about him that kind of creeped Andy out.

Maybe Elsie was right to be leery of Lance Robeson.

Chapter Seven

"Of course, I've read all about how you saved that woman's life a couple of months ago," the professor said to Andy. "And the role that King Harald there played. But what's your back story?"

Andy didn't want to share too much with the guy. So he kept it very short. "Well, I drove my own limo down in the Cities. The business flopped. Came back here to work for my sister."

"I'm curious. Did you ever drive any famous clients?"

"A few CEOs you might recognize. Sports stars. Senators and an ex-vice president. A pretty well-known film director. Big name musicians and actors."

"Such as?"

"Well, I really had a lot of fun with Dustin Newell. I drove him five or six times."

Lance looked impressed. "Dusty Newell? Of the Blitzers?"

"The very same."

"Was he as wild as they say?"

"Oh yeah," Andy confirmed. "Dusty was off the hook. He tipped me ten grand one time."

"And the drugs?"

"Yup, pharmaceuticals were deployed. But not by yours truly. I only survived by taking catnaps in the Town Car and munching on energy bars."

"Well, I'd love to hear more," Lance said, putting his espresso cup down on the redwood table between them. "But this is a business negotiation, right? You come as the Shelstad sisters' representative."

"The *who*?" Andy asked, quite confused.

"Emma and Elsbeth Shelstad, whom you know as Emma Nelson and Elsie Bjorklund. Are they willing to sit for an interview?"

Although the conversation had been pleasant up to this point, Andy was prepared to play hardball.

"Afraid not, Lance. You see, whoever you're looking for, Elsie and Emma aren't them. You've simply got a case of mistaken identity."

Lance smiled and nodded. "That's exactly what Elsbeth said when I went to her house." He leaned forward. "How much did the sisters tell you about my project?"

"Only that you have some bizarre notion that they had something to do with Chicago gangsters decades ago." Andy snorted, doing his best to sound dismissive. "Well, you are entirely barking up the wrong tree."

He paused to stare pointedly at the professor.

Lance leaned back in his chair and crossed his arms. "I don't know how much you've heard about my work, Andy. I like to say my day job is keeping my master's degree program ticking along. But my specialty is the history of crime in America. I've written dozens of articles, several books, consulted with the FBI, made media appearances. I was just on NPR, in fact, talking about the history of terrorism and drug trafficking. I was saying that—"

Suddenly, Harald jumped to his feet and started barking. He charged off after a squirrel that was just vanishing into the bushes.

"Harald, stop that!" Andy yelled. "Get back here! Sorry about the interruption, Lance."

The professor looked amused. "Can't blame him. I do tend to ramble on a bit. Anyway, I'm under contract to do a book on America's forgotten bank robbers. *The Heirs of Dillinger* is my working title. One of them was a guy who was born up in Herkimer County. Ole Bredahl."

"You aren't going to tell me that Emma and Elsie stuck up banks?" Andy asked incredulously.

Lance chuckled. "No, no. Not at all. Ole and his crew—there were two other guys—operated in the 1950s. Eleven good, clean bank jobs around the Midwest. Somehow Ole and his guys holed up in Cicero, Illinois, outside Chicago, and he caught wind of a big currency shipment there. They managed to hijack the armored car and they drove away with two million in cash. That would be about twenty million bucks today. It was the most epic American bank job that no one has ever heard of."

"What do you mean, no one's ever heard of it?" Andy asked.

"The money was never reported stolen," Lance answered.

"That makes no sense."

"True. But what Ole didn't know was that the cash belonged to a criminal syndicate in Chicago. A local Polish gangster was handling the transport on their behalf. Needless to say, that poor guy vanished pretty quickly. Sleeping with the fishes, probably. You don't screw up that badly with the big boys and survive.

"Now, why Ole didn't retire at that point and move to Brazil with the loot, who knows? But he pushed his luck too far a while later, and got nabbed during a bank raid in Dubuque. Both his guys died in the gunfire."

"Fascinating stuff, Lance," Andy said, "but what's it got to do with my neighbors?"

"We're getting to it, Andy." Lance paused, as if relishing the suspense of his tale. "Ole got twenty years in the joint. But he didn't even make it to one. No one knows for sure who did it, but Ole took a shiv in the gut. Maybe the Chicago mob got to him, maybe it was just an altercation with another con. Before he died, though, he'd made a friend in the slammer. And he told this guy a lot."

"Like where he put all that loot?"

"First things first, Andy. I was able to track down this ex-con through an online crime history forum. His name is Vernon. I saw him in April and we talked for hours."

"I hope this story has a punch line, Lance." Andy was getting impatient.

Just then Harald returned, ambling nonchalantly through the brush, back onto the patio. He plopped down between the two men, not seeming a bit embarrassed by his outburst of squirrel hysteria a few moments before. Andy could see that some burr removal would be necessary.

"Oh, it does have a punch line," Lance said. "It turns out that after each heist, Ole always went back to a little shack in the woods in Osceola County, Iowa. Chief among his amusements there were what Ole called his 'Twin Angels.' Twin blond sisters. Lovely young things, apparently. A double act."

Finally Andy understood. Flies could have flown into his open mouth.

"And that's who you think Elsie and Emma were?" he scoffed. "Twin hookers?"

Lance nodded smugly. "I do."

"That's just ridiculous. For starters, they aren't twins."

"They're close enough in age and they could have passed for twins."

"And you think they have the loot?"

"Not necessarily. But they might have some inkling

of where Ole stashed it. I'd love to ask them about that and the time they spent with him."

Andy was trying to come up with a suitably disdainful response, when his mind focused on something else. That thousand-dollar bill, floating out of the old *National Geographic* Harald had mangled. Elsie quickly snatching up the banknote, and cutting the encounter short.

Lance didn't seem to notice his rumination. "Let me tell you how I found them," he said. "Vernon remembered their first names. Emma and Elsbeth. My researcher went through over two hundred high school yearbooks from northwestern Iowa. From the late '40s, early '50s. It was just some old-fashioned detective work. Pretty amazing that now they live only a mile or two from me."

Fantastic luck for Lance, thought Andy. Rotten luck for Elsie and Emma.

"Still don't believe me?" Lance looked like a poker player holding a straight flush. "I want to show you something. Just hang on."

The professor hopped up, went into the house, and returned a minute later with a red folder. He sat again, pulled out two photos, and handed them to Andy. "Here, take a gander."

Andy examined them. They were high school graduation portraits, clearly copied from a yearbook. Two very pretty young women who looked a lot alike. They could have been twins. Their light-blond hair was done up in styles that were all the rage back during the Eisenhower administration.

Andy read the text beneath the first photo in a quiet voice. "Emma Shelstad. 'Still waters run deep.' Choir, Home Economics Club, Girls Basketball."

Then he read the other one. "Elsbeth Shelstad. 'Just a butterfly.' Band, Home Economics Club, Cheerleading Squad."

Andy felt a pain in the pit of his stomach. Sixty, sixty-five years is a long time for a human face to evolve. Time and gravity do their dirty work. There could always be some doubt. But those two girls sure did look like Elsie and Emma.

"Lance," he finally said, looking up, "even if these are pictures of Elsie and Emma, it proves nothing. Just because an ancient ex-con gave you their names and claimed they were Ole's hookers, you can't assume that he was telling you the truth. I'd call your evidence pretty flimsy, at best."

The professor shrugged. "This isn't a court of law, Andy. I don't have to meet a legal burden of proof."

Andy sniffed. "It will be in a court of law if they decide to sue your patootie for libel and defamation."

Lance made an exaggerated sigh. "Andy, I promised them I wouldn't ID them. I said I'd protect their identities."

"But it would get out," Andy protested. "Someone would figure it out."

"Listen, Andy. All I want to know is what they recall

about Ole Bredahl. About that huge payday out of the Chicago heist. Where did it go?"

"Lance, I gotta tell you, they are *not* going to talk to you."

The professor's handsome features darkened. "Then they are making a big mistake, my friend. A really big mistake."

Chapter Eight

"So what do you think, Harald?" Andy asked as they cruised out of town. "Could Elsie and Emma be sitting on two million bucks in cash?"

Harald responded with a sotto voce woof and a cocked head.

"My thoughts exactly," Andy agreed. "They would *not* be living in our neighborhood if they had that kind of moolah."

Andy's next stop was Oman's Organic Produce Farm. He let Harald out of the cab so the dog could cavort a bit with the resident black lab.

Andy grabbed two boxes of squash for that evening's butternut ravioli special, and a re-supply of late-season heirloom tomatoes. This time of year, Kirsten insisted on heirlooms for everything that needed a fresh tomato. Today's load included Brandywine and Mr. Stripey. Andy treated himself to a Brandywine, eating it like a very sloppy apple.

Then he dropped off Harald at Kirsten's place. His

parents said they missed having a pooch and wanted some quality time with their favorite and only granddog.

At Ansel's, Andy seated diners and cleared tables during a very busy lunch hour. He was loading up a tray with dirty dishes near the front of the restaurant, when someone shouted, "Hey Andy."

He looked up and saw an old high school friend, Ken Young, grinning at him by the front door. Ken had been the star quarterback on the New Bergen Muskies when Andy was a bench-warming defensive lineman. He'd been handsome, tall, smart, and an irresistible chick-magnet. Since then, he'd put on a few pounds and an extra chin. But he still had some of that old alpha male magnetism. He was on the New Bergen city council, and Andy had heard that some folks were talking him up for a state senate run.

"Hi, Ken. How you doin'?"

"I'm doin' great, Killer," said Ken, pumping Andy's hand.

Andy's fellow Muskies used to call him "Killer," heavy on the irony. Even though he stood a sturdy six foot four, Andy was known for his reluctance to hit players hard during games or practice.

"Business is booming. People gotta have coverage." Ken was an agent for Farm Owners' Mutual. Andy had his vehicles insured through him, as well as his renter's policy.

"So, table for one?"

"That's not why I stopped," Ken said.

There was no one waiting for a table, so Andy didn't mind chewing the fat for a minute. "What can I do for you, Ken?"

"Andy, I got a visit yesterday from Beverly Engebretsen."

Uh-oh, Andy thought. "Aunt Bev came to see you? That's nice."

"Fun lady, and a bit of a talker."

"And how," Andy agreed.

"She gave me this." Ken pulled a folded sheet of paper from his suit jacket pocket. He handed it over.

With a sense of foreboding, Andy unfurled it. Why was he not surprised?

The headline read:

Keep New Bergen in good hands. Appoint Anders Skyberg interim mayor.

There was a snap of Andy, looking a little tipsy, from a recent party at Aunt Bev's house. But instead of holding that bottle of Biberschwanz Kölsch he remembered savoring, he was gripping a badly Photoshopped package of Lovely Lena Mac 'n' Cheese. Below that was a testimonial to Andy's sterling character. And, as the coup de grâce, came another headline:

And don't forget. You'll get King Harald, too... The most famous dog in Beaver Tail County.

Andy distinctly remembered telling Aunt Bev that he'd give the mayor's run some thought. But she had jumped the gun on him. And she was going to hear about it.

"Ken," he groaned, "I'm sorry about this. It wasn't my idea."

"No problem, Andy. No problem." The former quarterback clapped him on the shoulder. "Great timing, in fact. The council is meeting on Tuesday evening to make the call."

Andy was shocked. A few minutes ago he thought he had all the time in the world to ponder his move. *Now he only had four days?* Things were spinning out of control, thanks, as usual, to Aunt Bev.

"I'm behind you, Killer, and so's Lon Uppgren," Ken continued, oblivious to the astonished expression on Andy's face.

"So you only need to pick up one more vote, and the job's yours. But you sure better bring Harald to the meeting. He's the real star. Charisma to burn, huh? Gotta run, pal. See you Tuesday."

"But..." Andy finally managed to blurt, as Ken scurried out the door.

"Was that Ken Young?"

Andy turned around and saw Kirsten standing there, with menu inserts for the evening's specials.

"You won't believe this," he fumed. "Aunt Bev gave him a flyer promoting me for mayor. I never told her she could put my name out there. And now it sounds like I could actually get the job."

Kirsten read the flyer. "Well, Aunt Bev seems to think you gave your stamp of approval," she said, handing it back to Andy. "I wouldn't sweat it. The job mainly involves going to council meetings and turning up for photo ops."

Andy was feeling a little panicked. "But how can I handle being mayor and keep up with my work here?"

"You can take time off whenever you need to. I've been mulling it over, Andy, and I think having you as mayor could be good for Ansel's, good for The Nordic. Didn't I tell you that we need to be more involved in the community? Well, if they vote you in, we'll be more involved."

"So, it's part of my job description now?"

"Basically, yes," Kirsten nodded. "It can't hurt our business to have you in there. If there are any licensing or regulatory issues with The Nordic, you'll be in a great position to lobby the appropriate parties."

"That reminds me," Andy said. "You seemed a little iffy about the figures that Peter Kamu came up with. Do you think we can work things out? Or are we gonna have to find another architect?"

Kirsten gave him a puzzled look. "What *are* you talking about? Of course we're going forward with Peter's design. Having that guy do our project is a coup."

"But you acted like you were ready to back out."

"Oh, Andy, that's just the negotiation process. I'll give a little more, he'll take a little less, and we'll get the deal done. We should end up just about where I figured we would. No reason to lose any sleep, little brother."

Then Kirsten arched an eyebrow.

"And don't worry. Trina Makkonen's not going anywhere. I've been jotting down some notes and I want you to meet with her and go over them. Just remember, though—look, don't touch."

* * *

As Andy drove over to Kirsten's place to pick up Harald, he mulled over what had just happened. A perfect storm of circumstances seemed to have trapped him into tossing his chapeau into the mayoral ring.

It was an ironic twist of fate for someone who had little interest in politics. But as Thor had suggested, maybe the time had come to accept his civic responsibility and do what needed to be done.

After chatting a bit with his folks, Andy loaded Harald into the truck and made a pit stop at Engkvist's Liquor, where he grabbed a six-pack of Biberschwanz Weissbier. Back home, a pint of potato salad, whole-wheat buns, and four fresh bratwurst—two for himself, two for Harald—awaited him in the fridge.

After that, the plan was to binge-watch *Firefly* until he fell asleep in front of the plasma screen. His niece Rory had loaned him the DVDs and said it was way better than even *Star Trek*.

As he and Harald climbed out of the Silverado back home, Andy heard an insistent voice calling to him.

"Anders, Anders," Elsie Bjorklund shouted over the fence. "Emma and I are wondering if you have any news for us."

Andy had almost forgotten about his weird encounter with Lance Robeson that morning. And, sitting in Elsie's kitchen with the two sisters a few minutes later, he figured his "news" wouldn't go over well.

It didn't.

Both sisters looked crestfallen.

"Did you tell this Robeson fella that we couldn't possibly be the women he's looking for?" Emma asked.

"I did," Andy said.

"And you tried to persuade him that he was wrong?" Elsie asked. "You tried *real* hard?"

Andy nodded firmly. "I did."

As Elsie slumped back in her chair, a dark look came over her face.

"I said to do *anything* you had to do, Anders."

There was actually some anger in her voice. And that rankled Andy. What more did the two sisters think he could do? He wasn't going to play the fall guy here.

"Listen, ladies, here's the deal. Short of beating him up, I couldn't have done much more. Lance Robeson is determined to write about Ole Bredahl and his two angels. And he thinks those girls were you."

"But what's his evidence?" Emma demanded.

"He's got the word of some ancient ex-con who knew Bredahl in prison. This guy said the two angels were twin sisters named Emma and Elsbeth."

"But Emma and I aren't twins," Elsie objected.

"Well, you two sure looked like it in your yearbook photos," Andy replied.

Elsie gasped. "Yearbook pictures? You saw them?"

"Yes, I did. Pictures of Elsbeth and Emma Shelstad. That's you, right?"

"That was our maiden name, yes," Emma confirmed dismally.

"I gotta say, you two were lookers." Andy sensed a big misstep there and hastened to add, "And still are, for that matter."

Emma sighed. "Nice of you to say so, Anders. But that really doesn't help us much."

"I don't know what to do," Elsie said, wringing her hands. "If this gets out, our names will be mud. We might as well be dead."

"Now, it's not as bad as that," Andy reassured her. "The people who count know better. And those who think the worst—well, you don't want to know them anyway."

"Anders is right, Elsie. You're being overdramatic, as usual." Emma sniffed. "At our age, what does it matter what people think?"

Andy was all for forgiving folks their old indiscretions. But he had to admit that now he was really wondering about that stray g-note of Elsie's. Still, there could be a totally innocent explanation for it. It might not have anything to do with Ole Bredahl's heist.

Just then, Elsie's screen door swung open and in walked Emma's younger son, Earl Nelson. On his heels came his girlfriend, Bonnie Bohonek. Andy knew both of them. They clerked at the FillerUp Truck Oasis near the Flèche Droite Nation Casino south of New Bergen, on the Interstate. Earl also drove a van part-time for a local delivery service. They commiserated on their lousy lotto luck with Andy whenever he happened to encounter either of them at the FillerUp.

"Hi, Mom. Hi, Elsie. Hey there, Andy," Earl said.

"Mother, Auntie, Andy," Bonnie echoed. The stocky woman with short red hair put a brown paper bag on the counter. "Brought you some lettuce and carrots, Elsie. Fresh outta the garden not an hour ago."

While Bonnie set about fixing some instant coffee, Earl, a scrawny guy of medium height, sat down at the table. To Andy, he always looked like a carny—with that brown, weathered face and missing teeth that signified a life lived hard and fast.

"So, Andy," said Earl, pushing the bill of his red Gardill Seeds cap up an inch or two, "you have any luck with that professor guy?"

Andy shook his head. "Naw, Earl. Robeson won't budge. He's going ahead with his book."

"You know," Bonnie said, measuring out a teaspoon of instant coffee, "maybe you two gals should just do the interview and make up stuff. He said he wouldn't use your names, so what would it matter? He'd be happy and you'd be rid of him."

"But I just don't trust the man," Elsie fretted. "We could still end up with our names in print as prostitutes."

Earl's face darkened. "Well, maybe it's time for me and Dennis to go pay this jerkwad…"

"Earl!" Emma snapped. "Language!"

The convenience store clerk flinched at his mother's rebuke as his girlfriend gave him a light slap on the side of the head.

"Sorry, Mom. Anyway, Dennis and I could pay him a visit, and give him an attitude readjustment. Betcha he'd sing a different tune then."

That didn't sound like a good idea to Andy. No how, no way.

Earl's brother Dennis was a security guard up in Herkimer County. Before that, he had been a deputy sheriff out in Reno, where he'd earned a reputation as a "thumper," a cop who liked to beat up suspects. He even shot a couple of unarmed perps. The department out there got sued several times, thanks to Dennis. For his part, Earl was known to be pretty feisty when he'd had a snootful.

Andy could think of few things more boneheaded than sending those two to the professor's house. But the negotiation with Lance Robeson was not Andy's responsibility. He had more than enough to worry about, with Aunt Bev's mayor mess coming straight at him.

Chapter Nine

King Harald lolled in the shade of the little maple in Elsie Bjorklund's backyard, gazing intently at a chipmunk that was loitering twenty or so feet out on the lawn. Harald knew he didn't have the slightest chance of ambushing the tiny rodent. But still he pondered how a dog as large and noticeable as himself might get the job done. His tactical scheming was interrupted when the back door of the house creaked open, and Elsie came out bearing food and drink.

The chipmunk, of course, skedaddled—gone in a wink.

"Here's some fresh water for you, Harald."

Elsie poured water into the bowl by the back stoop. Harald rose and trotted over to take a few laps.

"And a nice big dog biscuit." Elsie reached out her hand and Harald delicately took the doggie treat with his teeth.

He wagged his tail a few times to show his gratitude. To tell the truth, he wished she would give him something *really good*, like beef jerky or meat sticks. But any food offered ought to be consumed. He tumbled the biscuit farther back in his jaws and crunched vigorously, as Elsie vanished into the house.

He was heading back to his spot beneath the maple when he noticed the chipmunk, now out in the alley, gnawing on an acorn. Harald approached the wood-slat fence, managing to not spook the little critter. The dog hoisted himself up and put his paws on the top of the fence. Before he realized it, he had hauled himself over the thing, plopping back down onto the asphalt on the other side.

The startled chipmunk darted down the alley, with Harald in hot pursuit.

Just before the alley opened up into the street, the tiny rodent took a sharp right into someone's backyard, beneath another fence—vanishing from sight.

Harald slammed on the brakes. Foiled again.

But it was a beautiful, warm afternoon and it had been a while since Harald had gone on a ramble. For a dog, there was no time like the present.

A few minutes later, he was sniffing trees several blocks to the north. He could smell that a number of his canine comrades had passed and peed this way before. In an open green space down at the end of the street, he could see a pack of children running back and forth, shouting and yelling and kicking a ball. It looked like fun, so he trotted in that direction.

When he got there, Harald stood in the shade of a

basswood tree and observed.

He and the boss sometimes played with a ball. The boss tossed it and Harald fetched it, much to the boss's delight and high praise. But the ball these children were playing with was much larger. First, they kicked it in one direction and then in the other. Whenever that happened, they howled at each other.

Harald liked to howl, too. But not in the house. The boss did not like howling in the house. Harald had learned this the hard way.

He watched for another moment, then couldn't resist.

Charging across the lawn right into the scrum of small boys, he tried to grab the gaily-patterned ball in his capacious mouth. But it was way too big to fit. And it spurted off to the side. He scampered after the thing and pounced on it, covering it with his forelegs.

The ten or so boys gathered around, glaring at Harald.

"Oh man!" one of them whined. "That stupid mutt stole our ball."

Another lad came pounding breathlessly up from the far end of the turf.

"It's okay," he yelled. "It's okay. It's just Harald. He lives three houses down from us. He's a good guy. He won't bite."

Harald brightened and woofed his greetings. He knew this kid, who had patted his head many a time and even given him food. Harald never forgot anyone who gave him food.

"Now, Harald," the boy said, standing right in front of him, "you can't have the ball and you can't play soccer with us."

He bent over, patted Harald on his bristle-brush head, and gently extracted the ball from between his paws, handing the drool-covered object to another boy. Harald considered the youngster a friend, so he didn't resist.

"C'mon," the boy said, grabbing Harald's collar and tugging him upright. He led the dog back under the basswood tree. "You stay here, and I'll take you home when we're done."

As the boy ran back to his friends, Harald promptly pranced away, not in the least offended at having been kicked off the pitch for unsportsdoglike conduct.

Like most canines, Harald had a way of proceeding purposefully even when he had no particular idea of where he was going. It was a gift. After ten or fifteen minutes of ambling, Harald came upon a spot that proved to be familiar.

The boss had brought him to this place not too long ago. They had gone into the house, then back outside, under some trees. He remembered that he had chased a squirrel here. And he had seen something outside in the hostas that he had carried to the boss. Harald had found that thing oddly appealing.

Harald went around the side of the house to the place where he and the boss had been. He sniffed the chairs and the table, and could still smell the boss. That smell always made him feel safe and happy.

Then he stepped carefully over to the colorful little objects that had caught his attention that day. There were several to choose from, but he could carry only one.

Harald looked from one to another to another. Then he picked, plucking the object from its place in the dirt.

Now it was time to find his way back to Elsie Bjorklund's backyard.

Chapter Ten

Kirsten Skyberg lived with her husband Alan Vanska and two kids in a big brick house on a sprawling five-acre lot that overlooked one of Elbow Lake's more picturesque coves. Tucked away in the expansive back-yard was a one-bedroom guesthouse, also of red brick, newly built by Kirsten for her parents and other visitors. That was the first place Andy stopped when he drove out there for supper Saturday evening, after letting Harald loose to roam the fenced yard. The lindens and ash trees around the lot were starting to turn, and the dusky, spicy smell of autumn was in the air. Andy loved this time of the year.

It was about six in the evening when he knocked on the guesthouse door and heard a woman's bright voice from inside.

"Just a minute."

A few seconds later, the door swung open and Andy's mom grabbed him and gave him a hug.

"Good to see you, hon," Susie Skyberg said, hauling

him inside. "Your sister has a terrific meal planned."

"What's on the menu?" Andy asked, surveying the tidy living room.

"It's some kind of Mexican thing called pa-lel-la." Andy's dad stepped out of the bedroom, combing his thick white hair into place. He had on tan slacks and a blue plaid, short-sleeved shirt. Like Andy, he slouched a bit at the shoulders.

"Nope, Dean," his wife corrected. "It's called pie-ay-ah, and it's a Spanish dish. Sausage, chicken, shrimp, mussels, scallops, rice, tomatoes—quite a production, Kirsten tells me."

Dean Skyberg was a tall guy with a square, friendly face that frequently carried a look of bemusement, as he peered out at the world through his aviator-style glasses. He'd been a solid dad, a good provider, and a hearty laugher.

For her part, Susie Engebretson Skyberg was a tidy bundle of energy and enthusiasm—much like her sister-in-law Beverly. But unlike Aunt Bev, Andy's mom had a pronounced distaste for nutty schemes and garish hair coloring. *Her* gray was tastefully covered in a buttery blond tone.

Andy and his folks walked up the brick path to the big house, arriving just as a maroon Ford F-350 came rolling up the driveway. The pickup pulled in right next to Andy's Silverado, and an unfamiliar, middle-aged couple piled out.

The man caught sight of the Skybergs and waved.

"Dean, Susie, hi there."

Andy's dad waved back. "Joe, Mona. Good to see you. Welcome."

Leaning down, Andy whispered in his mom's ear. "Who are they?"

"The Coreys," she whispered back. "They were having their Airstream worked on, too. Up at Bilson's RVs in Hobartville. We got to talking with them. They're new to Beaver Tail County, and we're kind of showing them the ropes. Kirsten said it was okay to invite them."

The Coreys marched over to the Skybergs, grinning. Mona Corey was kind of short and stout, and walked with a spring in her step. Her husband had the build of an old football player, with a long face and piercing dark eyes. In addition to her purse, Mona was carrying what looked like a plastic container of food.

"Joe, Mona, I'd like you to meet our son, Andy," Dean Skyberg said.

"Howdy, nice to meet you." Andy shook Mona's hand, then Joe's.

"Likewise," Joe replied.

"Dean and Susie speak so highly of you," Mona said. "It's practically like meeting a living legend."

Andy gave her a slight smile, then looked at his mom quizzically: *What's she talking about?*

Andy was not the super-achiever sibling—that would be Kirsten. Nor was he the ne'er-do-well, loser sib—that would be Karl, currently dodging alimony payments in Nevada. Andy fell solidly in the middle—not entirely a disaster, but certainly not a living legend. He wondered if his folks had a higher opinion of him than he had realized.

"Will we be meeting your son-in-law tonight?" Mona asked.

Susie Skyberg shook her head. "No. Unfortunately, Alan's in Kuala Lumpur for a few weeks. Mergers and acquisitions work entails a lot of travel."

It seemed to Andy that his sister and brother-in-law spent only a few days together each month. He had a hard time understanding how a marriage could work that way, but theirs seemed to.

As they walked toward the house, Andy sidled up to Mona Corey.

"Whatcha got in the container, Mona?"

"Grandma Gorski's goblaki," she said.

Andy's eyebrows shot up. "Say what?"

Mona hooted. "Cabbage rolls. My grandma's recipe from the old country. Something for your sister."

"Wow, that sounds great, Mona," Andy said. Actually, he didn't like cooked cabbage, but why rain on anyone's parade? "My sister loves trying new ethnic dishes. Maybe she'll steal the recipe and put it on Ansel's menu. Only we'll call 'em Mona's Cabbage Rolls."

"Oh, then I'd be famous throughout New Bergen," Mona said with a grin.

Andy's dad opened the black-enameled door that led

into Kirsten's house and gestured for everyone to enter.

The first thing Andy saw was his niece Aurora, huddled in the nook by the staircase, engrossed in her iPhone, tapping and swiping with an index finger. As the two retired couples peeled off to the left, heading for the kitchen, Andy went right. He stood in front of Rory, waiting for her to acknowledge him.

"Ah-hmmmm," he rumbled in his throat. "Nathan Fillion is pretty hot, huh?"

Rory started and blinked up, like an abruptly awoken sleeper.

"Oh, hi, Uncle Andy." Her eyes went back to her iPhone, her thumbs tapping away on the little screen. "How'd you like *Firefly*?"

"You were right," Andy replied to the top of her head. "Excellent show. Like a sci-fi western in outer space."

Rory focused back on him, her thumbs still going. "Exactly."

"You joining us tonight? Bet your mom's paella is gonna be fantabulous."

She gave him a jaded, teenaged eye roll. "Not a chance. We're going to karaoke night at the casino."

It seemed improbable that a Goth-ish girl dressed in black from head to toe would be into singing Abba and Elton John tunes. But Andy knew Rory was not one to be typecast—she was as independent and sharp as her mom.

"Well, anyway, have fun," he said.

"You toooo-ooo," Rory replied, her sweet young voice dripping with sarcasm.

Andy was about to walk away when Kirsten's two cats approached from the living room, making a beeline for him. Ellie was the black cat, Kammers the calico. They knew he was a total sucker for petting, behind-the-ears scratching, and tummy-rubbing. Rory called them lap sluts. Andy squatted down for a minute or two and gave them what they wanted.

Andy's parents and the Coreys were already seated in their tall bar chairs around the granite-topped island in the middle of Kirsten's vast, fully equipped kitchen. Kirsten was pouring '09 Caymus Special Selection Cabernet into their wine glasses.

Climbing onto one of the tall chairs, Andy lifted his empty stem glass toward her. His sister poured the profoundly purple fluid into his glass. He took a sip, swishing it around in his mouth. The stuff was fantastically rich and dancing with subtle flavors.

Kirsten emptied the remains of the bottle into her own glass. Then she went out to the screen door and yelled, "Dylan! We're going to eat soon."

A couple of minutes later, Andy's twelve-year-old nephew climbed onto the chair next to him.

"Hey, Dylan," Andy greeted the sandy-haired, freckled kid, who was clad in camo shorts and a red Iron Man T-shirt. "How's school going?"

"It sucks, Uncle Andy," whispered Dylan, apparently not wanting to be overheard by his mom.

"Sorry to hear it. Having a tough class or something?"

"Naw, that's not it. I get mostly A's. I just don't like it. You know, I only want to draw. I want to be an artist like you."

Andy felt flattered—very briefly.

"Well, maybe not *exactly* like you, Uncle Andy. I don't want to paint pretty pictures. What I want to do is draw graphic novels. Like *The Sandman* and *The Walking Dead*."

Andy deflated a bit. "Well, you've got a lot more school to get through. But that doesn't mean you can't work at cartooning and get better at it. If you want, I'd be happy to check out your stuff."

Dylan brightened. "That'd be great. But keep in mind, I'm just learning. I'm only a kid."

One by one, Kirsten filled up every plate from the big paella pan and set them in front of her guests.

After a few bites, Andy turned to his sister across the granite counter top. "This is awesome, Kirsten. Are you going to put it on the menu?"

"It's a possibility," his sister replied. "The recipe is labor-intensive. Lots of expensive ingredients. It's up to Troy. He'll have to make it and make it pay."

Troy Dahlgren, Ansel's head chef, was a real catch for Kirsten. Trained at the big culinary institute down in the Cities, he had wanted to move to Beaver Tail County, where his dad had grown up. Troy's mom was Vietnamese, and he was starting to add some Asian fusion touches to the menu. Unfortunately, his spring rolls made with lefse, instead of rice paper wrappers, didn't go over so well with the natives. But Andy thought they were pretty tasty.

"Gotta say it's darned good," Joe Corey said, smiling agreeably. "But I'll tell you, the best paella anywhere is in this little hole-in-the-wall Spanish place just off Times Square. We celebrated our twentieth anniversary in Manhattan. Now *that* was paella."

Even Dylan seemed to enjoy the dish, except for a reluctance to deal with the several mussels on his plate. He very deliberately set those aside.

"So, Joe," said Andy, wiping his mouth on the napkin, "Mom tells me that you and Mona are fellow RV nuts."

"Yup, we're full-timers," confirmed Joe. "We both retired from government jobs in Nebraska. About a year and a half ago? Right, Mona?"

His wife gave a single nod, chewing on a big piece of chicken.

"Mona got out a little younger than me."

Mona swallowed. "Put in my time. That was enough."

"And the dream," Joe continued, "was always to hit the road with our Airstream and our Ford three-quarter ton."

"We sold our house in Lincoln and bought a cute little condo for a home base," Mona added. "One of our daughters lives in Lincoln with two grandkids. We get back to see them every few months. I've got some pictures. I can show them to you later."

"That would be great," Andy lied. "So where have you been lately?"

Joe put his elbows on the granite. "We've been to the Canadian Rockies, spent a good amount of time in Florida, a long stretch in Tucson, the big parks in Utah and Wyoming."

"We were just out at Zion a couple of months ago," Dean Skyberg put in.

"Aren't those red cliffs just gorgeous?" Joe said.

"And we've done so much that we never had enough time for," said Mona. "Bird-watching, photography."

"Sometimes we'll just hang out at a trailer court for a week or two," Joe said. "Get to know the people and the area. That's how we met your folks. We were having a little trouble with the electrical in the Airstream and brought it into Bilson's RVs in Hobartville. Saw their billboard up the Interstate. Susie and Dean were there, and they persuaded us to stick around Beaver Tail County for a little while."

"And now we can look forward to seeing a lot more of all you Skybergs," Mona gushed.

* * *

As Andy was heading out the door two hours later, his mom caught up with him.

"I'll walk you out to the truck, hon," she said, hooking her arm through his. "Didn't Mona's goblaki look delicious? I'm going to ask her for the recipe. It would be one way to get your father to eat his veggies."

Andy knew all too well that the only vegetables his dad willingly ate were creamed corn and tater tots. Things like broccoli and Brussels sprouts rarely sullied his taste buds.

"You know, Mom, even though I eat more veggies than Dad, I have to admit I've never been that fond of cooked cabbage. But it was real sweet of Mona to bring them."

His mother gave him a probing look. "Dad and I have been wondering about this mayor thing that Aunt Bev's trying to rope you into. Do you know what you're going to do?"

"Looks like I'm set to appear before the city council Tuesday evening. Could be by Wednesday morning your son will be mayor."

Susie Skyberg scrunched up her face in that concerned look of hers. "But do you really have it in your heart to take on the job?"

Andy's mother had always been sensitive to his moods and insecurities. As glad as she was to see the back of Tracy, her ex-daughter-in-law, she had been worried sick about Andy after the divorce. That was one of the reasons he had decided to stop licking his wounds back in the Cities, and rejoin the world. He just didn't want Mom to fret about him anymore.

"Kirsten thinks I should be mayor, too," he replied. "Anyway, it'd only be for a few months."

His mom looked up at him. "As much as you may

love them, you don't have to let either of those ladies railroad you, you know. It wouldn't hurt you to say no a little more often." She suddenly looked a bit embarrassed. "Except when I'm asking you to take the Coreys out to a few of your scenic spots for some snapshots. Could you, *please*?"

Trying hard to make a scowl, Andy grumbled, "No. Absolutely not."

Susie Skyberg wasn't buying it. She reached up and patted his cheek. "You're still as adorable as you were when you were five."

Andy grinned at her. "Sure, Mom, have 'em call me," he said, giving her a quick hug. This was one lady he could *never* say no to.

Chapter Eleven

"Want me to set up for the bookies?" a voice behind Andy croaked.

Andy looked up from the crossword puzzle he was filling in, and turned around to see J. J. Lindquist, empty serving tray in hand. The head waitress's froggy voice, she had explained earlier, was the result of a volleyball game yesterday up in Hobartville. J. J. had led her crew to a narrow victory. They celebrated in a sports bar only slightly less noisy than a roaring jet engine, yakking the evening away. "Guess I talked too much," she had whispered to Andy.

J. J.—named after two grandmothers, Joyce and Janet—had been a volleyball star in high school and junior college, and still played on the local circuit. She also played softball in the spring and did the occasional half-marathon. But Andy wondered how she managed to survive the post-game celebrations.

Fortunately, he wasn't her daddy. Andy had more than enough on his plate, with the upcoming appearance before the city council. Still, he worried just a little about J. J. and her drinking.

"Yeah," he told her, "go ahead and get the tables ready."

The fourth Sunday of the month was when the book-ies arrived and filled up several tables, after the brunch crowd had gone. They were the book clubs that Kirsten had approached about her "Eat and Critique" promo-tion—a special discount for dedicated book readers.

"Okay," J. J. croaked. "We got Doris Schattenheimer and her bodice rippers. Red wine and chocolate cake for them. Then there's Perry Elvik and his military history brigade. Beer and pizza guys all the way. The vampire erotica group is headed up by Marybelle Hillman. Red wine again, of course, and steak tartare on flesh-colored crackers. The cozy mystery bunch wants tea and *smør-brød*. Their fearless leader would be your Aunt Bev."

Andy scowled. "I hope she gets here early. I have a few choice words for the old dear."

Aunt Bev owed him big time for that slick preemp-tive move of hers on the mayoral business—handing out that flier even before he had agreed to her cockamamie scheme. But as Andy started to fashion his "few choice words," a familiar figure walked in through the door.

Lance Robeson. It had been a couple of days since their little kerfuffle over Elsie and Emma.

"Hi, Lance," Andy said. "Table for one?"

"Two for lunch, actually. Expecting a friend in a few minutes."

"Sounds good. Follow me, please." Andy led him to a quiet table right by the front window, away from the jabbering bookies. "Is this okay?"

"Fine, thanks," Lance said, looking at his watch. "By the way, I hope there are no hard feelings about our discussion regarding the two ladies."

Andy shrugged. He was still sorry about the pickle Elsie and Emma found themselves in, but there was nothing more he could do. "No, Lance, no problemo. I was just the messenger boy, after all."

"Good, good. And I wanted to tell you that the editor at *Cavalcade Weekly* definitely wants to include you and Harald in my article on canine crime busters. That puts you two in a hundred-fifty Sunday newspapers. I'd like to interview you some more, maybe get Cass Conlin's contact info. A professional shooter will call you about photos."

Andy placed a menu in front of Lance, and another on the opposite side of the table, and then went back to help J. J. The book club members were starting to filter in, and Andy directed them to their respective tables. When Aunt Bev arrived, he walked her to her group. "I want to talk to you when you're done with your group."

"Oh, what about, honey?" she asked innocently, clutching her hardcover copy of some M. C. Beaton mystery with a cranky, eccentric sleuth.

"You know perfectly well *what*."

She smiled sweetly at him. "Okay then. Later."

After all the bookies had been served their drinks,

Andy headed back to the lectern, just as the door swung open. He didn't recognize the woman who entered. She was quite attractive in a gamine way, looking to be in her late twenties or early thirties. Her dark brown hair was short and choppy, and she wore red capri pants and a black knit top, with a brightly patterned scarf tied around her neck. Andy grabbed a menu, but before he could speak, she put up her hand.

"I see my party right there," she said, and proceeded to Lance's table.

The professor stood up, seemingly determined to be welcoming and charming, despite his companion's tardiness. The lady, however, did not return his warm greeting. She sat with a plop and immediately crossed her arms over her chest, in the classic defensive posture. Andy couldn't see her face, but he bet she wasn't smiling.

J. J. nipped over, took a drink order from Lance's companion, and returned shortly with a glass of red wine. Then she quickly jotted down their orders and left.

A quirk of acoustics at the front of Ansel's allowed Andy to hear most of what Lance Robeson was saying, along with much of the woman's response. Andy wasn't a nosey parker. He tried to focus on the crossword he was working, but the conversation at the professor's table was just too juicy to ignore.

"I know you think I screwed you over, Brooke," said Lance. "But the situation changed after we made our arrangement. I had no other choice than to do what I did."

"Then why the hell didn't you tell me beforehand that you'd taken my name off the article? I didn't have a clue until I saw the journal. You relegated me to a footnote. A single, damned footnote!"

Her voice was as cold as dry ice and sharp as a scalpel. Andy wished he could see the expression on her face.

"Come on, Brookie. You're a competent young scholar and a pretty good research assistant. Don't get me wrong. But in this particular case I felt your work was weak and added little to the argument of the piece."

"Oh, spare me, Lance. You can't stand to share the spotlight with anyone. You want all the attention, all the glory." The woman paused a second. "And don't call me Brookie!"

Lance looked as if he were already getting bored with the conversation. "Well, *Brooke*, need I remind you that only one of us sitting at this table has had a book on the national bestseller lists. And only one of us has been on more TV and radio shows than any other history professor in this state." He gave her a little smirk and shook his head. "Be patient, my dear. If you put in your time for a few more years, you could earn some real recognition in the field."

Brooke leaned in toward the professor. To Andy, it looked as though she was ready to spit.

"It won't take me a few more years, Lance Robeson. If a journal won't publish my research, I know a major history blog that will. And I'm going to make it good and clear that you stole my findings and gave me one lousy footnote." She leaned back and took a gulp of her wine.

As the two antagonists were jousting, Aunt Bev approached the lectern.

"Anders, I want you to come over here and say hi to the girls," she bubbled. "They're so excited to meet the new mayor."

"Aunt Bev!" Andy groaned. "That's what I wanted to talk to you about. You know I didn't agree to…"

She grabbed his left arm and began hauling him toward the table of cozy lovers. Naturally, he couldn't air his irritation with his aunt in front of them, so he just nodded companionably to everyone. To a woman, they said that they would support his candidacy.

Back at the lectern, Andy tried to pick up the thread Lance and Brooke were spinning.

"And I'm going to help you get your first assistant professorship," Lance was saying in a soothing tone. "Just don't mess it up by jerking around the guy who can make that happen. Let this one slide. It's in your best interest."

"I'll decide what's in my best interest, thank you very much," Brooke hissed. "Now that I know how you really operate, I'm going to…"

The door to Ansel's opened again and a handsome young couple walked in, holding hands, grinning at each other—obviously very much in love.

Andy felt a twinge of jealousy. He wanted some of what that young guy had.

"Could we possibly get that snug little booth in the back?" the woman said. "We just love that spot."

Andy said of course, and led them back, catching a snatch of conversation at the vampire erotica table about the amatory virtues of vampires versus werewolves.

Normally, Andy would chat with each new table and give them some recommendations from the menu. But right now he wanted nothing more than to get back with the professor and Brooke. He seated the couple, left them their menus, and scurried away.

By the time he arrived at the lectern, the food had been delivered to the window table. Brooke was stirring her steaming vegetarian chili, while the professor nibbled on his butternut ravioli.

The two ate in silence until Lance finally spoke. "Brooke, if nothing else, consider the good times we shared. I'll never forget that little getaway to Napa, after the convention in Frisco. Not to mention those weekends down in the Cities."

She was evidently unmoved by his romantic reminiscences.

"I am going to report you to the ethics committee, Lance. I am going to write to the journal editor. I am going to publish my own paper. And I am quitting as of this moment."

She stood up. Lance stared at her with a look of anger mixed with surprise.

"You're making a big mistake, Brooke," he said, his voice as cold as a snake's belly.

"I could kill you, you bastard," the woman spat.

She grabbed her half-finished glass of red wine and threw it in his face.

Then she turned on her heel and stalked out of Ansel's.

Andy stood there with his mouth wide open.

All he could think was that Lance was darned lucky Brooke hadn't heaved her bowl of piping hot chili at him.

Chapter Twelve

Still marveling at Lance's baptism in wine, Andy left for home at four. He had been dreaming all day about throwing a frozen lasagna in the microwave and sitting down in front of ESPN for the evening. But he also felt a little guilty about not airing out Harald. He had left the dog in the house today, not wanting him to overstay his welcome in Elsie's backyard.

Harald didn't get all neurotic and barky about being inside all day, let alone chew and pee on stuff. Harald was a trooper, and he deserved a reward for waiting so patiently. A brisk walk would no doubt make him happy. But Andy had a better idea.

He went out to the back hallway and reached up onto the shelf above the coat rod. Groping around for a bit, he found what he was looking for.

Andy thrust the well-chewed yellow Frisbee in Harald's direction. "Whadaya think, big guy?"

Harald's eyes widened, he woofed, and his tail went into hyperdrive.

Twenty minutes later, the two of them were out on the big open field at Fred Barnes County Park, on the north edge of New Bergen, under a perfectly blue sky. They had the place to themselves.

Andy had seen plenty of YouTube videos of scrawny little pooches leaping high into the air to snatch Frisbees in flight. But Harald, frankly, didn't have the right stuff for airborne acrobatics. Except, it seemed, getting over a backyard fence—and that was more like climbing than jumping. He was too big and too slow. So Andy didn't put much juice or altitude on his tosses—just enough to set Harald a good pace. The dog caught most of them. When he trotted back, Andy always had to wrestle the yellow disk out of his jaw as the dog pretended to resist. It was a game Harald liked playing: *This is my Frisbee, puny mortal. Take it at your own peril!*

It was almost time to go home, after six-thirty, when Andy's phone rang. His first inclination was to ignore it and catch the voicemail later.

But not many people had Andy's cell number. Kirsten. J. J. Mom and Dad. Aunt Bev. Thor. A few other friends. It could be something urgent, though he didn't recognize the number.

Harald was standing in front of him, awaiting the next toss, looking impatient.

"Just a second, Harald," Andy said. Then he tapped the phone. "Andy here."

"Hello, Anders? This is Trina Makkonen."

Andy's heart jumped up into his throat. "Well, hi,

Trina. What's up?"

"I hope it is okay to call you at this time on a Sunday evening."

Man, Andy thought, that accent of hers sounded so sexy.

"Not a problem, Trina. Not a problem at all."

"Kirsten gave me your mobile number and she said you would not mind."

"Heck, I don't mind a bit."

Andy wished he could have said something a little more debonair. But thinking about those gorgeous lips of Trina's pressed close to the phone made him go all tongue-tied.

"Anders, I have spent some time reviewing the plans for The Nordic," she said.

"Yup, me too." Andy had, in fact, studied the notes that Kirsten had given him. He knew what had to be done. He felt well prepared to discuss some budget improvements.

"I know it is very last-minute," Trina continued, "but I am wondering if we could get together this evening. I am at the Medallion Suites in Hobartville. It should not take more than an hour or two to hammer things out. Peter called me this morning from Warsaw and he is very eager to finalize the deal with Kirsten."

Andy had known that a meeting with Trina needed to happen soon. But now that it was a reality, he actually felt a bit of stage fright. He didn't want to screw it up.

"All I need to do is get home and change clothes," he

said, trying to sound cool and collected. A super quick shower was in order, for sure. "I can be up there in about an hour, maybe a bit more."

"Excellent. I look forward to it."

As Andy disconnected, he turned to Harald, who seemed to be anticipating bad news.

"Sorry, boy," Andy said. "I've got some high-level negotiations to conduct, and we gotta go home."

Harald stared at him with sad brown eyes—like one of those old paintings of the huge-eyed waif children. It was pretty clear that the dog knew what was going on and was saying: *Please, let's stay.*

"I really am sorry," Andy told him, starting to back away. "Come on now."

Harald seemed almost to frown, then let loose a pitiful vocalization that sounded eerily like *Nooo!*

"Aw, don't be like that," Andy pleaded. "I mean, I got a chance to earn some major brownie points with Kirsten and hang out with a bodacious babe for a few hours. And I'm not gonna let *you* guilt me out."

Andy put a leash on the dog, and the two companions tramped back to the Silverado—one of them bubbling with anticipation, the other slouching in defeat.

* * *

Andy didn't know what to expect when Trina opened the door of her suite.

But he liked what he saw.

Woo-hoo, did he like it.

She was wearing a gray miniskirt with stylized black

94

cats printed on it. The skirt revealed her legs, glorious and firm, long and shapely right down to her bare feet. Above the skirt, a cropped white T-shirt clearly revealed the outline of a black bra underneath it.

Something in Andy's primitive male brain kicked in and he was unable to utter a word.

"Anders, hello," Trina said.

Andy hadn't noticed before that she had the slightest lisp. And it made her even more adorable.

"You are very prompt. One hour, just as promised."

He finally managed to say something. Something stupid.

"So, you like cats?"

Trina looked a little confused. Then, glancing down, she seemed to catch on that he was talking about her skirt.

"Yes, very much. I used to have them when I was a child. Now with all the travel…" She shrugged. "Maybe again someday. Do you have cats?"

"No, just a big ol' dog. King Harald."

Her expression brightened. "Your crime-sniffing canine. Yes, Kirsten told me about King Harald. I would like to meet him some day. Is he Norwegian then? With a name like that?"

Andy laughed. The girl had a sense of humor. "No, just a mutt. Maybe some Chesapeake in there. That's all we know."

Realizing he was sounding a bit like a dolt, Andy decided to bring the conversation around to the serious matter at hand.

"Guess we've got our work cut out for us. Kirsten really doesn't want to have to pull the plug on this little project."

He had taken that phrase right from Kirsten's notes. She had given him a road map of how to negotiate what she needed for the deal.

Trina's face registered concern. "Pull the plug? Oh no, Anders. I am sure we can come to an agreeable solution. Here, sit down and we will talk."

The gorgeous architect pointed to a streamlined, contemporary loveseat, and Andy nervously took his place there.

She sat next to him, curling her legs up under her. Andy noticed that she gave off a light floral scent. The lady smelled very good.

"You know," Trina said, leaning toward him, "we both work for alphas. Mine a male, yours a female. They like to have things their own way."

Having spent most of his life as the beta twin, Andy couldn't disagree about Kirsten's alpha personality. He'd been on the receiving end of it forever. But she *was* his sister, and his boss. And he was utterly loyal to her.

"Well, Kirsten has had quite a successful business career, and I think she feels pretty confident in her decisions."

"Of course. But your sister is fantastically lucky to get Peter for something this small," Trina continued, toying with a strand of her blond hair. "I hope she realizes that. And Peter is lucky to have a client with vision and the finances for what he sees as a very important project at this point in his career. I worry, though, that Kirsten is too budget-minded to appreciate this."

Andy nodded. That was not an unreasonable assessment. But Andy's job was to follow Kirsten's negotiating plan.

"You and I can make this thing happen," Trina said. "So let us put our heads together and see what we can come up with."

"Okey-dokey," Andy replied, then flinched at his colloquialism.

He pulled an iPad from the courier bag he had brought, along with copies of the budget and general schematics. He set everything on the coffee table in front of them.

By the time they had finished, three hours later, well after eleven, it seemed that a détente of sorts had been reached. Trina had identified certain features that Peter Kamu would probably agree to forgo, reducing cost overruns. In return, Andy slowly revealed his sister's concessions, granting each of them as a reward for every cut Trina agreed to. He was amazed that the final figures came so close to what Kirsten had predicted.

Trina gave a great sigh of relief. "Anders, we must toast our efforts to save this wonderful project. I bought a bottle of ice wine yesterday and chilled it, just for this occasion. What do you say?"

Andy had heard of ice wine—a kind of dessert wine made from frozen grapes—but had never sampled any. He knew it was fussy to make and quite pricey.

"Absolutely. I'd love to try it."

This had gone very well, he thought, as Trina went into the kitchen nook, where she pulled the tall, thin bottle from the fridge. He was satisfied with the results and pleased, above all, that Kirsten had trusted him to conduct himself in a business-like manner and not go all weak at the knees over the Finnish beauty.

Trina brought back two little juice glasses about half full of the chilled amber liquid.

"I propose a toast to The Nordic," she said, sitting down next to Andy.

"To The Nordic," he seconded, clinking his glass lightly against hers.

The wine was quite sweet, too sweet for Andy's taste. But he enjoyed being next to Trina, and he wasn't about to complain.

They sat silently for a moment, sipping. Then Andy spoke up.

"What was it like, growing up in Finland?"

"No different than coming of age anywhere in Europe or America, I suppose."

She told Andy about her family—father a teacher, mother a psychologist, sister a physician—and her experiences growing up in a small town near Helsinki. How she joined Peter Kamu's team when he was working on an opera house in the capital. How it was her dream to someday have an architectural studio of her own. She had already designed several cabins and houses out among the forests and lakes north of Helsinki, as well as a townhouse in the city center.

"And I suppose every one of them has a sauna," Andy said, feeling the distinct warming effects of the ice wine.

"Of course," Trina answered. "A house wouldn't be Finnish without one. Have you ever taken a sauna?"

The way she caressed that word "sauna," and made it dance and lilt, almost intoxicated Andy. In fact, he had never been in a sauna.

"It is best, Anders, if you are naked." She stared deep into his eyes.

Just for a moment, Andy imagined himself in a sauna with Trina, and not a stitch of clothing between them. *Whoa*, he thought, *best not to go there right now*.

He knew it must be getting late, but when he glanced down at his watch, he was surprised to see it was well past midnight. He stood, preparing to make his exit. Trina rose, too, and gave him a questioning look. Her perfect oval face and striking green eyes seemed disappointed.

"Do you have to go so soon?" she asked with a little frown.

Is this really happening? Andy thought. *Am I getting her vibe right?*

"Well, seems to me we've covered just about everything," he said, raising his eyebrows expectantly. "Or have we?"

She gave him a teasing look. "There is one more thing that needs to be *uncovered*, don't you think?"

"Well, I, uh…"

With a glint in her eye, Trina grabbed the bottom of her T-shirt and slowly pulled it off.

Andy was transfixed.

She tilted her head a little sideways. "You see, it is this bra I am wearing. I need some help taking it off, and I think you are just the man to do it."

Chapter Thirteen

Wearing a grin that threatened to crack his cheeks wide open, Andy tottered toward his back door at about four in the morning. His good fortune quite astonished him.

First, he and Trina had indeed hammered out the cost-cutting measures that culminated in a workable budget for The Nordic. The final details favored Kirsten a bit more than she might even be expecting. *Bet Big Sister will be pretty happy with my business smarts*, Andy thought with satisfaction.

Better yet, after the removal of that pesky black bra, Andy and Trina had come to another sort of culmination.

And Trina had definitely been the instigator. She made it clear that she wanted Andy in the sack with her.

But as great as the sex had been—and Trina was steaming hot—Andy hoped this would be the start of something bigger.

His affair with Cass Conlin had certainly been fun. But as for a deep connection with the swaggering lady cop… Well, it just wasn't there.

What Andy wanted, despite the scars that his ex Tracy had left, was a real lasting relationship. He wanted to feel that he was on the same page with his lady. Hopefully for many a long year. They'd worry about the m-word when they got there.

Of course, he didn't know Trina that well yet. No point in jumping the gun. But he had his fingers crossed.

As Andy stepped inside his house and flipped on the light, Harald stirred in his doggie bed just by the door. Looking a bit wobbly, he woofed quietly and heaved himself to his feet.

"You need to get out, buddy?" Andy asked apologetically. "Of course you do. Sorry to be gone so long."

Harald headed for the door, which Andy held open. The dog made quick work of it and plopped back onto his bed a couple of minutes later. Soon after, his master was fast asleep on his own mattress.

Even though he had only four hours of shut-eye—not much sleeping had been done at the Medallion Suites—Andy woke feeling refreshed and raring to go. He showered, shaved, let Harald out, fed him, and gulped down some bran flakes. Then he parked the dog in Elsie's backyard and headed to work.

It was Monday, so Ansel's was closed. But Kirsten had booked a lunchtime catering gig at Lovely Lena's headquarters. The setup was buffet style with some of Kirsten's most popular entrées—smoked salmon torte, beef goulash, and spinach ricotta gnocchi. There was a big Caesar salad bowl, trays overflowing with breads and desserts, and urns of Blue Mountain coffee.

As the Lovely Lena's guests started to stroll in, Andy caught sight of CEO Bud Storbakken and gave a wave. Andy knew he hadn't put enough time in on that painting that Bud had commissioned. The rendering of the North Woods cabin was to be a Christmas gift for Bud's wife, and Andy made a mental note to grab some studio time that evening.

A couple of hours later, he and Kirsten were back at Ansel's, unloading the chafing dishes and serving trays from the back of the Plymouth Voyager. Andy unaccountably found himself whistling.

"You're in an unusually chipper mood," Kirsten said, eyeing him suspiciously.

"Yeah," he replied, "I feel pretty pumped today. I think you'll like the deal that Trina and I hashed out last night."

Kirsten's eyebrows went up. "Wow. Working for The Nordic on Sunday night? That's dedication."

Andy gave a modest shrug. Fact is, he would have ridden a lame mule to Timbuktu with a blister on his butt to spend an evening negotiating with Trina Makkonen. Of course, he didn't tell his sister that.

"Do you have details for me?" Kirsten asked.

"They're on my iPad at home. I'll get 'em to you tomorrow, if that's okay."

She nodded. "And how is Ms. Makkonen?"

"Just peachy." Andy grinned a goofy, guilty grin that

he couldn't help, and his sister's expression darkened.

"And you looked, but didn't touch?"

Andy had never been able to lie to Kirsten. Even when they were kids, she always could tell when he was fibbing. But just as he started to reply, she put up her hand.

"On second thought," she said, "I retract that question. I don't want to know, okay?"

"Okay," he peeped, unbelievably relieved.

Changing the subject entirely, Kirsten asked, "So are you all ready for tomorrow night?"

What with Trina taking up his headspace, Andy had almost forgotten he was appearing before the city council Tuesday evening, to seek the post of interim mayor.

"Yeah, I've gone through denial, anger, bargaining, and depression, and now I've accepted the whole darned situation. It's like you said. The mayor doesn't really have to do much except show up."

"Sounds like the perfect attitude for a politician. And don't forget—if you run into any flak, I've got your back."

"Thanks, Sis," he said. "Hopefully it won't be filled with shrapnel before you arrive."

* * *

"Anders, could you please come here?"

Andy had barely climbed out of his truck, when he heard Elsie's voice. *Uh-oh*, he thought, *hope Harald didn't get into trouble again.*

"Be right there," he shouted. He jogged around his

garage and into Elsie's backyard. Harald met him at the gate, tail wagging. Andy gave the big mutt a pat on the head, then walked up to the back stoop, where Elsie stood, holding something wrapped up in newspaper. She wore a wry expression.

"Hi, Elsie. Whatcha got there?"

"Something I found tucked away in the hostas over by the garage. I don't want to point fingers, but I think one of us here put it there."

Elsie handed Andy the item she'd been holding.

Mystified, Andy unpeeled the crumpled newspaper, his eyes going wide, and quickly rolled it up again.

"Aw, Harald!" he scolded.

There in the day-old *Chronicle* was the very same pantless, aroused garden gnome that Harald had bonded with at Lance Robeson's place. Only someone seemed to have gnawed on the little fellow rather energetically. Not only did the dog steal the thing, he tried to eat it.

"So, Anders," Elsie asked, "do you know who that, um, *object* belongs to?"

He nodded. "I'm sorry, Elsie. I'll get this back to Lance Robeson. And I'll have a good talk with this guy about his behavior." He glared down at Harald, who was looking pretty sheepish, for a dog.

Harald, Andy realized, was starting to roam a bit too far from home. He always made it back okay, but something could happen to him. Next time Andy took him to the vet, he was going to ask about those invisible fences.

"Well, no harm done," Elsie said. "If I had known it

belonged to that awful man, I would have just tossed it. By the way, you don't need to worry about him bothering Emma and me anymore."

"What do you mean?"

Elsie crossed her arms. "Emma and I have pursued other measures. I think Mr. Robeson will find it's in his best interest to drop this whole matter."

"Fine with me," Andy said, puzzled but happy to no longer be a part of the Ole Bredahl drama.

Back in his own house, Andy pulled out his cell phone and called Lance Robeson. The professor seemed more amused than angered by Harald's thievery. He told Andy to bring the randy gnome over on Saturday about eight in the morning—the prof was booked solid until then.

"And I might have some interesting news to share with you," Lance said. "Something that could blow this whole Bredahl story wide open."

Andy was intrigued. "Can't you give me a hint?"

"No, I need to check through a few more sources. But I should have everything confirmed by Saturday."

"Sounds interesting," Andy said. "See you then."

"Oh, and one more thing, Andy," Lance added. "Tell the Shelstad sisters to call off their pit bulls."

"Their what?"

"Earl and Dennis Nelson paid me a visit yesterday evening. If they ever come onto my property again and make those kinds of threats, I'll call the cops on them. And I'll let the whole world know that I have evidence their prim and proper mother and aunt were teenaged hookers. Would you tell them that for me?"

As he clicked off the connection, Andy closed his eyes and shook his head, picturing the pair of blundering brothers confronting Lance.

"Those two fricking idiots!" he groaned. "They're only going to make matters worse!"

Chapter Fourteen

Andy had Tuesday off and he didn't want to spend it worrying about the city council meeting that evening. Frankly, he'd be relieved if someone else got the interim mayor's job. Still, he knew a couple of the folks on the council and he wanted to make a decent showing before them.

The best antidote for a case of nerves, he always felt, was to load Harald up into the truck and head out for a hike. On the off chance that the Coreys might be available—Andy's mom had asked him to show the couple some of the local scenery—he called them. Joe Corey answered and said he and Mona would be delighted to spend a couple of hours tramping through the woods with Andy and Harald.

Andy picked them up at Hopperstad's RV Haven, just outside the little burg of Apple Creek, and headed for Jonsrud State Park, not too far up the Interstate from New Bergen. The woods in the park were thick with oak and maple, and a picturesque stream ran through one of its loveliest parts. Moreover, Jonsrud had some of the best bird-watching in this part of the state.

The Coreys certainly came loaded for bird, so to speak. Both wore pricey Swarovski binoculars around their necks. Over his shoulder, Joe had a hefty digital Nikon with a big zoom lens—easily five grand worth of camera. Those two, Andy thought, apparently didn't mind spending their kids' inheritance.

Andy, his old film Nikon around his neck, led the Coreys into the woods. And the three headed down one of the prettier trails, with Harald on the leash.

Mona Corey, a bubbly woman with laugh lines around her eyes, peppered Andy with questions about life in New Bergen. She said she found the area charming, but couldn't imagine living there through the long, cold winter. Nebraska was bad enough, she observed.

Andy soon realized that Joe, a big, lumbering guy who huffed a bit as they walked along, was what a friend of Andy's used to call a "one-upper." Everything that Andy had done, Joe had done better. Everything that Andy enjoyed, Joe enjoyed more. Everything that Andy owned, Joe owned something nicer.

"So, Andy, you said you ran a limo service before you moved back to New Bergen," Mona said, as they trod along the hiking path by the stream.

"That's right," Andy replied. "Still have my Town Car in the garage. Use it for special occasions now and then. I call it the Black Beast."

"Mona and I have a Caddy Coupe de Ville convertible in storage," Joe quickly one-upped. "A 1965. Cherry red. Beautifully restored by yours truly."

"We could never bear to part with it," Mona added. "I imagine you made some good money in the limo business, what with all the big tippers you must have chauffeured around."

Andy had, in fact, made a lot of good tips. But it wasn't enough. "Actually," he said, "I pretty much lost my shirt. Making a go in small business is awful tough."

"That's why working for the state suited Mona and me just fine," Joe said. "No liabilities, no payrolls to meet, and a pretty cushy pension. Without it, we would not have been able to retire when we did. Right, Mona?"

"That's right, honey," Mona concurred.

At that point, Harald lurched off the trail and rooted around in some of the vegetation, no doubt searching for evidence of his evil adversary, the dreaded gray squirrel.

"I was a bookkeeper for the Nebraska Department of Roads," Joe continued. "Mona was an assistant to an assistant department head in natural resources."

"A glorified secretary," Mona laughed. "But most of my bosses were pretty decent guys. And there was one gal, too. Oh, look, a pileated!"

There, about forty feet down the trail, a big red-headed woodpecker was indeed perched up on a partially dead ash tree. Joe brought his Nikon up to his eye and quickly clicked off a few shots. Mona had her Swarovski binocs on the bird as well, and Andy focused on the creature through his zoom lens. The three of them stood there watching for a couple of minutes, until the woodpecker flapped off over the stream and into the woods opposite.

"That's a sight you don't get to see everyday," Andy said, smiling.

"One time Mona and I were out on a trail on the Keewenaw Peninsula," Joe said, "and we saw three of those little buggers. Separately. Though maybe it was the same one, coming back 'cause he liked having his picture taken."

Mona laughed. "Say, what kind of lens have you got there, Andy?"

Andy puffed up a little bit. "It's a Nikkor 70-300 zoom, one of the old ones. I just love the sharpness of it." He had taken lots of good pictures with that thing.

"I had one of those back when I shot film," Joe said. "It's, umm…" He shrugged. "…not bad. But this baby just blows it outta the water, Andy." He held up his digital camera to display the big zoom lens. "It's an 80 to 400 with vibration reduction. And I'm really sorry, but that old film camera of yours has gotta go. Get with the times, buddy! Full-frame digital. Only way to go."

Yeah, buddy, when I can afford five grand for a camera and a lens, Andy wanted to snap.

But instead he said, "Yeah, I'll have to do that someday."

He was ready for the hike to be over.

Suddenly, Harald started barking up a storm. Andy saw a deer darting across the path about one hundred feet ahead. "Too big for you, Harald," he advised his agitated mutt. "If you caught it, you wouldn't know what to do with it."

"I'm not so sure about that," Mona said. "He's one jumbo puppy. What the heck is he?"

"Mostly unknown, Mona. But we think some Chesapeake had a romantic tryst with a moose."

The couple burst out laughing. That line always got a good chuckle.

"We never had a Chesapeake," Joe Corey quickly interjected. He made that sour pickle look again. "Not a bad animal, I guess. But give me a chocolate lab any day. Now *that's* a dog. We've had three of them."

Andy was tired of being one-upped, so he decided to give Joe a little of his own medicine.

"Well, not to brag, but have any of your chocolate labs saved two people's lives? Discovered murder victims? Been in a national magazine?"

Joe looked at a loss, as if he wasn't used to having the tables turned on him.

"So Harald's been in a national magazine?" asked Mona, sounding impressed.

"Not yet," Andy said, leaning over to give Harald a pat. "But this big-shot history professor up at St. Magnus College is putting my crime-sniffing pooch into a story about animals that help police investigations. In *Cavalcade Weekly.*"

"That's in the Sunday paper, right?" Mona turned to her husband. "We'll have to keep our eyes peeled for it. We can send it to the grandkids. They just love dogs."

Andy stopped and squatted down face-to-face with

Harald. The dog attempted to slurp his nose, but Andy just managed to dodge that long, slobbery tongue.

"Well, I just hope Professor Robeson doesn't cut you out of the article," he said to Harald, "since you stole one of his garden gnomes."

"He *what?*" Joe asked.

Andy stood back up. "Harald likes to go roaming. He got over my neighbor's backyard fence, headed north about a mile to the professor's house—it's right south of Fred Barnes County Park—and grabbed the thing. The professor collects X-rated statuettes. You can imagine how my sweet old neighbor lady reacted when she found a naughty gnome hiding in her hostas."

Mona giggled, but Joe seemed to be struggling for a response.

"You should have seen how great our Christmas decorations looked," he finally blurted, obviously hoping to reclaim his lost momentum, "back when we had a house."

"Oh, Joe," Mona teased. "Andy doesn't care about our old Christmas decorations."

"Well, I'm sure they were very nice," Andy said graciously.

A half hour later, everyone piled into the truck and Andy headed back to the trailer court.

"That was great, Andy," Joe enthused. "Haven't had such a good hike in a long time. Thanks a lot."

"I hope we can have a repeat performance soon," Mona put in from the back seat. "We'd love to see some of the other places around here that you like."

Andy didn't really want to see the Coreys again, but they *were* his parents' friends. He had to be polite. Besides, most everyone had annoying tics. And if you could manage to get past them, you very often found lots of good qualities. Andy was sure the Coreys were no different. He just needed to get to know them better.

"Sure, guys, you betcha," he said. "We can do that. I know this great spot up in Herkimer County. It's absolutely stunning."

* * *

In all his years driving a limo around the Cities, Andy had little need for any sartorial distinction. He had started with one black suit, added another, retired the first, and purchased a third later on. Generally, he wore the cheapest white shirts he could find, paired with a small selection of black and red ties.

But with his appearance before the city council just hours away, he had been thinking about how he would look in a droopy, ancient black suit with a shiny trouser bottom. Much to his surprise, he found that he wanted to make the best impression possible on his friend Ken Young and the other four councilors.

So, after he dropped off the Coreys at their Airstream and took Harald to Aunt Bev's for a thorough washing, he tooled back up the Interstate to Hobartville. It was a little after one, and he made a beeline for Main Street and the county's only decent clothing store for business wear—Schwartzwalder's for Men.

Probably the last time he'd been in the store was about twenty-two years earlier, when he bought his suit for high school graduation. He could honestly say that the place hadn't changed a single iota.

There was dark wood paneling all around, and walls filled with suits, jackets, dress shoes, ties, and all the other accoutrements. The joint smelled of fresh furniture wax and shoe leather, and felt as classy as heck.

Greeting Andy when he came in was Phil Schwartzwalder, Jr., now well up in his fifties. Farther back, under one of the two glittering art deco chandeliers, stood Phil Schwartzwalder, Sr., easily eight-five, hands clasped behind his back. Both men were as trim and straight and dapper as ever. There was also a pretty young woman in a skirted business suit, whom Phil, Jr., introduced as his daughter Angela.

"Three generations on duty," Andy observed to Phil, Jr. "I remember when I bought my graduation suit from you guys."

Phil, Jr., studied Andy for a moment, his brown eyes darting up and down the lanky restaurant worker. "Hmmm," he said. "A 46 extra long. Dark blue with a light blue pinstripe. Am I right?"

Andy whistled. "That's impressive. You remember everyone you fitted?"

The gray-haired clothing retailer gave a slight nod. "More or less. Now how may we help you today?"

Andy explained that he needed a nice suit in a big hurry—like in two or three hours. Could they do it?

"Of course," Phil, Jr., replied. "As long as the alterations are simple."

He handed Andy over to Angela, who helped him select a dark gray, three-button suit with plain-front trousers. To Andy's dismay, the trousers needed letting out. That's what came of working amid all that great chow at Ansel's, he rationalized. Angela said the suit would be ready by three-thirty, if not earlier.

After she marked up the trousers with her little slice of soap, Andy changed back into his hiking duds and went out for a burger. He had more than enough time to come back and browse through Schwartzwalder's for a new pair of black tassel loafers, a light blue dress shirt, and a red-and-black striped tie. And the suit fit perfectly.

But it was the *guy* in the suit who had to close the sale tonight. Andy wondered if he was up to the job.

Chapter Fifteen

That evening, Andy had a simple supper of tuna salad on rye, creamed corn, and coffee. He put on his new suit, shirt, tie, and tassel loafers. He ran a comb through his hair. Harald, freshly scrubbed and tubbed himself, watched his master like a hawk. When Andy grabbed the fancy red nylon leash, the dog's tail started to wag. He knew something was up. Something more interesting than a walk around the hood.

"You wanna go for a ride in the Lincoln?" Andy said. "The Black Beast?"

Harald gave an eager woof to indicate his approval.

The New Bergen City Hall was a handsome limestone structure on the south end of Skjegstad Street. It had been built back in the 1950s, funded largely by a generous gift from old Georgia Dardenson, the chicken-brooder magnate. In her dotage in the 1940s, she had come to commune with New Bergen's old-fashioned, teeth-rattling winters. She was famously quoted as saying she was sick and tired of roasting to death in

Scottsdale. It was noted to be an ironic point of view for a brooder millionaire.

Andy expected the council chamber to be packed with supporters of the various candidates for the interim mayor's job, but in fact only twenty or so folks had shown up. At the front of the windowless, walnut-paneled room—festooned with framed photos of former mayors and council members—stood the tall, wide desk where the council held court. About a dozen rows of pew-like benches faced the desk. None of the council people had arrived yet.

Andy spotted Aunt Bev and Uncle Frank up in front, sitting with his parents. And God bless him, Thor Hofdahl was hunkered down in the back row with his wife Sonny. Andy's best human friend hooked a finger and signaled him to come over.

Heads turned and Andy could hear a few murmured words.

"There he is, that's King Harald."

"Oh, isn't he just *darling*? And he saved a woman's life."

"Wow, that is one big pooch."

Suddenly there came a piercing wolf whistle.

It was Aunt Bev, famous for deafening children with her ear-splitting whistles. Twisting around, she gave Andy the thumbs-up. "You look great, honey," she shouted. Dean and Susie Skyberg repeated the gesture. Andy's dad, in particular, was beaming proudly.

Andy went and sat down next to the Hofdahls.

"Thor, Sonny, thanks for coming to witness what may be the beginning and the end of my political career." He shoved Harald's rear end down into a seated position. The dog swiveled his head around, trying to see over the top of the next pew.

"I wouldn't be so negative," Thor said quietly. "I finally sussed out who your competition is. And I think you've got a pretty good shot."

"They're that weak?" Andy asked, surprised.

"Up there, just behind your folks is Derek Laska."

"Bill Laska's kid?"

He spied a skinny young man with a baby face and ramrod posture. He appeared to be going over some notes on recipe cards.

"Yup. Former president of the Responsible Young Americans Club at New Bergen High. Back from the university with a master's in public policy and not a snowball's chance in hell of getting a real job. I hear he's trying to catch on with Tim Steinhaufen's congressional campaign. He'd make Joe McCarthy look like a flaming liberal. And over there is Olive Van Houten. You know her story, right?"

Nodding, Andy shifted his gaze to the right and spotted a sturdy, middle-aged woman with short, curly brown hair. She was well known around the county not for her day job—a dispatcher in the sheriff's office in Hobartville—but as a perennial losing political candidate. She had even run write-in campaigns for governor a few times. Andy recalled that the primary plank of her statewide candidacies was to prohibit young people from skateboarding on public property.

Andy turned back to Thor. "That's it?"

"That's it. Unless someone comes out of left field, I'd say you're a shoo-in."

Andy gulped. The palms of his hands were starting to feel moist. What in heck had he gotten himself into?

"I'm gonna go sit up front, Thor. Say a prayer for me, so I don't make a fool of myself."

"Can't help you there, Andy," Thor said as Andy rose. "I'm an atheist."

"You'll do fine, kiddo," Sonny assured him. "Just relax and enjoy yourself."

Andy and Harald got up and ambled forward, sitting down next to Aunt Bev, who seemed to be bubbling and fizzing even more than usual.

"Isn't this just the most exciting thing ever?" She grabbed Andy's moist hand and gave it a squeeze. Then she reached over and tousled the dog's bristly head. "Aren't you just so proud of your master, Harald?"

The friendly mutt shut his eyes and leaned in toward the little henna-haired lady, apparently having forgiven her for the soap-and-rinse ambush in her backyard that afternoon.

"Are you nervous?" Andy's mom asked him.

"Well, a teeny bit," he confessed.

"Your boy's a sharp one, Susie," Aunt Bev declared. "He'll knock it out of the park."

There was a murmuring in the small crowd and

Andy twisted around to see his old teammate, Council-man Ken Young, striding up the aisle. The former quarterback spotted Andy and came over.

"Hey, Andy. Looks like you brought your fan club with you."

"How do you think our Anders is going to do?" Aunt Bev asked. "I hear that Lon Uppgren's on our side. Anyone else?"

"You can forget about Sara Higgins," Ken replied. "She wants to keep the chair empty until the election. She thinks that it doesn't make much difference."

Andy knew Sara Higgins only from her visits to Ansel's with her clients. A rail-thin blond, the attorney was a fierce advocate for women seeking divorces. Not a few ex-husbands from Beaver Tail County resembled flattened road kill after their courtroom encounters with her. According to New Bergen scuttlebutt, one of them had been Lance Robeson.

"How about Lars?" Andy's mom asked.

Lars Ostberg, the oldest council member, well up in his seventies, was also the longest serving. He had taught history at New Bergen High, a particularly weak subject for Andy. Mr. Ostberg had despaired of Andy's stubborn inability to make sense of the French and Indian War. For the would-be mayor, one battle had seemed pretty much like any other.

"We didn't get along great in school," Andy said. "I can't imagine he'd go my way."

Ken shrugged. "You never know, but you're probably right."

"So that leaves Jackie Morales."

"I'm optimistic she might put you over. Big supporter of the animal shelter up in Hobartville. On the board, in fact."

Andy brightened. That was where he had found Harald those two years before. Ken's idea of bringing the crime-busting canine into the council chamber was looking pretty smart.

"Seems my colleagues are starting to arrive," Ken said, making a sideways nod to Andy's left.

Andy took a peek over his shoulder.

Lars Ostberg and Jackie Morales were ambling up the other aisle, chatting. Behind them came Sara Higgins. No sign yet of Lon Uppgren.

"Before I take my seat, Killer, could you do me a little favor?"

"Sure, what do you need, buddy?"

Ken reached into his coat pocket and pulled out his smartphone.

"Would you take a picture of Harald and me? I'd love to have it up on my office wall. I got a spot open between my selfies with Chuck Norris and Alec Baldwin."

After Ken's photo, Andy joined his family. His mom and aunt jabbered at him, but he wasn't really listening. This was like some surreal dream. He felt as if he was being swept out to sea in a rudderless boat. The whack of a gavel on wood broke him out of his trance.

"I'm calling my last council meeting as mayor to order," proclaimed Sherm Bergholt from behind the raised desk. "Among the items of business are consideration of contractors for repair of worn playground equipment, two new liquor license applications, and the selection of an interim mayor."

Andy's hands started to tremble a bit.

There was no turning back now.

Chapter Sixteen

It was just after closing at Ansel's. But when Andy marched into the restaurant, still feeling disoriented after the council meeting, he found Kirsten, J. J., and Troy gathered around a table at the front of the café.

On the table sat a chocolate-frosted cake decorated with a bright orange cartoon dog and script that read "Congrats Mayor Skyberg!"

Aunt Bev came in right behind Andy, leading King Harald on his leash. Susie and Dean Skyberg followed, along with Thor, Sonny, Ken Young, Uncle Frank, and soon-to-be ex-Mayor Bergholt.

Kirsten hoisted a magnum bottle of Taittinger, already uncorked. "Everyone get in here and grab a glass. We've got bubbly and cake and we'll happily whip up a pizza, in case anyone's got the munchies."

Within two minutes all the revelers had a champagne flute in hand, filled to the rim—except Mayor Bergholt, a lifelong teetotaler, who had apple juice in his glass. Aunt Bev stood on one side of Andy, his mom on the other. Harald had been attached to a chair leg, given his proclivity for trying to inspect Ansel's kitchen.

"I must admit," Kirsten began, "that I never thought my twin brother would rise to such a high station in life."

Andy grinned along with his fans.

"But he did," Kirsten continued. "So, without further ado, a toast. To Mayor Andy Skyberg. May his brief term in office be rewarding and scandal free."

Everyone laughed, and raised their flutes. A flurry of additional toasts filled the air, as glasses clinked merrily against each other.

"Cheers to the new mayor."

"Skål there, Andy."

"To the big guy, go get 'em."

"Sláinte."

"Good job, sweetie."

Harald, who liked to party as much as the next dog, seconded the sentiment with a resonant *woooof*.

"I think the First Dog of New Bergen deserves a beer," Aunt Bev shouted.

Most everyone, it turned out, *was* feeling peckish, so Chef Troy Dahlgren, a quiet young fellow with a head of jet black hair, headed back to the kitchen to build a few chorizo and roast pumpkin pizzas. Andy ended up at a table between Ken and Mayor Bergholt. Right across from them sat Thor and Sonny. Nearby, Harald was contentedly lapping up the non-alcoholic doggie beer that Kirsten had poured into a soup bowl. J. J. circulated around, refilling the champagne flutes. Andy noticed that she already seemed a little buzzed herself.

"When are the reins of office handed over?" Thor asked, sipping on his freshly refilled flute.

"Andy and I are meeting at the city manager's office tomorrow morning," the old mayor said. "Judge Alstrup's coming down from Hobartville to give our young friend here the oath of office."

"So, Killer, how's it feel to be the new mayor?" Ken asked.

"Not too bad," Andy said. "It's still sinking in."

But the lanky restaurant host was filled with mixed emotions. He had been thinking about his future in New Bergen a lot lately. Opportunities had been dropped into his lap. The job at Ansel's, managing The Nordic and curating its gallery, the mayor's gig. There were plenty of good reasons to stick around, not the least of which was being near his family.

But what to do about that yearning for a repeat engagement with the big city? That dream of making it as a painter? Was it too late for Andy Skyberg? Why did it seem that everything he wanted was just out of reach?

As if some celestial being was hearing his thoughts—and saying "Not *everything*"—Andy looked up to see Trina Makkonen come through the front door.

She had on a black leather jacket, tight blue jeans, and high, high red heels that made her legs go on forever. She looked positively good enough to eat.

Andy jumped up and went over to greet her. About

Trina he had no doubts.

"Hi there," he grinned. "How'd you find out about this little clambake?"

She kissed him on the cheek. Out of the corner of his eye, he could see his mom and Aunt Bev scope it out. Busted! Andy didn't even care. Let them start the Beaver Tail County rumor mill churning. He was going to enjoy the moment.

"I talked to your sister today," Trina said. "She told me she was throwing a little party, whether you won or lost. She invited me to come."

Wow, Andy thought. That was really considerate of Kirsten. Did it mean she had given him a green light to pursue Trina?

"That's great," he gushed. "Why don't you come over and I'll introduce you to everyone."

As he took Trina around, Andy was careful to describe the lovely blond as the project manager for The Nordic's architectural firm. But both his mom and aunt were still giving him that look: *Is this the one?*

Andy parked Trina in between Sonny and himself at the table, safely away from Aunt Bev and his mom's sneaky questioning. He turned to Mayor Bergholt, who was tucking into his pizza. "So, Sherm, any words of wisdom you want to share with a newbie?"

The mayor was a round little man with a baldpate, pink complexion, and fringe of white hair. A highly respected CPA, Sherman Bergholt had always been a big booster of the town and played a mean cornet in the New

Bergen Community Band.

"You know, Andy, this is kind of a bittersweet moment for me. I've been mayor for almost twenty years. And I've had a blast. I've been proud to tell people, 'I'm the mayor of New Bergen, the greatest little town in our wonderful state.'"

He paused. "I know I'll miss the job. But the wife and I bought that condo in Sarasota and I'm seventy now, so it's time." He looked wistfully at Andy. "You might realize you're going to miss it, too, when you leave office next spring."

"And you did promise not to run for reelection," Ken interjected.

"You can count on it," Andy assured him.

"Until then, you'll have lotsa fun," the mayor said. "I've made up a list of events that you're scheduled to attend this fall and winter, in addition to council meetings and such. Any questions, just get on the horn to Florida. I'll help however I can."

"Sherm, what are your favorite memories?" Thor asked.

"You know, I started the tradition that for the Muskies' homecoming game every October, I bet the opposing mayor a buzz cut. His guys win, I shave my head. We win, he gets clipped. Right out on the field, after the game. We lost most of those games, but it's all in good fun."

"We're up against Hobartville this year," Thor observed. "And they've been mopping up the competition all season."

Andy thought his dark blond hair was one of his best features. But he couldn't really get his undies in a twist, fretting about losing it. Right now, his long day and unbelievable evening were finally catching up to him. Even a hint from the fair Trina that she would be happy to spend the night with him was gently declined.

Interim Mayor Anders Skyberg just wanted to go home with Harald and crash.

Chapter Seventeen

Thor and Andy were seated at one of the tall tables along the sidewall of Ansel's the next morning. Thor was working on a black coffee and a scone, Andy a cappuccino.

"You have any official gigs scheduled yet?" the older man asked with a grin. "*Mr. Mayor.*"

"Yup. Couple of interviews," Andy said. "Madge Juntenen called. Wants to set up something for next week."

Thor gave a single nod. "Editor of *The Beaver Tail County Chronicle*. Check."

"Then I make a visit tomorrow morning to Billy's Tacklemania."

"Billy Whitaker rang you up? He's gonna sing you a song, too?"

Billy Whitaker had been a staple of the local radio airwaves for decades, doing his down-home chat show from the bait and tackle shop he owned near the Flèche Droite Nation Casino. He also played twangy guitar and sang tunes of his own composition. Every one of the ditties sounded pretty much alike.

"Good grief, I hope not," Andy muttered. "But he gives a creampuff interview, so he's just about my speed for the first official Q and A."

"Sounds like you're off to a running start."

"Yeah, it'll be a hectic couple of days. We have a big catering job up at St. Magnus College tomorrow afternoon. A garden party shindig honoring Mrs. Steinhaufen for a million-dollar donation to the college."

Thor gave a mock shiver. "That is one tough old mama, I'll tell you that. You live in Beaver Tail County, you don't mess with Virginia Steinhaufen. I understand she's trying to buy a congressional seat for her grandson."

"Well, she's supposedly worth close to a billion," Andy observed. "So she probably can afford it."

"Andy! Good morning!"

Andy looked toward Ansel's front door and saw Bob Ludeman, one of the stalwart antique dealers of Skjegstad Street, march in. Bob was a diminutive guy who always dressed sharply, today in a beautifully tailored blue tweed jacket and crisp khaki trousers. He specialized in Art Deco and Art Nouveau jewelry and had loyal customers all over the world.

"Hey there, Bob," Andy said, hopping off his tall chair. He grabbed the man's soft little hand and shook it.

"I wanted to be one of the first on the street to congratulate you, Mayor Skyberg." Bob beamed at him.

Andy gave him a sort of *aw-shucks* shrug. "Well, thank you, Bob. I'm just about as surprised as anyone."

"You know, I think you'll be a darned fine mayor. Don't you agree, Thor?"

"I do indeed," the old socialist concurred.

"And this is for you, Mayor."

Bob reached into his pocket and pulled out a little red leatherette case that showed a certain wear and tear. He popped it open, and there on red velvet sat a lovely silver Art Deco tie clip with mother-of-pearl inlays.

"Bob, you shouldn't have," Andy exclaimed, touched by the gift.

"Oh, I beg to differ. Wear it in good health. And if I may just say one more thing?"

"Say away," Andy replied.

"We really need those new streetlights installed on Skjegstad, Andy. I hope you'll do your darnedest to make them happen."

Andy nodded. "Yeah, everybody on the street wants those. People are talking about bronze light posts with LEDs and Prairie School-style detailing."

"Precisely. And it would be awfully nice to update our Christmas decorations, too. They're state of the art—for 1965."

Over the next half hour, the new mayor was lobbied twice more by Skjegstad Street merchants.

Jill Robeson apologized again for the scene with her "bastard" husband, who still hadn't "found" her lost Custer letter. And she wondered if Andy could do something about the tardy emptying of the overflowing public trash bin in front of her store. She left him with the gift of a "Goldwater for President" pin.

Before she headed out, she asked, with a perfectly straight face, if Andy could order the cops to frog-walk her ex-husband down Skjegstad Street and pelt him with rotten bananas.

Andy said he wished he could help, but he doubted that fell within the mayor's purview.

For her part, Tonia Gilchrist, of Tonia's Trollhaven, wanted a four-way stop sign at the intersection of Perch and Spruce Streets, instead of a two-way. She said she had nearly gotten broadsided there twice in the last three weeks.

"These idiots just roll through stop signs," she fumed. "Like my red Hummer is invisible!"

Andy finally went to work at eleven, happy to take off his mayor hat and put on his host cap. During a pause in the lunchtime action, he popped back to his sister's cramped little office. She was tapping madly away on one of her spreadsheets.

"Kirsten?" he said.

She swiveled her chair around. "Yeah, Mayor Bro? What's up?"

"Haven't had a chance to touch base with you today, and I just wanted to thank you again for the party last night. It was great."

"Well, you deserved it, Andy. I think everyone enjoyed themselves."

"And thanks for inviting Trina."

"Seemed like the thing to do. And by the way, she just called this morning. Peter Kamu's okayed the terms of the agreement you two hammered out. We're good to go. Now we've gotta sign the deal and schedule the groundbreaking."

* * *

On the drive down the Interstate to Billy Whitaker's Tacklemania Thursday morning, Andy knew he should have been practicing his sound bites. But his mind was somewhere else.

Not only had Trina popped by Wednesday evening at Andy's house—where she fell in love with Harald, and he with her—but she had also stayed the night.

Climbing out of bed at five-thirty that morning, she had kissed Andy on his stubbly cheek, and started to get dressed.

"Hope you can stay for breakfast, Trina," Andy had said, sitting up in bed. "I make a pretty mean cheddar-and-spinach omelet. And I've got this terrific Tanzanian peaberry coffee."

"Oh, it sounds wonderful, Anders," she had replied. "But you cannot possibly imagine how busy my day is today. I have to get a PowerPoint finished, and then drive down to our offices in the Cities, for a ten o'clock meeting. I really have to go right now. You do not mind, do you?"

Andy did mind. As love affairs went, he enjoyed sitting around over a good meal nearly as much as the stuff

134

that happened in bed.

"No," he had lied as brightly as he could manage. "Of course not. You just drive safely."

Andy arrived at Tacklemania with five minutes to spare, a little before eight-thirty. The joint was a classic tourist trap of the type he had loved as a kid. In addition to fishing tackle and bait, Billy sold souvenirs, locally made foodstuffs and candy, the full line of Winnewashe Moccasins, gag gifts, and country western CDs. He featured a full wall of cheesy paperbacks and comic books. In front of the shop, under the awning, were some coin-operated kiddie rides—a little rocket, a dinky race car, a bucking bronco, a choo-choo train, a tiny motorboat.

Billy stepped outside the moment Andy pulled into the lot. He was in his full regalia. Cowboy hat, brightly colored cowboy shirt, boot-cut jeans with a bit of a gut hanging over the top, big shiny belt buckle, and alligator cowboy boots. His sharp features were lit with delight.

Billy's studio was at his desk in the back office. He had a standing mic hooked into his computer, which connected him via Internet to the station in Hobartville. Andy rolled his chair right over next to Billy.

Andy answered questions about why he ran for mayor, not alluding to the facts of a wily aunt and a jumbo martini. About his plans for his term in office. About his own history in New Bergen. About his sister's restaurant, and her new deli and gallery. And finally about King Harald's crime-busting adventure. He was pretty pleased with his answers.

"Now before you go, Mayor Skyberg," Billy finally said, "I got a teeny treat for you."

"Really? That's great," Andy replied, suddenly very afraid.

Sure enough, Billy rolled his chair a little sideways and grabbed the beat-up guitar that he had on a stand by the desk. He strummed the strings with his thumb, and nodded—apparently the thing was in tune. After a twangy little guitar intro, he launched into his brand-new song.

"I told you that I love you,
But still you want to go.
You said you couldn't stand it.
Your heart's broke, yes, I know.
If you knew good days were comin',
Would you change your mind, my dear?
The word is out, the people shout,
'Mayor Andy's finally here!'"

And that was just the first verse. There were three more, and an appalling chorus.

The truly awful thing was that Andy couldn't get the "Mayor Andy" melody out of his head for the whole drive home.

Billy Whitaker had given him a dreadful earworm.

Cruising back up the Interstate, he turned the radio to a rock station and cranked up the volume. It did no good.

He visualized himself in bed with Trina. And Billy was right there, singing in his ear.

He tried to focus on the thorny problem of Elsie and Emma and Lance Robeson. Had his neighbors really been hooked up with an old bank robber? Or was Lance some kind of persecutor of innocent old ladies?

And what was it that Lance had uncovered about the legend of Ole Bredahl? What was it he wouldn't tell Andy on the phone? Was it something that would implicate Emma and Elsie? Was it something that would inflame the Nelson brothers even more?

But as Andy pictured Earl and Dennis pummeling the persistent professor, their punches were delivered to the beat of Billy Whitaker's dratted tune.

Chapter Eighteen

Andy pulled up into his driveway and hopped out of the Silverado, still whistling that damned ditty. As he came through the back gate, King Harald welcomed him with a chorus of barks that broke the spell of the pernicious melody.

"Now *that* is music to my ears," Andy said, squatting down and giving Harald a vigorous two-handed rub on the neck. "Good to see you, too, Harald. You'll be glad to know your meal ticket acquitted himself pretty well on the radio."

Andy was scheduled to work the catering job up at St. Magnus College, but he didn't need to be there until two o'clock. Enough time to take Harald on a nice, long walk and make a dent in that pile of bills on the kitchen counter. With that new monthly check for his mayoral duties, he could pay the things a little quicker.

As he and Harald were heading inside, Andy spotted Dennis Nelson next door, working on the foundation of his mom's house. Andy detoured toward the white

picket fence. This might be a good opportunity to coun-
sel the former cop about the dangers of beating up
prominent professors.

"Hey Dennis, how you doin'?"

Emma's older son glanced up from the patching job
he was doing and stood. He swaggered over to the fence.

While his brother Earl was scrawny and wiry,
Dennis was built big and beefy. He had a bulldog face
and a pugnacious air—definitely not as amiable as his
little brother.

"Hi there, Andy, what do you say?"

He offered his hand and Andy took it, knowing his
knuckles would be squeezed hard. And they were.

"Not much, Dennis. Haven't seen you in a while."
Andy squelched the urge to rub his sore hand, not
wanting to look like a wimp.

"I hear congratulations are in order. Mayor Skyberg,
huh?"

"Just a weird set of circumstances, Dennis. What
have you been up to lately?"

"Still doing night guard work at the bank in Pinetop.
Part-time."

Andy didn't know what else to do but launch right
into his well-intentioned advice. "I hear you and Earl
paid Professor Robeson a call."

Dennis's expression turned sour. "Yeah, we read that
pencil-necked egghead the riot act. He's been harassing
Mom and Aunt Elsie. As good as calling them whores.
Me and Earl told him that if he ever contacted them

again, we'd beat the snot out of him."

Just what Andy was afraid of.

"Can I give you a little advice?" he asked tentatively, noting that the man's face was going red.

"It's a free country," Dennis snorted.

"You won't make things any better by messing with Lance Robeson. He's a well-connected guy. And if you touch him, you'll just bring a world of hurt down on your mom and your aunt."

Dennis glared at Andy. "Okay. You said what you wanted to. Anything else?"

"Guess not," Andy mumbled.

The security guard, without another word, turned and swaggered back to his patching job.

What a jerk, Andy thought, heading to his own back door. He and Harald had just made it into the house, when his phone rang.

"Is this Andy?" asked an elderly voice.

"Sure is," Andy replied.

"Cappy Briggs here, Andy."

"Hi, Cappy. It's great to hear from you."

Capitola Briggs was a retired teacher up in Herkimer County, who had helped Andy track down a legendary ebelskiver recipe a couple of months earlier.

"Well, I wanted to congratulate you on your new job as mayor. Didn't see that coming. Heard you this morning on Billy Whitaker. Wasn't that a nice tune he wrote for you?"

"Sure was, Cappy," Andy lied. "Can't stop whistling

it." That, at least, was the truth.

"And hearing you on the radio, Andy, reminded me of something. I want to get you up here for brats and beer before the snow flies, just like you promised. And ask your friend Thor and his wife if they'd like to come. There's no better time. The woods are just gorgeous right now. We're heading for peak color in a week or two."

Andy said he'd check with the Hofdahls and call her back. He did just that, and they set the date for two weeks out.

After his walk with Harald and a quick lunch, Andy put on a pair of black trousers and white shirt. He made sure Harald had plenty of food and water, and then locked the pooch in the house.

Andy arrived at the college just before two. The party supply company had set up a big canopy, beneath which tables and chairs were arranged. Big pots of multi-colored mums were scattered all around the roomy President's Garden, which was bordered by crisply trimmed hedges. The occasion was to honor Mrs. Virginia Steinhaufen and the big slug of cash that she had donated to the college.

Back in the dormitory kitchen they were using, Kirsten looked like a field commander, issuing orders to the troops. Andy stood waiting, while she consulted with J. J. and two of the other waitresses. Then it was his turn.

By the time the first guests started to arrive, Andy

was ready with his tray of wine and bubbly, wearing that fake grin that every food-service worker had to learn.

At least sixty folks had come to the alfresco buffet, and they all smelled of big bucks. Andy could see it in their clothing, in their hair, in their bearing. And most of them got face time with the president of the school. He was a short, fidgety man who had been a physics professor at St. Magnus in the nineties.

Andy loaded dirty plates and wine glasses on a tray to take to the kitchen. He was passing by the canvas back wall of the big rental canopy, when he heard St. Magnus's president through a gap in the material. He would have kept walking, except for the two words that caught his ear.

"Doctor Robeson..."

Reflexively, Andy lurched to a halt. He edged a little closer to the canvas. The president's voice was high-pitched, a bit adenoidal, unmistakable.

"...is one of our most popular teachers here at St. Magnus. And we wouldn't have our history masters program without him. I'm sure that he would never do anything that would be harmful to a leading family of Beaver Tail County."

"Perhaps you don't know the professor as well as you think," said an imperious female voice. "My grandson, as you know, is exploring a run for the U. S. House, and if Doctor Robeson's alleged findings are published, it could make that difficult."

A light bulb went on over Andy's head. He had a

good idea who this was. Virginia Steinhaufen herself.

Her family owned Steinhaufen Chemicals, a privately held firm that was estimated to have a market capitalization in the low billions. It had started up in Beaver Tail County over a century ago, but had moved its operations down to the Cities back before World War II. Tim Steinhaufen was an up-and-coming politico. His grandmother still lived in the family compound in the countryside near Bison Lake, and liked to throw her weight around.

"Has the professor approached you about his research?" the president asked.

"Heavens, no," the old lady snapped. "And if he had, neither I nor anyone else associated with Steinhaufen Chemicals would have spoken to him."

"Then how do you know what he's working on?"

"We have our sources."

"Can you give me any details about the professor's claims?"

"I hate even to say," the woman fumed, "but I suppose I must. The professor believes he has found evidence that a subsidiary of Steinhaufen Chemicals supplied the Nazi war machine in the months after Pearl Harbor."

"Ah, then I can understand your concern," the president said. "But here at St. Magnus, our scholars enjoy unfettered academic freedom. If what Professor Robeson has found is true and accurate, I don't know how we can stop him."

There was a brief silence, as Andy held his tray of dirty dishes steady. Wouldn't do to have wine glasses clinking against each other while in full busybody mode.

"I thought you might say that," Mrs. Steinhaufen said. "Consider my donation today for the new Steinhaufen Student Union as simply a down payment. I have also been thinking of two million for an endowed chair in chemistry."

Andy could almost hear the president licking his chops.

"But I think you know what has to happen," the old lady continued. "Or should I say, *not happen*?"

"You've given me some food for thought, Mrs. Steinhaufen."

"I hope that you and Professor Robeson make the right choice," she concluded. "In any event, you can tell him that it would be unwise to back the Steinhaufens into a corner."

On that cheery note, Andy tiptoed away, astounded at Lance Robeson's knack for raising hackles wherever he went.

Chapter Nineteen

The Friday lunch crowd at Ansel's was even heavier than usual, with diners waiting twenty and thirty minutes for a table. Luckily for Andy's parents and their friends, the Coreys, they had arrived early, a bit after eleven, and grabbed a spot by the window, just before the rush. Andy even had a few minutes to chat with them.

"Susie took me by your house the other day, Andy," noted Mona Corey. "What a cute little bungalow. Have you done any work on it?"

"Not really," Andy replied. "I'm renting it. The landlord had it in pretty good shape when I moved in." He didn't bother to mention that the landlord was his sister Kirsten, who had bought the house as rental property.

"And we saw King Harald in the backyard," Mona continued. "We always used to have a heckuva time juggling our chocolate labs with our work schedules and the kids' activities. So do you just leave Harald outside when you're off doing things?"

"It depends on how long I'm going to be gone.

Sometimes he stays in the house. And sometimes my next-door neighbor watches him."

"What a great arrangement," Mona said, just as the waitress brought a tray with four cups of black coffee. "And we heard that you've become a politician, Andy. Or should I say, 'Your Honor'?"

"Oh, no, please," he insisted. "Andy suits me just fine."

"We're darned proud of him," Dean Skyberg beamed. "How's the job going, son?"

"Too soon to tell," Andy replied. "I'm meeting with the city manager next Wednesday to get my marching orders."

"You know," Joe Corey interjected, "I was the secretary for our union in Lincoln. Very important job. Over three thousand in our local. I was instrumental in negotiating the contract in 2002."

Susie Skyberg reacted to Joe's comment with a smile about as real as a three-dollar bill. Even Andy's dad looked a teeny bit irritated—and it took a lot to irritate Dean Skyberg.

Joe, looking pleased with himself, had managed to bring the conversation to a dead halt.

"Well," Andy said, after an uncomfortable pause, "better get back to work. By the way, I really recommend the special. Cod and tomato casserole. Just *deee-licious*."

By now customers were starting to stream in and clump by the lectern. Andy spent a busy hour hosting.

Striding back to the front after seating a party, he bumped into his mom, heading to the ladies room.

"Oh, hon, I'm so sorry about Joe," she apologized. "He just can't seem to help himself."

"Don't sweat it, Mom." Andy patted her shoulder. "There are narcissists all over the place. I just don't know how you and Dad can stand to hang out with him."

"Well, they just kind of glommed onto us. And your dad's too polite to blow them off."

"And you are, too, Mom."

She smiled sweetly. "Guilty as charged. Anyway, every RV park and camp has a big blowhard like Joe. Just to give you a heads-up, there's a chance your father and I might be heading out to New England. Real soon."

"Leaving the Coreys in the dust?"

She nodded impishly.

"Pretty passive-aggressive of you, Mom," Andy kidded.

She shrugged. "Oh, and by the way, Bev's all excited. She's gotten herself a job as a part-time assistant events coordinator up at the Beaver Tail Lodge and Conference Center in Hobartville. She starts a week from Monday. The really good news is that she'll have a lot less time on her hands to dream up crazy schemes."

"Hallelujah! But why does she want to work? She and Frank don't need the money."

"You ought to know the answer to that. She's got energy to burn. She's gotta have something to do until she takes on Ronnie's mayoral campaign."

Back at the lectern, Kirsten was removing the daily-special insert from the menus. The cod and tomato casserole had sold out.

"What was that little pow-wow with Mom about? She had on her guilty face."

Andy leaned over, and whispered in his sister's ear. "Seems that Mom and Dad have had an ample sufficiency of the Coreys. They might head out to New England PDQ."

"Just to get away from those two?" Kirsten shook her head. "Where in heck did my pushy, Type A personality come from? It wasn't from Mom or Dad."

"Probably from some ancient Viking marauder," Andy blurted out, before he could stop himself.

His twin sister mock-glared at him, then grinned. "So I get my best qualities from Dagnar the Dreadful, huh?"

"Makes sense to me," he teased.

Andy's eyes wandered to the bar, where he caught sight of J. J. picking up a couple of lattés from Calvin, the bartender and barista. She was well out of earshot. He looked back at his sister.

"Kirsten, do you think J. J. drinks too much?"

She raised her eyebrows.

"We went to the new brew pub after the gig last night," he recounted, "and she just about floated away on the suds. I had to drive her home."

Kirsten looked over at the head waitress. "Well, J. J. always says she likes to work hard, and play even harder. So far, though, I've got no reason to complain about her performance."

Just then, Andy's parents and the Coreys got up from their table and started to head for the door. Mona made a beeline for Andy.

"Joe and I were wondering if you'd be able to take us on another bird-watching expedition," she said. "Maybe to that spot you mentioned in Herkimer County. It sounds just wonderful."

Andy grimaced inside as he smiled outside. "Sure. Why not? I've got your cell number, and I'll give you a call with a date or two. How's that sound?"

She grinned and gave him a quick, unexpected hug. "Andy, you're a gem."

She started to leave, but did a quick U-turn.

"You know, I never did get to show you those pictures of our grandkids," she said, pulling her smartphone out of her purse. "I got a whole gallery of them on this thing."

* * *

At a quarter to eight on Saturday morning, Andy tapped out Lance Robeson's number on his phone. Come by at eight with the filched figurine, the professor had said. Andy had wanted to reconfirm.

There was no answer, just his voicemail. But Andy was eager to get shed of the lewd gnome, so he loaded Harald up in the back seat of the Silverado. The obscene lawn ornament was boxed and sitting on the front seat. If necessary, Andy would plant the blasted thing in

Lance's backyard and leave a message.

A few seconds before he pulled onto the narrow, wooded lane that led to the professor's house, another vehicle came zooming out—a gray Chrysler van that was making like a drag racer. Andy had to slam on the brakes.

As the soccer mom-mobile roared past him, kicking up dirt and dust, Andy caught sight of the driver.

It was Jill Robeson. Scowling and red-faced. Gripping the wheel like a fiend.

"Looks like she just had an unsatisfying encounter with her ex," Andy said to Harald.

They pulled up onto Lance's gravel-covered driveway. Andy climbed out of the pickup, grabbing the box that contained the salacious statuette.

"Want to say hi to the prof, Harald?" he asked.

The dog gave a quiet little woof and wagged his tail. Andy released the hound, who jumped around for a little bit, sniffing everything within reach.

Stepping up onto the handsome stonework stoop, Andy punched the doorbell button and heard a gong sound inside the house. Juggling the box under his left arm, he waited for about thirty seconds. He pushed the button again, holding it down.

Dong. Dong. Dong.

Still no answer.

Andy sighed and glanced down at his ginger-colored mutt. "Think we've been stood up, Harald."

Harald snorted and headed for a clump of bushes.

Andy set the box down on the stoop, and pulled out a little spiral notebook from his shirt pocket. He flipped it open to a blank page and held it up to the doorframe. With a mechanical pencil, he jotted down a note.

Hi, Lance... Sorry I didn't catch you at home. I returned your risqué garden gnome and stuck him back by your patio with the others. Harald says he's real sorry and he'll never do it again. Thanks for being so understanding. See you at Ansel's...
Andy Skyberg

Andy ripped out the sheet, folded it in two, and opened the screen door. He slipped the note beneath the fancy brass doorknocker.

"Okay, Harald, let's go dump this thing where the sun don't shine." Andy snatched up the box and headed around the side of the house.

From the edge of Lance's patio, Andy regarded the little garden gnome orgy going on amid the hostas, then shook his head. Didn't Lance ever entertain people out here who might not be amused by such lascivious doings? Well, it wasn't Andy's problem.

He opened the box and extracted the lecherous little guy from the crumpled newspaper. Where to put him? He spied a good spot, near an amorous gnome couple.

"What do you think about a threesome?" Andy asked the two diminutive lovers.

Setting the bottomless figurine down next to the

acrobatic couple, Andy pressed its base into the dirt. He straightened up and backed away, checking out his handiwork.

"I think that's fine, Harald, don't you? A cozy little love nest, I'd say."

He looked around, then did a three-hundred-sixty.

"Oh, dogdammit," he groaned. "Harald? *Harald*?"

The big canine had silently vamoosed. And now Andy had to go find him.

Chapter Twenty

King Harald never got lost. The very concept of "lost" would have astounded him. His ancestors were hunters, trackers, wanderers—they always found their way home. The DNA that made him a canine gave him the remarkable ability to always be right where he expected to be.

Without giving it much thought, Harald was able to navigate himself pretty much through any part of New Bergen. Sometimes it was a matter of smelling or hearing something distinctive along the path. Such as that big cottonwood tree that always reminded him to have a pee and turn left to get home. Or the bunches of kids shouting near that place with the sprawling brick building and playground and the bell that rang.

So Harald decidedly was not lost after he left the boss on that shady patio. He had been in these woods before. He had even found that lovely little toy and taken it back home for the kind lady who looked after him when the boss was gone. Harald wondered why the boss had put the toy back in the ground. Maybe he wanted to play with Harald and wanted Harald to fetch it again. But Harald was bored with that particular game.

Out in the woods, he filed new information away, for future use when he visited this spot again.

There, on his left, was a crooked tree that he would definitely remember. And right near the bottom of it was a flicker of something bushy and gray that was moving back and . . .

Squirrel!

All logic and reason that Harald normally possessed evaporated in a wink. That ancestral instinct went *boom!* And he took off.

Harald was, for the most part, a pacifist. He was an extremely good-natured dog who had never bitten any-one in anger. True, there had been a few playful nips as a puppy, but no one had been hurt. It was all in good fun.

For some mysterious reason, though, he felt deep inside himself that squirrels deserved to die. It was not an idea, not a thought, not a fancy, but some instinct bred deeply into his bones.

Two times he had actually gotten a squirrel in his mouth. *Ooooh,* it felt so good.

As usual, his best chance of scoring depended on finding one of the little gray rodents out in the open, far away from the safety of the trees. But this certainly wasn't that kind of place, with trees and bushes and shrubs packed in tight. Squirrels had all the advantages here. Harald would need incredible luck.

And he very nearly had some, after he lost sight of the little gray vermin after the first twenty seconds of the chase.

He had dropped down on his haunches, listening and sniffing very intently—perfectly still, camouflaged by the shadows under the tree canopy. There came a very, very slight crunchy noise from his right, like tiny feet pattering away. Harald didn't even move his head, but shifted his brown eyes to the right.

Nothing there.

Then a tiny, twitchy nose poked out from a low wall of green leaves, followed by a nasty, twitchy gray face. The squirrel sniffed the air.

Harald held his position, but tensed up the muscles in his legs, ready to pounce.

The squirrel tiptoed out into the open space, looking about. Because the dog was in the shade and stock-still, the critter didn't notice King Harald, cruncher and muncher of vile gray rodents.

The squirrel came out fully in the open, walking as if on very tiny eggshells.

Without even thinking, Harald lunged and snapped his rather impressive jaws together, fully expecting to feel the mushy-crunchiness of a living thing in his mouth.

But all he caught was a mouthful of air.

The squirrel had vanished.

Harald huffed and growled a bit, then sat down to

scratch himself behind his right ear.

He could have continued his pursuit. But for Harald, the hunt was truthfully much more fun than the catch. Head held high, he decided it was time to rejoin the boss—if he could figure out where the boss had wandered off to.

Harald hadn't gone a hundred yards when he smelled something familiar wafting around him, something in the dirt and on the leaves. The scent of a person he had recently met. He followed the aroma into the weeds and shrubs on the downslope of a small hill, snuffling insistently. He bulled his way through brush and vegetation, until he came to a giant log.

Harald walked slowly around the log, stepping very delicately. He was on high alert.

When he saw what he saw, he went over and nudged it with his snout.

Nothing moved. Nothing happened.

While a dead squirrel was a very good thing, this definitely was not.

The jumbo mutt threw back his head and began to howl.

Chapter Twenty-One

Andy had put down the back gate of his Silverado, and was sitting on it with his legs dangling. Harald was lying in the truck bed next to him, covered in mud and burrs, wearing his leash, which Andy had wrapped firmly around his right hand. There would be no more impromptu excursions through the woods today.

The Chev pickup was still parked in front of the professor's house. But now people from the sheriff's office were scurrying all around the place, inside and out. Yellow crime-scene tape had been put up around the property and into the woods, which extended right into Fred Barnes County Park. The driveway and the road were full of official vehicles—squads, unmarked cars, the county medical examiner's van. Doc Hilgenberg's old black Caddy was there, too, parked up on the shoulder of the gravel-topped lane, a blue light winking on the dashboard.

Andy tried, but just could not get the image of Lance Robeson out of his head.

Homing in on the sound of Harald's howling, Andy had found Lance lying face down in the moss and weeds. The professor's arms and legs were splayed out. A deep, dusky red stain covered the back of his head, matted in his thick, auburn hair.

Someone, it seemed, had finally had enough of the professor.

As bad as Andy felt about what he had witnessed, Harald seemed even more dejected. The picture that went with the adjective "hangdog" in the dictionary might well have shown Harald just then, slouching miserably, as if he had done something really bad. Andy kept reassuring him that he was a good boy, but the dog would not be consoled. Andy could only wonder if canines were as traumatized by the sight of a dead body as humans were.

When Andy found Lance, he had immediately called 911 on his phone and given the operator the GPS coordinates. That's about when he started to feel a sudden nip in the air, as gloomy clouds moved in—that cold front the TV weatherman had promised. All Andy had on were his jeans, a khaki work shirt, and his New Bergen Muskies baseball cap. He was already starting to shiver.

The first cop to arrive on the scene, about twenty minutes later, was Barb Jorgenson. She was the deputy who had replaced Cass Conlin, and was an old pal of hers from the police academy. Barb's people skills were vastly superior to Andy's old girlfriend's.

"Cass told me about Harald's special little talent,"

Barb had said. "I didn't believe her. Gotta be kind of a pain in the rear for you, though, huh?"

Andy had nodded. "Oh, yeah. It was never my dream to have a murder-sniffing pooch. But then again, there's no telling how long Lance would have lain here before someone found him. Harald did you guys a favor."

"So, you know the vic?"

The new deputy was as darkly attractive as Cass Conlin had been prettily blond—curly black hair, deep brown eyes, olive skin. Andy might have even considered a run at Deputy Sheriff Jorgenson. If she had been single. And straight. As it was, he simply enjoyed chatting with Barb whenever she dropped by Ansel's. And through her, he caught up on the latest news about Cass and her new job with the FBI.

"Yeah, I do," Andy replied. "Long story, which I expect the sheriff will want to hear."

"Wouldn't surprise me," Barb said.

Soon, several other officers had come crunching through the woods, and Barb had taken Andy and Harald back to the Silverado, with instructions to wait. It was like watching some kind of army operation, seeing all the units and personnel that showed up. There were five deputies, a detective, plus the sheriff and assistant sheriff, as well as a couple of crime-scene technicians that Beaver Tail County shared with Herkimer County and another adjacent county. Doc Hilgenberg was the associate medical examiner—the county's part-time and only coroner. Down the lane, out on the county road, Andy could see a TV news van lurking, like a hungry vulture.

Fortunately, Andy wasn't scheduled to work the noon shift, so he didn't bother to call Kirsten or J. J. After about an hour of sitting on the truck's gate, he stopped Ed Vandegraff, the assistant sheriff. Andy asked if he could leave. Ed said no, not yet. Then Andy asked if he could use the bathroom in the house. That morning coffee needed somewhere to go.

Ed grumbled, but took him inside, leaving Harald tied to a maple next to the house. Andy had to put on paper booties and cheap rubber gloves. "Can't have you contaminating the scene," Ed growled.

"But I'll have to touch the handle, maybe the seat," Andy said. "I might blot out a fingerprint."

"Not a problem. The toilet's touchless. Just wave your hand over the sensor on top."

Andy was astonished at the condition of the front rooms, where Lance had his research library and office. It looked like everything had been tossed. Cabinet drawers were sticking out. Files and papers lay all over the floor. Books and journals had been taken off shelves and thrown around. The bulletin boards had been stripped of their clippings, notes, and pictures. Andy had remembered seeing a computer and hard drives on the desk. They were gone. A crime-scene photographer was tiptoeing around with his fancy rig, shooting every nook and cranny.

Out back, through the sliding doors, Andy could see Sheriff Delmar Mandsager and a detective hunched over a section of the brick patio. One of the crime-scene technicians was squatting down, picking up something from the surface of the bricks and putting it in a small plastic bag.

As the morning dragged on, Andy's patience wore thin—especially when the slate-gray clouds up above began to spit a light drizzle. He was about to move himself and his mutt into the cab when Barb sauntered by, carrying an evidence bag.

"Hey, Barb," he griped, "I've been here three hours. Can I just tell you guys what I know, and go home?"

She gave him a sympathetic look. "Yeah, you probably don't need to hang around. We're thinking that we got a burglary here, gone real bad. I'm not even sure we need much more from you. But let me find someone who can take your statement, okay?"

A few minutes later, Andy stuck Harald in the Silverado's cab, and went to sit in the front of a black-and-white with Ed Vandegraff. Ed started a little digital recorder, but had a pencil and pad at the ready.

"This is Assistant Sheriff Ed Vandegraff," he said into the device, "and I'm taking a statement from Anders Skyberg involving the Professor Lance Robeson case. Mr. Skyberg is the mayor of New Bergen."

Andy blinked in surprise. He still wasn't used to his new title.

"If you would, Mayor Skyberg, just tell me about today's events and your discovery of the victim." Ed hastily spoke the date and time.

Andy described everything that had happened. How he was returning the garden gnome that Harald had nicked. How Harald had taken a powder, and how Andy found him and the late professor.

"And you saw nobody else around here when you came?" Ed asked.

While he had been sitting on the gate of his Silverado, Andy had been calculating how much he ought to tell about the people who had it in for Robeson. He had performed some mental triage. He knew just what he wanted to say.

"For what it's worth," he answered, "I saw Jill Robeson coming out of the driveway as I was just about to turn in. Don't know the circumstances. But she was driving like a maniac. She looked awful mad."

Ed started to scribble.

Andy had decided he wouldn't mention Jill's operatic encounter with Lance at her store, unless he was asked. But he thought her lunatic driving and demented expression that morning were fair game. Naturally, a bitter ex-wife would be suspected in any event.

"Anything else to tell us?" the assistant sheriff asked, looking up from his pad.

Andy cleared his throat nervously. "You know that I work at Ansel's in New Bergen."

"Of course. I took the wife there for our anniversary. Just had our twenty-fifth." The lawman beamed.

"Well, congrats. Quite an accomplishment."

"Great chow. Pretty pricey, though."

At that, the assistant sheriff looked down at the recorder, and his voice took on a more professional tone. "You can continue, Mayor Skyberg."

"The thing is, I saw Professor Robeson get into a heated argument there with a former research assistant of his called Brooke. Don't know her last name. I overheard them and got the impression that he'd screwed her. A couple different ways. Had an affair with her and didn't come through on some professional favors he'd promised."

Ed jotted energetically. "Any more tidbits?"

"I got 'em coming out my ears. I understand that the professor was doing historical research on Steinhaufen Chemicals and old Mrs. Steinhaufen wanted it to stop."

The assistant sheriff's eyes widened. "How the heck you know that? You don't look like a one-percenter to me."

"I am decidedly not of that ilk. But I couldn't help overhearing her speaking with the president of St. Magnus College, where Lance taught. I was working a catering gig, just Thursday evening."

Ed suddenly looked at Andy with narrowed eyes.

"By the way, how is it that your dog happened to come all this way and steal the professor's garden gnome in the first place?"

This was the part Andy had dreaded most. He would have to tell about his unwanted entanglement with Lance and Elsie and Emma. He wanted to avoid tagging the old ladies as hookers when they were young. But he had to say what he knew.

"Lance Robeson and a couple of old ladies I know, neighbors of mine, were having a dispute. Elsie Bjork-lund and Emma Nelson. They're sisters."

Ed's face showed a glint of recognition. "I believe they go to the same church my aunt belongs to. She thinks the world of those two."

"Well, the fact is that Lance Robeson believed they knew an old-time bank robber named Ole Bredahl when they were a lot younger."

"Ole Bredahl?" Ed exclaimed. "I haven't heard that name in years. I used to read about him in my dad's crime magazines. And those two old ladies knew him?"

"Lance thought so. He wanted to interview them. They were dead set against it. They said they'd never been associated with gangsters. And they were worried their names would be dragged through the mud. Elsie asked me to go talk some sense into the professor. That's why Harald and I came out here in the first place. And I guess something about those stupid gnomes appealed to my pooch."

Andy paused. Should he reveal what Lance had told him about the threats from Earl and Dennis Nelson? Should he risk putting Emma and Elsie even deeper into the soup?

He was tired and cold and damp and sick of the whole thing. Let the professionals figure it out. Andy Skyberg had helped them enough for one day.

Chapter Twenty-Two

By the time Andy hopped out of Ed Vandegraff's black-and-white, the drizzle had turned into a down-pour—soaking him to the skin in the matter of a ten-second dash to the Silverado. It was that kind of day. The roller coaster that was his life seemed to be dipping into another deep trough.

Andy didn't say a word to Harald on the drive home, though he usually liked to share his thoughts with the dog. For his part, Harald, quite uncharacteristically, stared straight ahead through the back and forth of the windshield wipers. He seemed bummed out, as well.

Back home—after another soaking, as he ran from the truck to the house—Andy changed into some dry clothes and drip-brewed a single cup of peaberry coffee. Sitting at the kitchen table, sipping his java, he thought about Lance Robeson's fate, lying there broken and bloody out in the woods.

We'll all end up horizontal like that someday, he thought dismally. Someone would have noticed that

Lance was absent soon enough, he supposed. They would have gone hunting for him.

But what if Andy were to get bonked dead on the head out in some remote spot? Who would even know he was gone? Let alone come looking for him?

Sure, Kirsten would notice if he missed a shift. But what if he had taken some time off? He could keel over right here at home and no one would think to look for him for days. He trusted that Harald wouldn't try to eat him. But there'd be no one to feed the poor guy.

The thing Andy missed most about his ex-wife Tracy—and there was a lot he did *not* miss—was thinking that there was one other person in the world to whom he was Number One. Everything. Best of the Best. The Whole Enchilada.

Of course, it turned out he wasn't that to his ex. Never had been. But he had enjoyed the illusion for several years.

It was way too soon to hope that Trina might be the one. He had known her for only a month. But what if she *was* that person? He suddenly had a deep need to connect with her.

"Harald," he said, pulling out his phone, "I gotta talk to someone who can talk back."

Harald, lying by the table, still rather morose, seemed unoffended. He didn't even bother to lift his head or look at Andy.

Andy tapped Trina's number in his directory and put the phone up to his ear. Somewhere down in the Cities or up in Hobartville her phone rang. Once, twice, three times, four times. And then her voice came on the line, distant and mechanical—a few million ones and zeroes recorded in some digital chip.

"Hello. You have reached Katrina Makkonen of Kamu and Associates. I am unavailable at the moment. Please leave your name and message after the tone, and I will return your call as soon as possible."

She disappeared, and a few seconds later the beep sounded.

"Hi, Trina, it's Anders," he said, trying not to sound too needy. "I just wanted to chat for a bit. Had kind of a…rough morning…and wanted to hear your voice. Call back when you have a few minutes."

He put the phone down on the table, realizing that after what he had seen in the woods, he just didn't have it in him to work the dinner shift. Punching his sister's number on his phone, he took a deep breath.

She answered in two rings. He told her what had happened and how crummy he felt. She said he should absolutely not come in, and asked if he wanted her, or Mom and Dad, to stop by. When Andy said no, she urged him not to crawl into a six-pack of Biberschwanz and blot out in front of the ESPN.

"Isn't there someone you can be with for a while?" she asked.

Andy instantly knew the answer to that.

He said bye to Kirsten and made another call.

* * *

Andy had gotten to know Thorstein Veblen Hofdahl about two years ago, only weeks after he had returned to New Bergen. They had connected when Thor was admiring some of the Ansel Adams photos that Kirsten had up on the walls of her restaurant. They were the real deal, printed by the master photographer himself.

Andy had sidled up to Thor as he was examining the famous image of the boulder field at Mount Williamson, and asked if he was interested in Adams. Thor amazed him by saying that in his younger days he had roamed Beaver Tail County with a 4x5 view camera, inspired by Adams and Edward Weston. After Thor had finished his lunch, Andy took him upstairs to show off his soon-to-be painting studio. The two men had been fast friends ever since.

Sonny Hofdahl answered the knock on the back door and ushered Andy and Harald in, as her Border collie Angus yapped away outside.

"I had no idea you were at the crime scene," Sonny said, with a look of concern. "Must've been awful, finding him like that. The grapevine's gone into overdrive, of course, with all the folks seeing the hubbub out there where the professor lived. But no one knows yet what happened."

"Well, now you and Thor do," Andy said. "But you need to keep it under your hats. Orders from the sheriff."

"Oh, you betcha," she replied, as they went into her kitchen, still being transformed by contractors. "Have you had lunch yet?"

Andy suddenly realized he hadn't eaten anything since the bowl of cereal that morning. "Nope, guess not."

"Well, let me whip you up a nice goat cheese omelet and some coffee. Thor's back in his office. I'll bring it to you in there. And I can give Harald some dog chow. Angus will never know."

The second Andy stepped into his friend's office-cum-library, the crusty old socialist looked up from his desk—stacked willy-nilly with papers and magazines—and tipped his gnarled features slightly sideways.

"Well, old bean, you and Harald seem to have stepped into the deep doo-doo once again."

Andy lowered himself into the straight-backed chair next to the desk, and Harald plopped on the floor beside him.

"Crap on a stick," Andy muttered. "We really have."

"Tell me what happened."

And Andy did.

He told about how Harald found the body. How *he* found Harald. How the cops think it might be a burglary gone bad. How he himself thought there would be lots of suspects. More than a few people hated Lance enough to want him dead.

"I didn't tell you this before, Thor, but you know those two old sisters I live between?"

"Sure. Emma Nelson and Elsie Bjorklund."

Andy sighed. "The late professor thought they had some association with an old-time bank robber named

Ole Bredahl. Back in the '50s, when they were young and pretty."

Thor's pale blue eyes widened behind his old horn-rimmed specs. "As in boyfriend and girlfriends?"

Andy's phone rang on his hip and he put up a finger. "Just a sec, Thor."

Maybe it was Trina.

He looked at the screen, but it wasn't her number. "I'm sorry," he said, putting the phone away. "You were saying?"

"As in boyfriend and girlfriends?" Thor repeated.

Andy shook his head. "As in hookers and their sugar daddy."

"Those two!" Thor exclaimed. "They always struck me as pretty darned straight-laced."

"Now, maybe. But not back in the fifties. At least according to Lance. He'd been bugging them for an interview and threatened to expose them if they didn't cooperate."

"Ah, the distinguished professor wasn't above a bit of extortion."

"Yup. Elsie asked me to go over and talk some sense to the guy. But it didn't work. So then she and Emma sent Dennis and Earl Nelson to see him."

"Not the best emissaries," Thor observed. "Those two like to mix it up, Dennis especially. Their dad was the nastiest bar brawler in Beaver Tail County, back in the '60s. Rumor had it that he roughed up Emma from time to time, too. No one cried much when that eighteen-wheeler creamed his pickup. A blessing in disguise for Emma. She got a good insurance settlement out of it."

Sonny came into the office carrying a teak tray with a steaming cup of java and a big omelet, along with a croissant and strawberry jam. Andy thanked her and dug in.

"I imagine Lance had some enemies in academia, too," Thor said as Andy ate. "Academic politics can be as nasty as anything."

Andy pictured research assistant Brooke's red wine flying into Lance's face. But his mouth was too full to describe the scene to Thor.

"And then we know," Thor went on, "that his ex wasn't particularly fond of him, either."

Another vision popped into Andy's head, this time of a crazed-looking Jill Robeson flying up the road that morning. But Andy was getting sick of talking about the life and death of Lance Robeson. In fact, he felt a bit miffed at the man himself. The professor had managed to thoroughly spoil Andy's weekend.

"You know, Thor," he said, wiping his mouth with the napkin, "it seems like whenever something good happens to me, something bad comes along to cancel out the fun. I mean, I was just thinking I might have found a new girlfriend. You saw Trina at my party, right?"

"She's hard to miss," Thor said. "Sonny had a good talk with her and hopes you have luck with the lady. The wife thinks she's a catch."

"From Sonny's lips to God's ears," Andy said, gazing toward the ceiling. "Tracy totally knocked the wind out of me, what with running away with that Pilates coach, and the divorce and all. Then I find Cass, and wouldn't you know? We break up, too. And I was just starting to feel like I'm getting my mojo back when, *wham*, I get sideswiped by this ugly business."

Thor leaned back in his old oak swivel chair and knitted his hands behind his head. He regarded Andy with that probing look he had whenever he was mulling something over.

"Andy, you're a big boy. And you ought to realize by now that life's just a process of two steps forward and one step backward. If you're lucky. Excrement happens, my friend. And Harald there knows how to sniff it out lately. It's just rotten luck that he's roped you into another murder case."

Andy looked down at Harald, who seemed to realize he was being talked about.

"Yeah," Andy said to Thor. "Sometimes I wonder if there isn't a little bloodhound and police dog mixed in there with that Chesapeake and that moose."

* * *

By the time Andy got home from Thor's, the rain had trailed off to the east and a cool, partly cloudy afternoon had taken its place. He had stopped at the Big Valu supermarket on the south end of town and picked up a couple bags of groceries, including a nice big rib eye for that evening. He grabbed one bag and took Harald into the house. Heading out to the Silverado for the other bag, he heard Elsie shouting for him. Feeling unenthusiastic about another chat with her, he walked through the damp grass to the fence that divided their two yards.

"Hey, Elsie," he said, "what's happening?"

"Earl just called me," she said excitedly. "He said that one of his customers at the FillerUp told him there were all kinds of police cars and vans out at Professor Robeson's place."

Andy wasn't going to tell Elsie that he and Harald had set off the whole dreadful rumpus. Anyway, he had promised Barb and Ed that he would keep his trap shut. And he was going to do it—at least with Elsie.

"Really? What happened?"

She tried to not smile, but couldn't quite manage it. "Earl said the rumor is that they found the professor out in the woods, dead. Poor man."

Then, oddly, she winked at him.

"Don't you worry, Anders. This will remain our little secret."

Andy stared at her, baffled. What was she talking about?

Then it hit him.

"Elsie, I talked to the guy a couple times. That's all. If he died out in the woods, it's nothing to do with me."

"I understand," she said, nodding slowly. "*You didn't do anything.*"

"I didn't. I really didn't."

"Of course you didn't."

Andy groaned. "Elsie, if the professor was murdered, *I didn't do it*. Have you considered that it might have been Earl and Dennis? You sicced them on the guy, after all."

"No, no, no, no, no," Elsie said, shaking her head. "Earl and Dennis swear they didn't touch a hair on that man's head. They just tried to reason with him. And besides, they wouldn't hurt a fly."

"But Dennis beat up a bunch of people out in Reno and shot a couple others."

"That was his job, dear. In-the-line-of-duty, they call it. That doesn't count."

"Really, Elsie. You have to understand that I would not kill somebody just because you didn't like him."

"I understand completely. I understand that you *did not kill that man*." Then came a little Cheshire-cat grin.

Andy was growing more and more peeved with his neighbor. What kind of person did she think he was? After all, she had cajoled him into this mess in the first place, and now she was all but insinuating that he had bashed a man's head in for her.

Andy narrowed his eyes. "Will you answer me a question, Elsie? Straight up?"

The smile faded and was replaced with a look of wariness. "If I can."

"Were Emma and you Ole Bredahl's two angels?"

Elsie stiffened and backed away from the fence a step. "That is a question that I will *not* dignify with an answer. It presumes things about us that are just downright insulting. And if that professor somehow persuaded you that these are the facts, I think that you should look deep into your heart, Anders Skyberg, and ask yourself who your friends really are."

And with that, she twisted on her heel and walked back across the grass.

Andy wasn't ready to let her off the hook. "Elsie, one more thing."

She stopped, turned around, and gave him a chilly look. "Yes?"

"Did that thousand-dollar bill that Harald found a few weeks ago come from Ole's armored car heist?"

Elsie glared at him, turned her back on him, and marched into her house.

"That," Andy said under his breath, "is definitely a non-denial denial."

Chapter Twenty-Three

Andy slept like a rock Saturday night, something he hadn't expected, given the events of the day. It had helped that he had his rib eye with only one glass of zinfandel, and had spent the rest of the evening reading a spy thriller until his eyelids grew heavy. He managed, briefly at least, to blot Lance Robeson and the Twin Angels out of his mind.

His phone had rung three times during the evening, and each time he glanced at the screen eagerly, hoping to see Trina's name and number. But it was Kirsten once, then his mom, checking up on him. And the Coreys the third time, wondering if he was free on Monday for that hike up in Herkimer County. He said he'd pick them up at Hopperstad's RV Haven bright and early. An amble in those woods actually sounded mighty therapeutic.

Harald still seemed a little downcast and clingy on Sunday morning. So Andy called his mom and asked if he could drop the dog off with her and his dad while he was at work. He figured some heavy-duty pampering and petting from the folks was just what Harald needed right now. It couldn't be easy, being a murder-sniffing pooch.

When he arrived at Ansel's a little before ten, Andy felt refreshed and ready to face a shift full of ravenous brunchers. J. J. and the other Ansel's staffers were abuzz about the murder out by Fred Barnes County Park. The name of the victim hadn't been officially released, pending notification of next of kin. But the rumor making the rounds had him pegged as Professor Lance Robeson.

Andy kept his trap shut. He was prepared for Harald and himself to be outed as the duo who had found the dead man, but he was glad it hadn't happened yet.

Business was brisk. It was one o'clock before Andy had time to take a break and check his voicemail. His heart jumped when he saw a message waiting for him from Trina. She said she was so very sorry to miss him, and that she had been terribly busy. She would be back in New Bergen on Wednesday, for the contract signing with Kirsten and the general contractor. She looked forward to spending time with Andy and giving him a nice, long hug.

He was disappointed he couldn't talk to her. But hey, at least she wasn't blowing him off. There was ample reason to hope this thing might go somewhere.

As the crowd was starting to thin out after one-thirty, Lance's old research assistant, Brooke—Andy still didn't know her last name—came in with a female friend. The glum, angry woman he'd observed a week ago was nowhere to be seen. She looked happy, almost giddy.

The young lady she was with appeared to be about college age. Pretty and blond and wholesome looking. But one thing struck Andy when he seated them. She was wearing what seemed to be a genuine Rolex, not some street vendor's cheap knockoff. And the watch face was ringed with little diamonds that glinted like the real deal. Not something your average co-ed would wear.

Brooke and her companion ordered champagne the minute they sat down. J. J. carded both of them and quickly brought out the bubbly. The two were soon clinking their champagne flutes together.

Andy wondered what they were toasting. He sidled over to jewelry dealer Bob Ludeman, who was having a Monte Cristo sandwich at the bar. Bob, one of the biggest gossips around, knew almost everyone in Beaver Tail County.

"Bob?"

The prim, impeccably dressed little man looked up from his *New Yorker*.

"Andy, hello. What can I do for you?"

"See the two ladies at the table by the window?"

Bob twisted around and peered toward the front of the restaurant.

"I do."

"Do you know who the pretty blond is?"

"Yes, Andy. Her mother is a regular customer of

mine."

"Great. Who is she?"

"Rachel Winslow."

That didn't help Andy very much. "She's wearing a real Rolex. A diamond-encrusted Rolex."

"Well, why shouldn't she? Her grandmother is Virginia Steinhaufen."

* * *

When Andy arrived at the RV park Monday morning, Joe and Mona Corey were waiting by their truck.

"You drove the first time," Joe said. "Let me be the chauffeur for this outing."

Their destination in Herkimer County was a corner of a tract of federal forestland, historically called Olander's Wood, after the old Swede logger who had owned it a century ago. But it was rocky and hilly and not an efficient place for a modern lumber operation. So its pines and spruces had the chance to grow old and gnarly and picturesque, scraping out their livelihoods amid haunting rock formations.

With Joe Corey piloting his Ford F-350, and Mona and Harald sitting in the backseat, Andy navigated them in on a series of narrow, muddy roads. They went very slowly, especially on a stretch of rutted track at the top of the gorge, where Swenson's Rapids had cut through the rock formations. For the big pickup, there was about a foot to spare on either side—thick trees to the right, sheer cliff to the left. They ended up in a clearing large enough for the pickup to get turned around in, for the trip back. From there, they walked to the gorge to shoot photos and watch for birds.

"We never could've found this spot without you, Andy," said Mona. "It's breathtaking."

"Whoa, that first step is a long one!" Joe laughed, gazing into the gorge. "How far down?"

"Forty, fifty feet," Andy guessed.

"Very pretty," Joe allowed. "Almost as scenic as Wildcat Brook in New Hampshire."

Andy stifled a chuckle. *Of course you've been to someplace more scenic*, he thought.

"Not many people know about it," he said. "Kind of a secret spot for hikers and rock climbers and photographers. And kayakers like the rapids. A word of warning, though. These trails we're going on are full of rocky patches, ankle-twisters. So watch your step. We don't want anyone limpin' out of here with a sprain."

They walked back to the clearing, and from there went off into the woods and rocks. They trod only a mile and a half. But the hike took them nearly two hours. The Coreys were in bird-watching heaven. They went nuts with their Nikons, shooting hundreds of pictures. They even saw a bald eagle swooping down to a nest atop a lightning-shattered spruce.

Even unleashed, Harald behaved himself beautifully. He didn't spook a single bird. The dog still seemed a little insecure, nudging Andy for neck rubs and petting along the way.

Back at the truck, Mona set up three lawn chairs on a

dense bed of needles beneath a big eastern white pine. Joe put a little propane grill on a wide patch of dirt out in the open, placing it so sparks would catch no tinder. Andy laid out four burgers on the grill—one for each human and canine. If needed, he had a few more patties in the cooler.

Over by the chairs, Joe snapped the caps on a couple of Biberschwanz Pilsners. Like a moth to the light, Andy headed toward the beer. The sun was high enough that he took off his jacket. It felt good to sit down after the short but arduous jaunt.

"I can't believe how lucky we were, meeting your folks," Mona said between sips of her pinot grigio. "They've just been the best darned hosts you could imagine. And we even got to make friends with the mayor of New Bergen." She reached over and patted Andy on the shoulder.

He shrugged modestly. "Well, fortunately, the job's only gonna last till next May." The beef was starting to sizzle, so he grabbed his beer and stood. "I think I'd better check those burgers."

He went over to the grill and flipped the meat patties. He was feeling pretty hungry after their hike, and the burgers smelled divine.

"Looks like they're almost done." Mona had come up beside him. "I brought some coleslaw to have on the side. I had a little bit of cabbage left over from a batch of goblakis I made. You know—Mona's famous cabbage rolls." She grinned.

"Oh, yeah," Andy said. "Kirsten told me they tasted fantastic. Didn't you say the recipe was your grandmother's?"

"Yup. I spent a lot of my childhood at Grandma's house. I loved her dearly, but she was not your touchy-feely kind of granny. We didn't get away with anything." She sighed. "Makes me realize how much I miss seeing my own grandkids. Sometimes I think it would be okay to spend less time on the road and more time near them."

The wistful tone in her voice made Andy feel sorry for her. Every marriage involved compromises, he knew all too well. Maybe Mona wasn't as keen about the nomadic life as her husband was. Maybe she wanted to see her grandkids grow up, and be a part of their lives.

"You know, we never did hear any of the details about that murder case you got involved in last summer," Joe Corey boomed from his chair. "Your folks said it was a pretty close thing."

"Yeah, I figured I was a few seconds from the Pearly Gates," Andy answered, keeping an eye on the burgers. "I'll tell you, Joe, nothing concentrates the mind better than having a big ol' .45 semi-automatic aimed at your chest. I thought, *this is it*. Rest in peace, Andy Skyberg."

"I was once held up by two hoods with guns," Joe said proudly. "If the good guys hadn't arrived when they did, I'd be pushing up daisies now."

Andy twisted around and stared at the retired bureaucrat. The man's black, beady eyes were dancing with delight at having once again topped Andy.

"Oh, Joe, would you just quit trying to outdo Andy all the time," Mona said, with some real irritation in her voice. "I think those burgers look done now. Let's eat."

* * *

Driving home from his outing in Olander's Wood, Andy popped on KTIL-FM for a spot of its classic rock. At the end of a Clapton tune, the two o'clock news came on.

"Sheriff Delmar Mandsager announced earlier this morning that the body discovered under suspicious circumstances near Fred Barnes County Park, just outside of New Bergen, was that of St. Magnus College history professor Lance Robeson," the announcer said. "The victim was found Saturday morning by the dog of a New Bergen resident. Foul play is definitely a possibility, the sheriff said. An official autopsy is expected to be completed by tomorrow. Now, moving on to the mystery of the missing outhouse…"

Reports of the death had been on the news since late Saturday afternoon. But this was the first mention Andy had heard of Lance's name, and the fact that a dog had found him. He wondered how soon folks would connect the canine reference to King Harald.

Andy headed his truck into the parking lot at Griak's Garden Store. Kirsten had asked him to stop and pick up some decorative items for the sidewalk in front of Ansel's—corn stalks, dried flowers, pumpkins, and gourds.

Just as he was about to climb out of the Silverado, his phone ding-donged.

"Yup, Andy here," he said.

"Andy, Barb Jorgenson. Got a minute?"

"Sure. What's up?"

"We got a little favor to ask."

"Meaning the sheriff's office?"

"Uh-huh. We're wondering if we could borrow King Harald for a couple hours tomorrow morning. God knows how, but he sure does have a knack for sniffing out evidence. And we haven't had any luck finding the murder weapon anywhere near the late professor's place."

Andy was actually kind of flattered. It would be Harald's first professional engagement.

"No promises," he said, "but we'll give it a shot."

It took Andy twenty minutes to get in and out of the garden store. He was loading up the back of the Silverado with his purchases, when he noticed Jill Robeson. She was heading for the beat-up Chrysler van that he had seen her driving Saturday morning, struggling with a big pumpkin.

Andy darted over. "Hey there, Jill, I'll get it for you."

He grabbed the pumpkin. It felt like it weighed fifty pounds.

"Oh, thanks so much, Andy," she panted. "I thought I was going to pop a seam."

She trotted over to her van and opened the back.

Andy loaded in the bulky orange fruit, causing the rear springs to creak a little.

"That's what the shopping carts are for, Jill," he observed.

"I know, I know. I'm just kind of distracted. Still distracted."

"I'm awful sorry about Lance, Jill. Just heard the report on the radio. Really sorry."

"I'm gonna be honest," she said, her features hardening. "I really hated him for what he put me through. But the girls loved their dad, okay?"

"Understandable," Andy observed. "They've got a very different perspective."

"Yeah, they do." She gave him a long stare. "You were the ones who found him, weren't you? You and your dog?"

"Yeah, afraid so," he admitted. "Harald found Lance when I went to drop off something for him." He looked her straight in the eye. "We saw you coming out from his house."

"And you told the police, didn't you?" she said, not sounding happy about it.

Andy suddenly felt defensive, but he wasn't about to apologize. "Yeah, Jill. I mean, you were driving like a maniac, and you looked mad enough to chew gravel. I told Barb Jorgenson and Ed Vandegraff. I had to."

Her mouth formed a scowl. "I wish you hadn't, Andy. I really wish you hadn't. The cops were going to talk with me about Lance, one way or another. It doesn't help that you saw me leaving the scene of the crime. They already know we had a pretty nasty divorce." She paused. "I'm curious, what were you doing out there?"

Andy didn't want to go into the whole naughty gnome story. "Lance had an interest in two elderly sisters who live on either side of me. He thought they had some association with the old-time bank robber Ole Bredahl. I was trying to persuade him to leave them alone."

"Oh, *that*." Jill rolled her eyes. "Bredahl was one of Lance's little obsessions. He always wanted to get Ole into a book. Thought that big heist of his was a great story."

"I got the impression you and Lance were barely talking to each other." Andy said. "So why were *you* out there Saturday morning?"

"It was about that damned Custer letter. Lance told me he'd found it. And he wanted to give it back to me. So when I knocked on the door and he didn't answer, I figured he was just screwing with me—a typical Lance stunt."

Andy wondered if Lance had taken out a big life insurance policy that benefited their daughters. That—plus Jill's animus for her ex—could be a motive to kill. But he didn't have the nerve to ask. Somehow, though, Jill seemed to know what he was thinking.

"Listen, Andy, I didn't touch Lance. I really didn't. But to be perfectly honest, if I knew who did, I'd buy the guy a drink and a nice, juicy steak."

Chapter Twenty-Four

Harald had been to this place before. Twice with the boss. Another time on his own. When he found that nifty gift for the old lady who sometimes took care of him.

But this morning, Harald did not want to be here. He remembered, all too well, what he had found out in the woods behind the house just a few days earlier. Someone dead, lying motionless on the ground. It was not a pleasant memory. It made him feel sad. Sad enough that his tail stopped wagging and his ears drooped and he slouched.

He sure wondered why the boss brought him here. He wished they'd gone to play with the yellow disk instead.

Even more baffling was the way the boss and the woman who was there kept thrusting those pieces of cloth at his nose, as he sat on his haunches. Of course, he knew the scent, which had belonged to the dead person. What did it mean?

The boss must have had a good reason to bring him

here. But danged if Harald could figure it out. The boss just baffled him sometimes.

"Okay, super sniffer," the boss said. "Let's go out in the woods and see what we can find."

He unclipped Harald's leash. "Go on, Harald. Vamoose. We'll be right behind you."

Harald blinked up at him, slouched a little deeper, and did not budge.

"Shoo, Harald. Go do your thing."

Of course, it was just gibberish to Harald. But he had an inkling of what the boss wanted, and he was having no part of it.

No more dead bodies. Nuh huh. No way. Not going anywhere.

"I think he doesn't understand," the woman said.

"I think maybe he does," the boss said. "And he doesn't want to do it. Maybe I need to lead by example."

He came over and clipped the leash to Harald's collar, then led him gently into the scrub and undergrowth.

Now Harald understood. They were going for a walk in the woods.

For a good hour and a half, Harald led the boss and the woman randomly through the trees and brush, stopping from time to time to mark a trunk. He attempted unsuccessfully to engage the boss in a game of fetch-the-stick. He quite enjoyed taking them through thickets and brambles.

Finally, the boss took charge. He started to lead

Harald back out of the woods.

"Well, I think that's enough of that, Barb," the boss said.

"Hey, we tried," the woman answered. "I really appreciate you guys coming. Can't expect a miracle every time."

A few minutes later, Harald came across a scent that brought him up short. He stubbornly refused to move a step farther, even as the boss tugged on his leash.

"You ornery ol' mutt," the boss said, a bit impatiently, "what is it?"

"Let him have his head, and let's see," the woman said.

Andy unleashed Harald, who stepped off at right angles to the path they were on. The boss and the woman followed him into the brush.

Leading his companions back and forth, around a certain spot thick with weeds and scrub, Harald sniffed the ground vigorously. It didn't take him long to find what he was looking for.

He stepped slowly over, bent down a little, and nudged the thing with his nose. Then he delicately picked it up with his mouth and turned around. He dropped the object he had found at the boss's feet.

"Holy cow, Harald, you found it," the boss said.

The woman squatted down and looked closely at the thing. "One of the professor's gnomes."

"A well-endowed lady gnome," the boss said.

"Andy, I see some auburn-colored hairs sticking

between her boobs, and some blood in the striations on the surface. This has gotta be the murder weapon."

Chapter Twenty-Five

Andy's first official meeting with the city manager on Wednesday morning was short and sweet.

"The mayor's job is really very simple," she told him in her city hall office, as she petted Harald's bristly head. The dog stood contentedly next to her chair while she gave Andy a rundown of his duties.

Nadine Rosenberg had done the grunt work of managing the New Bergen city government for the last five years and was well-respected around town. She was the one who made the trains run on time—that is, if New Bergen had had any trains. The middle-aged single mom had come from a similar job in Ohio.

"Your chief responsibility, Andy, is to show up for meetings and events on time. And to not say anything dumb." She handed him a sheet of paper. "Here's your schedule for the rest of the year. It's mainly officiating at ceremonial occasions. And city council meetings. You have no vote, of course, but you call the meetings to order, and close them. We also have a couple of visits set up down to the state capitol. Lobbying. We really need some dollars for those new street lamps we want on Skjegstad."

"Yeah," Andy said. "Those lights will really class up the downtown. People have been asking about them."

"Your first official gig is the ribbon cutting at the new Little Daizy Day Care next Monday," Nadine continued. "It's on your schedule. Of course, as you circulate around town, feel free to book dates on your own. But if you do, please let my assistant Wanda know."

"Okay, sure," Andy said. "I know Wanda from high school. She was in glee club with my sister."

"Now, I've got a question for you."

"Shoot," Andy replied.

"How much do you know about civic government?"

"Pretty much the stuff I Googled and found on Wikipedia."

"A good start. But I'd like you to bone up a little more."

She opened one of her desk drawers, pulled out a book, and handed it to him. "Read this."

Andy looked at the cover: *Civic Government for Dimwits*. Actually, not a bad idea. "Thanks, Nadine, I'll do that."

The city manager leaned over and let Harald lick her cheek. "Tell me, Andy, how the heck did Harald here go and find another body?"

Andy and Harald's names had been in the morning

paper, so the cat—well, *dog*—was out of the bag.

"Just doggone bad luck," he quipped.

As he exited city hall, Andy ran into Ken Young entering the building.

"Hey there, Ken," he said. "Just got my marching orders from Nadine. I'm going to open the new day care center next Monday."

"Good one," the councilman said. "But if I were you," he advised, eyeing Harald, "I wouldn't bring your dog. We sure don't need him to find another body, do we? Especially in front of a bunch of toddlers."

* * *

Inking the deal with Peter Kamu Associates and Helgerson Construction later that day seemed reason enough for celebration. Kirsten, Peter, and George Helgerson, Jr., had gathered in Kirsten's meeting room above Ansel's at mid-afternoon. Andy and Trina were in attendance, as well. After the three interested parties had jotted down their John Hancocks on the contracts, Andy opened the bottle of Dom Pérignon that he had chilled earlier that day. Toasts were made to The Nordic and everyone involved.

A bit after four o'clock, Kirsten ushered Peter and George down the stairs, leaving Andy and Trina alone in the meeting room. The blond architect drew close to Andy, giving him a look that married affection with a certain unease.

"I am so sorry I was not able to talk to you over the last few days, Anders," she said, taking his hand in hers.

"I know how difficult it has been for you and poor King Harald. What a terrible thing, finding that dead man. But you would not believe how jammed my schedule has been. Tonight, though, I am all yours. If you will have me."

"Oh yes, please," Andy grinned. "As much of you as you can spare."

"I can spare quite a lot. In fact, I would be honored if you will accompany me to dinner at Chez Louie in Hobartville. I have taken the liberty of making reservations. And it will be my treat, courtesy of Kamu and Associates."

Andy started to object. He was so darned happy to see her, he didn't mind picking up the tab.

"No, Trina, I'd really like to pay."

"I will have no protestations of male chivalry," she said firmly. "After all, you are a deductible expense."

* * *

After his braised leg of lamb and that lovely '03 Château Palmer at Chez Louie, Andy was amazed that he hadn't nodded off when they got back to Trina's suite. But having Trina next to him on the plush king-sized bed, in a state of total undress, was strong motivation to stay awake. He didn't want to miss a single minute of wonderful her.

In addition to being drop-dead gorgeous, Trina was whip-smart, funny, observant, and a great listener. One thing Andy found very refreshing about her was her apparent disinterest in his own romantic back story.

Most women whom Andy had gone steady with—as they used to say—wanted to know about the *other* women he had gone with. What were they like? Were they pretty? Why did he break up with them? Andy never understood the fascination.

Trina hadn't even asked if Andy had been married, let alone about Tracy and the divorce. And hurray to that. It would have been about as pleasant as ripping off a big scab.

The lovely Finnish architect seemed perfectly happy being in the moment—not ruminating about past and future. And that suited Andy just fine.

On the doggie front, Trina was equally copacetic. Harald, who was spending the night with Aunt Bev, had taken an instant shine to her. And she to him. Andy made a mental note to get a selfie of the three of them together—then do a little watercolor from the pic, to give to Trina for Christmas.

They lay there in the dimly lit bedroom, Andy on his back, Trina on her side facing him. She ran her hand over his chest, then back around over his stomach.

"Anders," she said, "you are quite muscular for a man your age."

Ouch, he thought. *That sentence started better than it ended.*

"Well, between all the stuff I haul around for Ansel's and wrestling with Harald on long walks—let's just say I don't need a gym membership." Andy surreptitiously tightened his stomach, hoping for something like a six-pack effect.

Trina looked him in the eye. "Anders, may I ask you a question? What were you and Harald doing in that man's backyard, the morning you found his body?"

Not exactly the romantic sweet nothings Andy was hoping to hear. He really didn't want to talk about the very unromantic subject of Lance Robeson's brutal murder. Most everyone found murder fascinating—except when they viewed the brutality of it up close and personal.

Still, it was quite a yarn and he shared it with Trina. All the details and all the unanswered questions. Who had motive to take out the professor? Were Andy's neighbors, Elsie and Emma, really the Twin Angels? And did they know anything about the missing loot from Ole Bredahl's last big heist?

"How much money did he take?" Trina asked.

"From what Lance said, it could have been a couple million bucks."

Trina's eyes widened. "Anders, do you think your neighbors might have that money? Hidden somewhere?"

Andy laughed. "Naw. Even if Elsie and Emma were the Angels, that was more than half a century ago. If they had gotten the money, they would have spent it all by now."

But Andy didn't believe his own words. He still could see that stray g-note Elsie had slipped into her pocket.

Just then, a rather daring idea popped into his head.

Elsie had stonewalled him when he had asked about the thousand-dollar bill Harald had found.

What if there were more Grover Clevelands in Elsie's basement? Hidden in her precious, mint-condition *National Geographics*?

Tomorrow was Thursday. And Elsie would be off to her weekly afternoon bridge party, which she attended religiously. She'd be gone for two or three hours. Andy had the key to her house, and he might just do a little harmless snooping. Bring along Harald and his sensitive schnoz.

They'd be in and out in a wink. Piece of cake.

Chapter Twenty-Six

Andy worked a split shift the next day, which gave him time to zoom back home before Elsie headed out to her bridge game. He kept an eye open through the mini blinds on his living room windows. And sure enough, about a quarter after one, a shiny new Buick pulled up in front of his neighbor's house. Elsie stepped out of her front door and locked it behind her. Speaking a few words to her friend, she climbed into the Buick and off they headed to their bridge game.

"Okay, Harald," Andy told his dog, who was standing guard right behind him. "Moment of truth. Let's go pull off our little caper."

Andy and Harald went out through the alley and into Elsie's backyard. Using the key she had given him, he unlocked the door, and the two unmasked intruders slipped quickly into the house. The place smelled faintly of lavender, as it always had. Flipping on the light for the basement stairway, Andy padded down, with Harald thump-thumping behind him. It was dim down here, but he could still see everything.

The basement had been a pine-paneled rec room when Elsie's husband was alive, a sort of prehistoric man cave. There was a bar in the back corner, which probably hadn't seen a martini mixed on it in the decade since Einar Bjorklund had passed. An old Zenith TV set was parked next to a beat-up gray file cabinet. And on the wall opposite was the heavy bookshelf containing the closely-packed, semi-famous collection of *National Geographic*s. Nearly one thousand issues. Elsie had told Andy once that she had subscribed since she was a teenager, and later on bought copies going back to the month she was born.

If that shelf should fall over on a guy, he'd be a goner.

Andy whistled quietly. He didn't even know where to begin. It would take hours to look through the blasted things, and Elsie might even notice that someone had been handling them.

Harald, though, was unintimidated. He walked right up to the bookshelf, sniffed it, and plastered his damp nostrils to some issues three shelves from the bottom.

"Whatcha got there, buddy?" Andy asked, as he eased Harald off to the side. He wiped the dog snot off one of the magazines and prized it from the shelf. He riffled through it. Somewhere in the midst of a story about African Pygmies he found a pristine thousand-dollar bill. He stared at Grover Cleveland's portrait, then tucked the bill back among the Pygmies and returned the magazine to the shelf.

"Now, Harald, are there any others?"

Harald sniffed some more, and fixed on a spot on the bottom shelf.

Andy pulled out two issues and looked through those. Each of them contained a single grand bill.

At that point, Harald lost interest and wandered over to sniff around the bar. But Andy kept at it, finding g-notes in almost every issue he examined.

The haul of cash that Ole Bredahl had taken from the Chicago mob's armored car was rumored to be two million or so smackeroos. Even if each magazine contained a bill, that would be less than half of the alleged haul. But it made sense that the sisters would have split it. So Emma's share could be squirreled away somewhere else.

"Mystery solved," Andy observed to Harald, feeling like a proper sleuth. "Now we know where Ole's money ended up."

But who else knew? Lance Robeson's killer had stolen his research material, which might well lead him straight to this basement.

Andy had to figure out what to do with this new information—obtained quite illegally. But this was neither the time nor the place for pondering his next move.

"Think we better go, Harald."

The two were halfway to the stairs when Andy heard the back door opening on its squeaky hinges—something he was tasked with oiling.

Damn, he thought, *Elsie's come home early*.

Doing a U-turn, he took Harald by the collar, scampered back down the stairs, and led him to the space behind the old, green sofa. There was just enough room for them to fit—Andy on his hands and knees, and Harald on his stomach. The dog, not liking the situation, started to whimper. His heart racing, Andy clamped a hand around the big canine snout. "Harald, shut up."

The dog knew what that meant, and ceased his fussing.

There were footsteps up above.

But not old-lady footsteps.

Grown-man footsteps.

"Looks like Elsie left the lights on again."

"Not to mention leaving the back door unlocked."

"A little dementia, maybe?"

Andy went from feeling relief that it wasn't Elsie, to being scared because it was her nephews, Earl and Dennis. He had no desire to get into a dustup with those two. But what were they doing here, absent their aunt?

"I want to take a look downstairs to see if everything's okay," Earl said.

"Yeah, fine, knock yourself out," came Dennis's voice from above.

Andy was starting to sweat now, worried that Harald—showing signs of wanting to wiggle—might give them away. He maintained a firm but gentle grip on the dog's mouth. Harald was giving him a plaintive look: *Why are you doing this to me?*

The ceiling light came on with a click. Footsteps clumped down the stairs and approached the sofa, stopped, shuffled, stopped, then began again, heading back for the stairs.

A droplet of perspiration rolled into Andy's left eye and he tried to blink it away. It had been only a minute, but it felt like an eternity.

Andy heard Earl mount the steps and flick a switch. The rec room ceiling light winked out. The only illumination now came from the tiny basement windows.

Andy heaved a sigh of relief. *Maybe*, he thought, *we'll get out of this alive.*

The brothers were standing at the top of the steps, near the kitchen. Andy could clearly hear them talking.

"I swear I remember seeing a snapshot once of Elsie and Mom, standing with some guy holding a big old shotgun," Dennis said.

"Elsie's got stuff hidden away all over the house," Earl replied. "We need to find the old photo albums and letters."

"Man, Earl, ever since that professor said Ole Bredahl could be my dad…"

"Or maybe Jack's dad," Earl put in.

Jack Bjorklund was their cousin, Elsie's son. Andy had never met him, but he knew that Jack and Dennis graduated high school the same year.

"Anyway," Dennis continued, "I wonder if the guy in the picture holding the gun was Ole Bredahl. I mean, was my real dad a bank robber?"

"So what are you gonna do about it if he was?"

"I don't know, Earl. But I'll never figure it out unless we dig up some evidence."

"Well, we better get cracking, 'cause I gotta leave for work in half an hour."

It was probably the longest half hour in Andy's life. His knees were aching from kneeling behind the sofa and Harald was starting to squirm. So Andy stood up, his knees creaking, and led his mutt over behind the bar, holding onto his collar. Back there, Andy sat cross-legged on the floor.

But their torment wasn't over yet.

"There's that file cabinet down in the rec room," Andy heard Dennis say, when the two brothers came back into the kitchen. "Go check it out."

Andy's heart began to race as he heard Earl's steps coming toward the stairs. Then there was a pause.

"I don't think there's enough time, Denny," said Earl. "I gotta get to work."

Dennis didn't argue. "Okay, whatever. Let's try again next week. But man, this's like lookin' for an effing needle in the haystack."

"Hey," Earl snorted, "don't be such a Debby Downer. At least we got rid of that a-hole Robeson."

Andy heard the door squeaking, then slamming shut. A key snicked in the lock.

Harald started whimpering. Andy felt like whimpering, too. What a close call! He stood and stretched out his arms. Harald ambled out from behind the bar and made a quiet woof.

A few minutes later, the two housebreakers were safely back inside their own domicile—after Harald had a bathroom break in the backyard. Andy drip-brewed himself a strong cup of coffee and rewarded Harald with a well-deserved meat stick.

As heart attack-inducing as their little break-in had been, it pretty much conclusively proved the case for Elsie and Emma's involvement with Ole Bredahl. And it introduced a new twist in the tale—what if Ole had gotten one of the sisters pregnant before he went to prison?

But what troubled Andy most was that ambiguous, off-handed comment about getting rid of the professor.

Had Earl and Dennis actually done the deed? Or did it mean they merely approved of the murder? Was this anything that he should tell Sheriff Mandsager about?

And how did you happen to overhear this highly incriminating little chat, Andy? the sheriff would certainly ask.

Well, I snuck into Elsie's house to look for thousand-dollar bills from a long-ago armored car heist, and Harald and I were hiding behind the sofa in the basement rec room.

Oh yeah, that would go over *real* well.

Chapter Twenty-Seven

"Thing is, Thor, I got me a bit of a situation."

"Sounds ominous."

The two men were standing out in Thor's yard late on Friday afternoon, both of them leaning against Andy's Silverado, arms crossed. Harald and Angus the Border collie were capering around, Harald barking and playing, while Angus tried to herd him back toward the truck.

"And I'm darned if I know what to do about it," Andy continued.

"Well, spit it out." Thor pulled a hankie out of his pocket to clean off his horn-rimmed bifocals.

Andy described how Harald had found the first grand-note a few weeks before, when he chewed up Elsie's old *National Geographic*. Andy hadn't given it much thought until Lance Robeson said he believed Elsie Bjorklund and Emma Nelson had been hookers in their youth. And that Ole Bredahl, the old bank robber, had left his final score of ill-gotten gain with the two young women of easy virtue.

"Although," Andy wondered out loud, "is it 'ill-gotten' if it was gotten from another crook?"

"Not sure about that," Thor said.

"Anyway, I go and have a brainstorm the other night," Andy said. "What if there are more g-notes down in Elsie's basement? Squirreled away in her collection of *National Geographic*s. So, knowing that she goes to bridge club on Thursday afternoon…"

Thor scowled. "Don't tell me you broke into her house."

"Not exactly. I have a key."

"You're pleading innocent on a technicality? Pretty darned ballsy, if I do say so. So what did you find?"

"The evidence was there. Harald sniffed out a few g-notes in the magazines, and I found some others. There were probably a lot more. But we didn't have that long to look."

"Interesting subject, those large-denomination bills," Thor said, crossing his arms again. "Tricky Dick took them out of circulation back in '69. The five hundred, the thousand, the five thousand, the ten thousand. They're still legal tender, of course, but any that turn up in the system go back to the Federal Reserve for destruction. Know why?"

Thor seemed to be in one of his lecturing moods. Andy hoped he would keep it brief.

"Nope, why?"

"They were the favored means of financial transaction for criminal enterprises. The bad guys couldn't be writing checks or doing wire transfers without the Feds looking over their shoulders. A briefcase full of thousands would do the job instead. From what you and Harald found, I'd say that Elsie at least has some of the Bredahl loot."

"Yeah, I think so, too." Andy sighed. "And I don't think it's safe for her—or Emma—to keep that money in the house. If whoever killed Lance knows about it, Elsie and Emma could be in their crosshairs."

"So that's your so-called situation?"

"No, there's more."

Andy recounted what Earl and Dennis had said, word for word. About the not-so-veiled reference to taking care of Lance Robeson. About Ole Bredahl fathering Elsie or Emma's son.

"You take a couple of oddly honorable pinheads like the Nelson brothers," Thor observed, "and they're trying to protect their mom and their aunt. Maybe not only were the old ladies hookers. One of them maybe had a bastard son with a criminal. It's another secret that has to be kept quiet. Another motive for killing Lance Robeson. And now one of the brothers has personal skin in the game, so to speak. It upsets his whole sense of identity. Who he thought was his pop *wasn't*."

Thor made a good point. Andy had to admit that Dennis and Earl were looking more and more like the guys who did it.

"So, Thor, do I go tell Sheriff Mandsager about it?

And confess that I snuck into Elsie's house? Or do I keep my trap shut and leave it to the law to sort it out?"

* * *

The best pal ever, Thor had agreed to take Harald for the night, so Andy could enjoy another hot date with Trina up in Hobartville.

They caught supper at the Tex-Mex joint on Main Street. Andy had a seafood chimichanga and Trina *arroz con pollo*, washed down with a pitcher of Corona. Then they took in a flick at the only movie multiplex in the entire county.

They ended the evening back at the Medallion Suites, where there was no sleeping, dozing, or snoozing until well after one a.m.

Trina had never been to Gustav's, the breakfast-and-lunch joint just down the road from St. Magnus College. Built from two old railroad passenger cars that had been joined side-to-side in the late '50s, the greasy spoon was wildly popular with students and faculty alike. Trina and Andy spent about twenty minutes waiting on Saturday morning, before they were seated at a table for two.

Andy adored diners and dives. Not just the rich, greasy, tasty chow, but the noise and the aromas and the people-watching. At Gustav's, there were tables of students talking animatedly about movies or politics or classes or sports. Young guys eyed co-eds, and vice versa. A booth of professorial types huddled over something undoubtedly very brainy. A pair of highway patrolmen wolfed down scrambled eggs and hash browns. Genial, energetic waitresses scurried about.

"How very American," Trina said, nibbling on her blueberry sourdough cakes. "It tastes appealing, of course. The mouth loves this sort of thing. But it really should be dessert, you know, not breakfast." She looked around the diner at plates stacked high with sausage and bacon and pancakes and cheese omelets and caramel rolls. "How many of these people will have heart attacks and strokes?" she asked, shaking her head. "You really must not eat much of this cuisine, Anders. Only as an occasional treat."

That was the first time anyone Andy had brought to Gustav's had given even the merest hint of disapproval. Of course, Trina made a good point. But it seemed a mite churlish of her to bring it up.

Andy ate on in silence for a few minutes, a bit annoyed. Then he offered Trina an invitation to something he felt would be very much to her liking.

"I'm going up to Herkimer County next Thursday. A friend's throwing a little party at her cabin in the woods. Just a picnic lunch, nothing fancy. She's an old retired teacher and she has this big, forested property. Wondered if you're free, would you like to tag along? That is, if you're gonna be in Hobartville."

Trina's face brightened. "I would love to. It sounds nice."

"Super! I'll pick you up at the Medallion Suites about nine on Thursday morning."

"How much land does your friend have?" Trina

asked, as she was entering the date on her iPhone.

"I think about four hundred acres."

"Is it very scenic?"

What an odd question, Andy thought. "Yeah, sure. Beautiful evergreen and birch forestland, with a pretty stream flowing through it. Why do you ask?"

"Peter happens to be looking for a property like that. He is designing a secure, gated vacation community for special clients. Every residence will be unique, and uniquely Peter Kamu."

Meaning a getaway spot with 24-hour security for multi-millionaires. Andy understood that Trina was an ambitious junior partner in a high-end architecture firm. But suddenly he felt very protective of Cappy Briggs and her roomy plot of paradise in the woods.

"That reminds me," he said, changing the subject. "I came up with three possible spots for your site office during construction. They're all on Skjegstad Street. Two are storefronts. A former beauty parlor and a lawyer's office. The other's a nice little bungalow on the south edge of downtown. The owner's trying to sell or lease it as a shop. It's not as close to the construction site, but it's…"

"Excuse me."

Andy blinked up to see a young woman with short, dark hair glaring down at him.

She had a familiar face.

Some recognition began to dawn.

Oh hell, he thought. *Not now.*

"Are you the maître d' from Ansel's?"

"Host," Andy corrected quietly. "We're not so grand as all that."

"Do you know who I am?"

"Yes, I do. You're Lance Robeson's research assistant. Ex-research assistant. I seated you and him a while ago. Your first name is Brooke. Don't know your last name."

The woman's scowl deepened. "I think you eavesdropped on a very private conversation I was having with Lance. Then you went and told the police. And do you know what?"

"What?" he squeaked.

"Since I don't have an alibi for the time of his death, and since you shared the fact that I had a blowout argument with him, now I'm a person of interest in that SOB's murder. Thank you very *fricking* much for sticking your nose into something that didn't concern you!"

"I couldn't help but overhear the conversation," Andy protested. "It's the acoustics of the place. But you know something?"

"What?" she snapped.

Andy didn't like her attitude and decided to return fire. "I was *not* able to hear you when you were at Ansel's last Sunday with Mrs. Steinhaufen's granddaughter. I could *not* make out what it was you two were celebrating, just a couple days after Lance was killed."

The woman's eyes flared even wider.

Andy narrowed his, trying to appear resolute. "Were

you toasting his murder?"

Trina made a little gasp of surprise. Taking her to Gustav's had seemed liked a good idea, but now he wished they had gone to the breakfast buffet at the hotel.

Brooke backed away a step, as if she thought Andy might be a little wacko. "Not that it's any of your business, but I was Rachel Winslow's nanny. She just turned twenty-one and I took her out for champagne and lunch. A little celebration."

Andy decided to take a leap. "So the Steinhaufens had you get the job with Lance to spy on him."

The former research assistant had clenched both her fists, her knuckles turning white. Andy hoped earnestly that she wasn't about to pop him in the nose.

"If you think that," she hissed, "you're an even bigger idiot than I thought. My association with Lance had nothing to do with the Steinhaufens. I worked my butt off to earn that job. But when I learned he was researching the alleged Steinhaufen-Nazi link, I told Mrs. Steinhaufen. And that is all that you need to know."

With an angry huff, she turned around and marched away.

Andy was appalled. He started to apologize to Trina for the scene, but she put up her hand. "Tell me, please, Anders. What just happened?"

Andy told her about the conversation he had overheard between Lance Robeson and Brooke at Ansel's. How it was clear that the young woman had felt used by the man, both professionally and sexually. She obviously had reason to want bad things to happen to Lance. Andy had felt obliged to inform the authorities about the confrontation.

"Well, you took the proper course, telling the police," Trina reassured him. "I am sorry for the woman. But it was her own stupidity that put her into this predicament. She was seduced by his power and then blamed him for using it. Did she think having sex with him would change his personality? That he would run after her like an eager little puppy? That their love would be eternal?"

Andy was a bit surprised by Trina's vehemence.

"Still," he said, "we shouldn't be too critical of her—being in such a weak position compared to him."

"Maybe not," Trina said, her lovely lips bending into a frown. "But it just embarrasses me when smart women make such foolish assumptions."

Chapter Twenty-Eight

Monday morning, driving to the new day care center out by the Interstate, Andy had to admit that he felt a few butterflies in his gut. This would be his first official act as mayor of New Bergen, and he wanted his little speech to go over well. He had agonized over the thing all day Sunday, and finally managed to get down a few hundred decent words. That was after another couple thousand or so had been crumpled up and tossed into the circular file.

The other guest of honor, Harald, rode along in the front passenger seat, sticking his snout out over the half-open window. He seemed to be bubbling with anticipation, as if he somehow knew his adoring public awaited him. Aunt Bev had agreed to meet them at the day care to hold onto the gregarious hound while Andy cut the ribbon and gave his little speech. It was only fair. After all, she had gotten him into this improbable situation.

It was a beautiful early-autumn morning, with a warm breeze, blue sky, and fluffy clouds up above.

Of course, everyone loved dogs and children. So with Harald and the diminutive day care denizens in attendance, Andy's debut appearance was bound to be a big success.

Little Daizy Day Care's new home was a brick building out on a frontage road, with a big fenced playground in back and lots of colorful equipment for little ones to cavort on.

People were already gathering. Donna Dirksen and her husband were both in their Sunday best. This was a big deal for them, a huge upgrade from their home-based day care near Elbow Lake. A clutch of children—three- and four-year-olds, from the looks of them—made like jumping beans, under the watchful gaze of Donna's staff. Several of the tykes were gotten up as cute little daisy flowers.

A clump of grown-ups stood chatting with each other out in the parking lot, near the front entrance where the rainbow ribbon was suspended. Among them Andy saw Barb Jorgenson, the sheriff's deputy. She was out of uniform, in jeans and a maroon sweatshirt. Hauling Harald by the leash, Andy ambled over.

"Hi, Barb. What are you doing here?" he asked. "Crowd control?"

"Nope, I'm just a proud parent today."

"One of those little ones is yours?"

"Yup," she beamed. "Second daisy from the left. Millicent, Millie. Our pride and joy."

"Well, cool," Andy said. He wondered if Barb or her

wife was the biological mom. Or maybe Millie was adopted. But he figured he had better not ask.

"Any news on the Robeson case? Did you find prints on the gnome Harald found?" Andy was still proud as punch of his clue-sniffing canine.

"Just the vic's," the deputy sheriff replied. "The hair and blood were his. The perp must have been wearing gloves."

"You need me or Harald for anything else?"

"Not now. But the detective may still want to talk to you. And the county attorney will for sure, when we have a perp in hand. Right now we're interviewing folks at the college, Lance's friends, and so on. We're trying to see if the gear that was stolen turns up anywhere. There wasn't just computer stuff, but fancy camera equipment, too. And some valuable artwork."

"Did they get the Custer letter?"

Barb blinked at Andy, looking surprised. "How'd you know about that?"

"His ex told me."

Andy glanced over Barb's shoulder and saw that the Dirksens were giving him the high sign. Time to get this show on the road.

"Gotta go, Barb," he said. "Duty calls."

Then he looked down at Harald. "Okay, boy. Showtime. But where the heck is Aunt Bev?"

As if by magic, the henna-haired dynamo, heretofore unseen, popped out of the scrum of grown-ups.

"You know, Anders Skyberg," she said, looking up a

great distance at her lanky nephew, "you clean up awful good. That suit is just real handsome. And I love a nice regimental tie."

"Well, if I'm gonna do very much mayoring, I better look the part. By the way, Mom told me you've joined the world of the gainfully employed."

"Yup," Aunt Bev nodded proudly. "It's just a part-time position at the Beaver Tail Lodge and Convention Center."

"That big spread up in Hobartville? The one on the lake?"

"Uh-huh. I'll be helping with conferences and special events. I know coordination backwards and for-wards. Been doing it for years. Just never got paid for it before."

It was no secret that Aunt Bev had indeed organized many a church and school function throughout the years. Her efficient, if somewhat bossy, approach always got the job done.

Just then, Andy heard Donna call his name.

"Here, you give me Harald," Aunt Bev said. "I think the children would really like to meet him."

She took the leash out of Andy's hand and led the dog over to the youngsters, who practically mobbed him. Harald endured all the petting and prodding in good temper, occasionally giving a little face a big lick. The children couldn't get enough of him.

"Andy!"

He turned around just in time for Donna to grab his

elbow and pull him toward the ribbon.

"Donna, howdy. What a great morning for you folks."

"If you knew good days were coming," she sang with a sly grin, "would you change your mind, my dear? The word is out, the people shout, 'Mayor Andy's finally here!'"

Good lord, Andy thought. *She actually memorized that preposterous song.*

But he grinned good-naturedly. "Yup, I'm finally here. And I wrote a little speech for the occasion."

A few minutes later, Andy was standing in front of the entrance, holding city hall's official ribbon-cutting scissors. Lined up next to him were Donna, her husband, and the councilman for this part of town, Lars Ostberg. In front of the officials, out in the parking lot, the friends and clients of Little Daizy Day Care waited for something to happen. The little kiddies fidgeted and jabbered beneath watchful adult eyes, while nearby, Aunt Bev kept a firm grip on Harald's leash.

After Donna welcomed everyone, she introduced Mayor Andy, who withdrew his printed speech from his inside jacket pocket. He unfolded the paper and cleared his throat.

"Welcome, everyone, to the grand opening of Little Daizy Day Care," he began, hoping no one noticed how the paper was quivering from his stage fright. "Ever since the first merchant opened his doors in our fair town, we New Bergenites have always been celebrated for our dauntless work ethic and—"

All of a sudden, Harald erupted in basso profundo barking.

Crazy-loud barking.

With his not-inconsiderable canine strength, he began towing Aunt Bev across the parking lot. She tried to restrain him, but was out-muscled by the determined pooch.

Andy instantly saw the problem, as a ground squirrel skittered off into the weeds.

For an instant, all the spectators watched the scene with their mouths open. Finally, Aunt Bev managed to subdue the agitated hound and gave Andy a thumbs-up.

But before Andy could continue his speech, one of the little daisies started to cry. Soon another began to wail, then another and another. Donna's staffers quickly started tut-tut-tutting the children, hustling them off the tarmac and into the day care center.

"Maybe we should just cut the ribbon, and have some punch and snacks," Donna said to Andy, sounding apologetic. "I'm sure your speech is wonderful, but you're playing to a tough crowd out here."

Not exactly an auspicious debut appearance for the new mayor, Andy had to admit. He bet that lots of folks would be snickering at him behind his back—or maybe even in front of it—for days.

Of course, it wasn't the dog's fault. Harald was just being Harald. But someone was definitely not getting a beef stick tonight.

Andy could hardly wait to shed his mayor's suit and get back to work. At Ansel's he knew what he was doing. At Ansel's he knew what to expect.

Chapter Twenty-Nine

The big table at the back of Ansel's had been reserved for a party of twelve on Wednesday evening. But it would be no ordinary party, Andy knew. The dinner was a political fundraiser for Tim Steinhaufen, and the business elite of Beaver Tail County were expected to attend.

The candidate arrived early, a bit before seven, with his campaign manager. A handsome guy in his mid-thirties, the chemicals-fortune scion schmoozed a bit with Kirsten, knowing that she was herself a multi-millionaire. Tim exuded a lot more charm than his grandmother had a couple of weeks ago at St. Magnus College. Andy remembered how the wealthy matriarch had read the riot act to the college president, trying to get him to squelch Lance Robeson's research into the family's shady past.

By seven-thirty the guests and their bulging wallets had arrived, and wine and drinks flowed liberally. Andy had no idea how many campaign dollars would be donated that evening. Tens of thousands, for sure.

Just after eight, two women came through the door. It took Andy a few seconds to recognize Jill Robeson, all dolled up. She looked a bit wobbly, though. A boozy smell wafted off her, as she introduced her friend to the new mayor.

"Gotta go to the little girl's room," Jill mumbled, making her way unsteadily past the political fundraiser.

Andy spent the next few minutes sorting out a party of six that included two in wheelchairs. It took a little effort, but he got everyone into a good spot and summoned J. J. over to take the drink orders.

As he headed back to his lectern, he noticed Jill Robeson returning from the restroom. But instead of joining her friend where Andy had seated her, Jill made a beeline for Tim Steinhaufen's table.

Sparks glinted in her inebriated eyes. She tapped the would-be congressman on the shoulder and began to growl out some unfriendly words.

"Uh-oh," Andy said, launching himself in her direction. He caught her in mid-invective.

"…your witch of a grandmother probably put out a contract on my ex-husband. Made it look like some messed-up burglary."

The accused, turning beet red, jumped to his feet.

"Ma'am, I have no idea what you're talking about."

In response, Jill stabbed him in the chest with her index finger.

"I'm talking about Professor Lance Robeson. Father

of my girls. He had the goods on your family."

Andy skidded to a halt, and put his arms on Jill's shoulders, intending to pull her back. But she was a big, strong girl and jabbed backward with a very sharp elbow into his stomach. Andy gasped, bending over double. It hurt like the dickens.

"Your great-grandfather consorted with the Nazis, you fascist millionaire scumbag!" Jill slurred.

By now everyone in the restaurant was staring at her. Andy groaned when he saw several diners whipping out their smartphones to make videos of the altercation.

"My ex was going to blow the lid off what your company did back in '42," Jill snarled.

"Ma'am, I think you're drunk," Tim Steinhaufen snapped, finally sounding something like a self-possessed congressman should. He turned his back to her and sat down.

Andy tried to pull Jill away, but she wasn't done. Easily breaking Andy's grip, she bent down behind Tim.

"But I'll be sober in the morning," she hissed. "And the Steinhaufens will still be a bunch of Fascists!"

Tim Steinhaufen shot up from his chair like a rocket, almost knocking Jill over, his eyes glaring fiercely.

"You miserable bitch," he growled. "I will crush you like a..."

And then he used the f-word, in the form of an adjective. His expletive came out loud and clear, and Andy wondered how long it would take for the whole ugly scene to show up on YouTube.

Finally, Andy managed to get a good grip on Jill and hauled her toward the front of the restaurant. "I think you should take the lady home and put her to bed," he told her friend. "She needs to sleep it off."

As the two of them exited, Andy saw J. J. and Kirsten rushing toward him.

"What the hell just happened?" his sister asked.

Andy recounted Jill's stealth attack on the wannabe congressman.

"Better go unruffle some feathers," Kirsten said. She took a deep breath and headed back to the Steinhaufen table.

J. J. stood by the lectern with Andy, a strange look on her face.

"You okay?" he asked.

"Yeah," she said. "It's just that I've never seen Jill like that before. I mean, I heard that she drinks a little too much sometimes." She blinked up at Andy. "I'm not like that, am I? When I drink?"

"No, not like that."

"Meaning?"

Andy decided to be brutally honest. "You're not a nasty drunk, like Jill. But a couple of times you've scared the hell out me when you've climbed into that Corolla of yours, and you wouldn't let me drive you home. You're lucky you haven't killed anyone."

She looked as if his words had hit home. "You're not the first person to mention that."

* * *

Just after breakfast on Thursday morning, Andy loaded Harald into the truck and headed for the Hofdahl farm to pick up Thor and Sonny for the picnic at Cappy Briggs's cabin. But when he drove up onto their property, it was just Thor who climbed into the Chev pickup.

"Where's the missus?" Andy asked.

"One of her nanny goats got sick. She needs to stay home and wait for the vet. Sends her regrets."

Andy realized he had forgotten to call Cappy and ask if he could bring Trina. But now that Sonny couldn't make it, Cappy would still have the same headcount for lunch.

They swung by the Medallion Suites up in Hobartville, and Trina emerged from the lobby. She looked very woodsy chic, with olive-drab slacks and hiking boots, topped with a heavy black hoodie and a gray canvas backpack.

The drive north to Herkimer County was interesting, as Thor and Trina felt each other out. It so happened that they shared a love of Nordic folklore and history. Andy was impressed that Trina actually seemed fascinated by Thor's work on translating that old Viking saga, *Skjorfjeld's Retreat from Vinland*, and asked some trenchant questions. By the time they pulled up to the big log house in the woods, at about a quarter to eleven, the geezer and the babe were practically old chums.

A moment later, Cappy Briggs came trotting out onto the front porch, wiping her hands on a dishtowel. Andy had come to know her as an absolute bundle of energy, even at the age of ninety. She was a sinewy little woman, clad in worn jeans and a heavy flannel shirt, with a close-cropped head of white hair,.

"You are here finally," she said with a warm smile. "I have so been looking forward to this visit."

She pattered down the steps and gave Andy a big hug. Then she bent over so Harald could deliver a slobbery kiss on her fuzzy cheek.

"Cappy, this is Thor Hofdahl," Andy announced.

Thor stuck his hand out and Cappy shook it. "Wonderful to meet you, Ms. Briggs."

"Cappy," she sniffed. "Call me Cappy and I'll call you Thor."

Then she caught sight of the lovely Trina and her eyes widened. "And this must be Sonny." She turned back to Thor and gave him a wink. "You sly old dog, you."

"No, no, no, Cappy," Andy hastened to correct her. "Sonny had to cancel, so I brought my friend. This is Trina Makkonen. Hope you don't mind. Trina's Finnish. She's an architect."

Cappy wasn't even slightly fazed by her error. "Oh, I don't mind at all!" She went over to the gorgeous Finn and gave her a hug, too. "Welcome to my humble abode."

"Thank you so much, Cappy," Trina replied. "You have a very beautiful place here."

"Well, come inside and see the cabin," Cappy said, shooing them up the steps. "I'm getting lunch ready.

You can meet my niece. Great-niece, actually. But why split hairs? She had the day off, so she came up to help out."

Cappy's niece, Becky Reingold, was in the kitchen buttering some whole-wheat buns. She was a nurse practitioner in the ER at St. Luke's Hospital in Hobart-ville. Her dark hair was cut short and practical, just like her aunt's, and she had an easy-going manner and a sharp sense of humor. Andy liked her right from the get-go.

Just as promised many weeks ago, Cappy had a heaping plate of venison brats for the grill, set up just outside the mudroom door. Thor, a grill master from way back, presided at the Weber propane, while Cappy and Becky loaded up the picnic table with homemade potato salad, oven-roasted Brussels sprouts, and refrigerator pickles. There were more than enough bottles of Biberschwanz Dunkles in the ice-filled cooler that Andy hauled outside.

They ate alfresco, at the picnic table behind the cabin, beneath several leaning birches, noshing and chatting away the noon hour. For his part, Harald enjoyed a couple of brats and scarfed up a pickle that fell off the table before anyone could stop him.

After dessert—apple pie and cheddar cheese—everyone moved from the table to a group of old-fashioned web chairs. Becky, sitting opposite Andy, took a sip of her black coffee.

"So you work in the ER, Becky," said Andy. "Must

be exciting."

"Too exciting, sometimes," she answered. "That's why I moved back here from Chicago. Got sick of treating gunshot wounds."

"Well," Thor put in, "you'll be seeing some of those when deer season starts in a few weeks."

Trina sniffed with obvious disapproval. "The American obsession with firearms is something I do not understand. Of course, the police should have them. But why are they so ubiquitous here? Even children use them. We have guns in Finland. But they are not so much out of control."

Thor shook his head gloomily. "That there, Trina, is one humongous can of worms. Hunting rifles you can understand. For some people, that puts food on the table. Consider those fine venison brats we just had. But handguns? Only one purpose for them. Killing people."

Andy cleared his throat. "True, Thor. But without Cass Conlin's 9mm, I wouldn't be here to enjoy this fine picnic."

"That's right," Becky said. "Aunt Cappy tells me that you and Harald were involved in a criminal matter."

It was bound to come up, Andy thought. But before he answered, Thor did.

"Yup, King Harald here has a peculiar knack for turning up dead bodies. The most recent being a history professor from St. Magnus College."

"Oh, my goodness!" Cappy exclaimed. "I didn't know you were involved in that murder, too, Andy."

"I wouldn't exactly say I was 'involved' in it," Andy said. "More like an innocent bystander. The killer or killers are still on the loose."

"So who do you think the leading suspects are?" Becky asked.

"No inside info, I'm afraid," Andy answered. "But I do know that Lance, the professor, PO'd a lot of folks."

Cappy leaned forward with interest, as if relishing the juicy details. "Such as?"

"Well, it's no secret that Lance and his ex had a nasty split, and she has a bit of an anger-management problem when she's been hitting the sauce." He shuddered, remembering the scene from Ansel's. "I saw her last night when I was working. She was totally polluted and she ripped into Tim Steinhaufen. Basically accused his grandmother of putting a contract out on Lance Robeson."

"Tim Steinhaufen? That young guy running for congress?" Cappy asked.

"His f-bomb from last night is already on the Internet, on the video sites," observed Thor. "It'll be interesting to see how it impacts his campaign." He pointed an index finger at Andy. "His honor here looked pretty good, trying to wrangle the recalcitrant Jill."

"For gosh sakes! Why would the Steinhaufens want to murder a history professor?"

"Tim's grandma is one scary old broad, and might have a good reason," Thor answered. "Have you ever heard the rumors about the way the Steinhaufens did business in Germany before World War II?"

"No," Cappy said. "Can't say that I have."

"Well, there've been stories for years about old man Steinhaufen and his brother having been big fans of Der Führer," Thor explained. "Nothing I've seen suggests they ever visited Herr Hitler himself, but they were pals of Fritz Todt, the first Nazi armaments minister. If Robeson had dug up specific evidence of them trafficking with the Nazis into 1942, that'd be pretty incendiary."

"It gets even more convoluted," Andy said. "There's Lance's former research assistant. Apparently he didn't come through with the byline he'd promised her on some published paper. Not only that, he slept with her and dumped her."

"Sounds like a pretty good motive to me," Cappy noted.

"But there's more," Andy continued. "Turns out the woman was a nanny for one of Mrs. Steinhaufen's granddaughters. And when she found out about the prof's research into the family, she spied on him for them."

Becky shook her head in amazement. "It's like a soap opera."

"Even my next-door neighbors had it in for Lance," Andy said. "For reasons I can't go into. Thing is, there are a lot of folks who wouldn't have minded the guy getting his skull cracked open."

Andy glanced around the circle of chairs. From the looks on people's faces, there had been more than enough criminology conversation. It was, after all, a pretty grim subject.

"Okay, now that we've covered murder suspects and Nazis," Cappy said, echoing Andy's thoughts, "let's go for a little amble through my woods and burn off some of that apple pie."

* * *

"This has been a darned near perfect day," Andy said to Harald, as he steered the Silverado left on Willow Street and headed for home. It was late in the afternoon and the October sun was low in the sky. Thor had given him his seal of approval on Trina—the old guy was quite impressed with her. For her part, Trina had charmed Cappy with stories of growing up in Finland. And, thankfully, she had not mentioned Peter Kamu's plans for a gated community in the north woods.

Andy had really liked Becky Reingold. It made him feel good that Cappy had someone close by to keep an eye on her. To be able to live alone in such a beautiful place at Cappy's age was a blessing, and when she finally passed, Andy hoped she went with her hiking boots on.

"Yep, Harald," he said, "it's been a darned good day."

That's when Andy saw the flashing lights of a squad car. Parked right in front of Emma's house.

Chapter Thirty

Andy quickly parked the truck and put Harald in the house. He rushed next door to Emma's just as Barb Jorgenson was leaving.

"Hey, Barb, what's going on?" he asked.

The dark-haired deputy slipped a small notebook into her uniform pocket. "You haven't seen Earl Nelson recently, have you, Andy?"

Not since I broke into Elsie's house a week ago, he thought.

"No, not in a few days," he replied. "Why? Can't you find him?"

Barb was silent for a few seconds. "If you do see him, Andy, let him know that it would be in his best interest to come to the sheriff's office in Hobartville for a talk."

There were no smiles from Barb tonight. She definitely meant business.

"Come on, Barb. Harald and I are practically honorary deputies by now. Can't you at least tell me if this has something to do with Lance Robeson's death?"

Barb gave him her best cop stare, and then relented. "We have several witnesses in a bar who heard Earl boasting about 'taking care' of the professor."

"Earl is like a lot of people, Barb. You get a little booze in him and he's bragging about all kinds of things he's never done."

"Maybe so. But that's not all. We followed up on a tip and found some vital evidence on Dennis Nelson's property. We've arrested him and we really need to talk to his brother."

Andy's heart sank. Though he was certainly no fan of Dennis or pal of Earl, he felt awful for what this news must be doing to Emma and Elsie.

Barb clearly wasn't enjoying this conversation any more than he was. "Listen, Andy, maybe you could go in and talk to the ladies. They're both pretty broken up over this news." With a tired look, she walked over to her black-and-white and drove off.

Dreading the task at hand, Andy climbed the steps of the little bungalow and rapped on the door. A moment later it swung open, and there stood a grim Elsie Bjork-lund, a wad of tissue in her hand.

"Oh, Anders," she sighed.

"Hi, Elsie, I just heard the news. How's Emma doing?"

"Come on in. We could use some company. I have coffee brewing."

Entering the living room, Andy saw Emma sitting on

the sofa, looking pale and dejected. He plopped down on the ottoman in front of her. Elsie came back into the room and handed him a mug of coffee. Then she sat down next to Emma.

Emma Nelson's house always seemed dark and dreary to Andy, not at all like Elsie's modern, bright décor. But right now, dark and dreary seemed quite appropriate.

He took a deep breath. "Deputy Jorgenson told me they've arrested Dennis and they're looking for Earl."

Emma gazed at him with strikingly blue, teary eyes. "Bonnie said that Earl was going to stop by here after work Monday night and drop off some tools. But I never saw him and nobody's heard from him since. I'm just worried sick."

Andy thought desperately of something to say that might comfort the old lady. "I know Earl likes to go bow hunting in the fall. Maybe he's just out at some hunter's shack and he hasn't thought to call."

It was a lame scenario, but it was the best he could come up with.

Emma dabbed her eyes with a tissue. "He would have told Bonnie. And he would have called me, too, Anders. I know he would have. He's always been very good about checking in with me."

Andy understood that Lance had set this whole dreadful mess in motion. But Elsie and Emma had done their part, too, refusing to talk with the professor, then bringing Emma's hot-tempered sons into the equation.

Over the last weeks, Andy had felt as if he were watching a train wreck in slow motion. He hadn't been able to help, but maybe it wasn't too late for the truth to do some good. The place to start was back in the 1950s.

He leaned forward on the ottoman, mug enclosed in both big hands, and looked from one woman to the other.

"I don't think you two have been entirely honest with me."

For an instant, Elsie looked indignant. But then Emma patted her sister on the hand, and Elsie's shoulders deflated.

"You really do have Ole Bredahl's money, don't you?" Andy probed. "You really are the Twin Angels, aren't you?"

Emma nodded. "There's been enough lying. It's trying to keep secrets that got us into this situation, and the boys, too. I think Anders should know what really happened."

"Right," Elsie said with a note of resignation. "No more deceit." She clasped her hands on her lap and collected herself. "You know, Anders, Emma and I were quite popular when we were girls. Might be hard to imagine that now."

"No," Andy said. He knew for a fact they had been fine-looking young ladies. "Not at all."

"Lots of boys asked us out. We enjoyed the attention and the little gifts. And the guys seemed to like spending time with us. But—" She gave Andy a firm look. "—we were never *those* kind of women."

Hookers, he thought. *She means hookers.*

"That's the honest truth," Elsie continued. "We met Ole in a café. Of course we didn't know who he was. We didn't know for a long time *what* he was. But he was charming. Tall, blond, very handsome, in a beautiful blue suit. He asked if he could sit with us, and we were feeling daring…"

"*You* were feeling daring," Emma sniffed.

"And so he bought our lunch and drove us home in a big green Pontiac. He asked if he could see us again, and we said yes."

"Didn't your parents object?" Andy asked.

"We made real sure that they never found out," Emma said. "Anyway, we were both out of school and over eighteen and living in an apartment in town. We were working at a factory that made car parts."

"Ole took us to nice restaurants and out dancing, and even to the Cities and Des Moines," Elsie recalled. "We stayed at his cabin, too. It was a scenic spot out on a bend in the river."

"But at some point, didn't you figure out he was a bank robber?" Andy asked.

"Not for a long while," Emma responded. "We never read the newspapers. All we knew was that he had to travel for his work, and was away for long stretches of time. We'd sometimes go for months without seeing him. He said he was an insurance adjuster."

"We did notice that some of his friends seemed a

little rough on the edges," Elsie put in. "But they were always perfect gentlemen around us. Ole was in the war, you know."

She meant World War II, of course.

"He had the most incredible stories about fighting his way through France and the Battle of the Bulge. About being on leave in Paris. He received a Purple Heart for his wounds."

"How long did you know him?"

Emma scrunched up her face. "Four or five years?"

"That's about right," Elsie said. "The last time we saw him, it was at the cabin. He finally told us who he was and what he did. He showed us where the money was hidden, and said if he should happen to die, doing his work, it was all ours."

"Two million," Andy said. "Right?"

"Yes," Emma answered. "Two million. Ole and his men took a few thousand each. For 'walking-around' money, he called it. The rest they left buried near the cabin, to keep it safe until they needed more. Well, as it turned out, his two friends were killed in Dubuque and he was captured. As soon as we could, we moved the money."

"We didn't know what would happen to the cabin while he was in jail," Elsie explained. "We might not be able to get to the money if the place was sold."

"And after he was killed," Emma continued, "we figured it was ours."

"He said we should never tell a soul that we had it,"

Elsie said. "Because the money came from bad men who might try to get it back."

Lance was right, Andy thought. What a heckuva story. "And all those years you kept the money in your *National Geographic*s?"

"Well, we split it, of course," Elsie said. "I put mine in different hiding places at first. Then later on I realized those magazines were the perfect spot. Nobody ever wanted to look at them or borrow them. And if they did, I just said I couldn't allow it, as they were mint copies."

"We were too worried to put it into banks," Emma explained, "in case the serial numbers were on record."

"Did Einar know about it?" Andy asked Elsie.

"Oh, you betcha. I told him all about Ole when we got engaged. I wanted to give him a chance to back out, once he found out that I was the friend of a bank robber. But he just thought it was kind of amusing."

"Weren't you ever tempted to use the money for a big house and fancy cars?"

"Oh, no. Einar always saw it as something like an inheritance, to be used responsibly. He did take a thousand or two, now and then, and invested in stocks. Lots of it he put into computer companies. My husband loved electronics and such."

"What stocks did he pick?"

"Back in the '60s, IBM. In the '80s, Microsoft."

Andy's jaw dropped. "You must have done pretty well."

"Oh, we did. We put Rose and Jack through college

with the IBM stock, and we were very happy with Microsoft. That's how we did all those wonderful trips, before Einar got sick."

Elsie glanced at her sister. "Now Emma took a different approach than I did. She gave most of her Ole money to charities."

"It was dirty money," Emma said. "If Earl or Dennis had wanted to go to college or start their own businesses, I would have used it to help them. As it turned out, I figured I might as well use it to do some good. Take the devil's money and put it toward God's work."

"More than a few poor families in these parts have received envelopes with a thousand-dollar bill inside," Elsie said. "They never knew who their anonymous angel was." She patted her sister's knee. "Not a Twin Angel, mind you, but a *good* angel."

Andy could only marvel at such generosity. She was practically a saint. "What did your husband think about that, Emma?"

"Never told him about the money. He would have just blown it on booze and gambling."

"You know, it's bound to come out now," Andy said. "Your history with Ole Bredahl. It can't be stopped."

Elsie's gaze pierced him as few gazes ever had. He could almost see that blond girl of the 1950s, that Twin Angel who had been so lovely.

"I realize that, Anders," she said with a rueful smile. "But our main concern is to make sure that Dennis and

Earl aren't convicted for a crime they didn't commit. That's the only thing that matters now."

Andy sure hoped the two old ladies could pull that off. But he couldn't see how Dennis and Earl were going to get out of this fix.

There was one more thing. Andy hated to bring it up. But he could still hear Dennis and Earl speculating about whether Ole could have fathered Dennis or Jack Bjorklund. He wouldn't blame the two women if they kicked his keister right out the front door. Still, he had to ask.

"What year did Ole go to prison?"

"It was 1956," Elsie answered. "I remember they arrested him the day after Elvis was on *The Ed Sullivan Show*."

"He sang 'Love Me Tender,'" Emma recalled, her expression brightening. "I always used to sing that to Dennis when he was a baby, to get him to fall asleep."

"So was Dennis born before Ole went to prison," Andy asked.

"Oh yes," Elsie said. "And Jack was a bun in the oven."

Andy did the math, then tried to figure out how to frame his next question. But it was as if Elsie had read his mind. Her eyes wide, she gave him a look of disbelief.

"Why, Anders, you aren't suggesting that Ole was the father of one of our sons?"

"Well, yeah," Andy answered sheepishly. "I guess I am."

But instead of the outrage that Andy was expecting, Emma and Elsie looked at each other and broke into smiles.

"Do you think we should tell him?" Emma asked her sister.

But before Elsie could respond, the doorbell rang. Andy popped up to answer it and ushered Bonnie Bohonek into the living room.

"Oh, Elsie, Emma," she blubbered. "The police came by the house to let me know that they're looking for Earl. They think he's involved in the murder of that professor fellow."

"Sit yourself down, dear," Emma said solicitously. "Let's keep each other company until we hear from Earl."

Bonnie slumped into a side chair.

"Bonnie," Elsie asked, "do you think there's any chance that Earl's gone hunting?"

Bonnie shook her head desolately. "No, he wouldn't of gone off without saying something. He wouldn't of missed work. And I called some of his buddies, and they don't know nothing."

She looked up at Andy, then back to Elsie and Emma. Her chin started to quiver.

"I'm scared for Earl," she whispered. "I'm real scared."

Chapter Thirty-One

Aunt Bev's older boy, Myron, was in his mid-forties and a lot thinner and fitter than he had been just five years earlier, when he suffered a mild heart attack. He still had the same earnest face and thick head of brown hair. But now he was built like a serious jogger—which he, in fact, had become.

Ronnie, as everyone called him, had driven up from Nebraska for a round of meetings at the Lovely Lena headquarters, and was staying in town through Monday. Andy's folks had offered to treat Ronnie and his parents to supper at Ansel's on Saturday. Kirsten couldn't come that evening, but Andy happily accepted the invite to join the party. With Trina out of town for the weekend, he had nothing better to do.

He worked until six, and then set up the big table in back. Ronnie was the first to arrive, promptly on time at six-thirty. By then, Andy had bellied up to the bar, and was working on a Beefeater martini. Ronnie perched beside him and ordered the same.

"So, how's life among the Cornhuskers?" Andy asked.

"Can't complain. Lots of nice folks down there. Olivia and the kids are finally acclimating. But we're looking forward to moving back home in the spring, when school's over."

"Well, super. Glad to hear things are going well in the world of gluten-free noodles."

Ronnie smiled at him. "And how's the mayor's job working for you? Are you still speaking to Mom?"

"Yeah," Andy groaned. "But I'm kind of glad she found that job up in Hobartville. It should keep her out of my hair for a while."

"And speaking of hair," Ronnie teased, "I hear you might be getting a buzz cut at the homecoming game on Friday."

"Wipe that smug smile off your face," Andy teased back. "You may be getting your own buzz cut a year from now, when you're mayor."

Ronnie squirmed a bit. "Fact is, Andy, I'm not going to run for mayor."

Andy's jaw dropped. "You're *what*?"

"I'm sorry, I really am. But this whole thing was one of Mom's weird ideas, not mine. She thought it would give me a leg up at Lena's. And I kept trying to tell her that I have just too much on my plate right now. I'm the guy they picked to launch the gluten-free product line. I'm the guy who's up for VP next year. I just don't have any time for politics."

He looked at Andy, frustrated. "You know Mom. She gets an idea in her head and bulls forward, no matter what. Sooner or later, everyone else just seems to fall in line." He shook his head. "But not this time."

Andy took a long, slow sip of his martini and let the news sink in. "So I guess I went through all this for nothing."

Ronnie gave him a pat on the back. "Look at it this way, cuz. Come springtime you'll be out of office. A mere footnote in the history of New Bergen. But you'll have been the mayor of a town. That's a *real* accomplishment. And you can thank Mom for it."

Andy hated to admit it, but Ronnie made a good point. "Mayor of New Bergen" was the most impressive title he could list on his résumé. It wasn't a bad gig. It just wasn't what he imagined he'd be doing at age forty.

"Hi there, guys."

Andy and Ronnie looked up and saw Andy's parents standing there.

Ronnie hopped off his bar stool. "Aunt Susie, Uncle Dean, great to see you."

He gave Andy's mom a quick hug and pumped his uncle's hand. "Might as well head back to our table, huh?"

On the way, Susie Skyberg grabbed her son's arm. "The Coreys are history," she said excitedly. "They left this morning for Nebraska. Mona was feeling lonely for her grandkids."

"You don't sound too broken up about it." Andy

said, taking his chair at the table.

His mom grinned. "Your dad is so relieved."

"That Joe Corey is *such* a braggart," Andy's old man groused, holding the chair for his wife. "He's just gotta top you every time. Whatever he has, or knows about, is bigger, better, faster, stronger. If I had a double bypass, I bet he'd have to have a triple one."

Everyone was laughing as Aunt Bev and Uncle Frank marched up to the table. More greetings were exchanged and more hugs administered, before the henna-haired firecracker finally plopped down in her chair next to Ronnie.

"And how is our new mayor of New Bergen?" she asked across the table.

"Just fine, Aunt Bev," Andy sighed.

"And how is our *next* mayor?" she asked, patting Ronnie's hand.

Ronnie looked at Andy, then back at his mother. "Mom, there's something we have to talk about."

"Sure, go ahead," she chirped. "I'm all ears."

* * *

Andy stopped right in front of Uncle Sam's Mercantile a bit after noon on Sunday. It was just four weeks ago that he had walked in on the kerfuffle between Jill Robeson and her dearly departed ex-husband. A lot of water had gone over the dam since then.

He popped inside with his Ansel's to-go bag. No one was in the shop except Jill, who was sitting on a tall stool behind the cash register, reading an old issue of

American Heritage.

She looked up and smiled. "Andy, hi. Know anything about Dan Patch?"

"Who?" Andy asked, setting her Monte Cristo sandwich and latté next to the cash register.

"The most famous horse in the world—that is, the world in 1900. Champion pacer. That's different than a trotter, you know. Dan was the first fully marketed sports hero in history. He and his owner lived down in the Cities. I'm thinking of bidding on a big lot of Dan Patch ephemera."

She put down the magazine and pulled a twenty out of the cash register. "Keep what's left. And before you go, I wanted to apologize again for that scene I made with Tim Steinhaufen. Wasn't fun for anyone. But it did some good. I just went to my first twelve-step meeting."

Andy felt a wave of relief. "That's great, Jill. I know it's helped lots of people."

"But I also wanted to tell you that Lance was right about the Steinhaufens. I have evidence."

Andy raised his eyebrows. "What kind of evidence?"

"Actual documents. They show the Steinhaufens' German subsidiary was actively doing business with the Nazis post-Pearl Harbor."

"Pretty inflammatory stuff. But how did you get hold of it?"

"Whoever killed Lance took his computer and paper files. But the last time he came over to get the girls, he transferred a bunch of stuff onto their computer. He did that every so often, as a backup. The girls didn't mention it to me after he died. I guess they didn't think it was important."

"But Jill, do you really, *really* think the Steinhaufens would have killed Lance over that material?"

Jill crossed her arms. "Yeah, absolutely. I've sent copies of his Steinhaufen material to Sheriff Mandsager's office. It's up to them to follow through on it. But I get the impression they're pretty convinced the Nelson brothers are the killers."

Andy thought about poor Elsie and Emma—fretting about Dennis in jail and Earl on the run. Elsie told him that Emma had become so distraught she had taken to her bed. Andy hoped, for the sake of the two sisters, that it *was* the Steinhaufens who did in the professor. Not Dennis and Earl, as boneheaded as the two brothers could be.

If not for a chance meeting with a minor-league bank robber six decades ago, Elsie and Emma wouldn't be living this nightmare today. Andy wondered if there was something he had done years ago that could come back and haunt him. The past, it seemed, was never really quite over.

"I'm wondering, Jill, did you see anything in Lance's material that dealt with Ole Bredahl, the old bank robber?" he asked.

"As a matter of fact, yeah. I sent those copies and scans to the sheriff, too. Would you like to see 'em? Give me your e-mail address and I'll send you the files."

"That'd be great." Andy hauled out his wallet and removed a business card, the one he optimistically had printed for his art studio. "Here it is. I'm gonna be curious to see what they contain."

He turned to leave, but looked back at Jill. There was one more thing he was curious about.

"Ever hear of a research assistant named Brooke?" he asked.

Jill's face darkened. "Oh yeah, I know who she is."

"Did you know that she's pals with the Steinhaufens? Used to be a nanny for one of the grandkids. She was telling the family what Lance was up to."

Jill looked astonished. "I had no idea." She was quiet for a few seconds, then smiled. "Well, how delicious. His little bed buddy was informing on him to the Nazi lovers."

* * *

When Andy was done working Sunday afternoon, he decided to take a chance and surprise Trina at the Medallion Suites. She had been down in the Cities over the weekend, but she should be back by now.

Holding the chilled bottle of ice wine that he had bought a few days earlier, Andy rapped on her door. He waited a little while, then rapped again. He was almost ready to give up and leave, when he heard the lock click open. Andy quickly turned around, his grin widening in anticipation.

The door swung open and there stood a tall, buff, brown-haired fellow of about thirty or thirty-five. With a big white bath towel around his middle and looking damp from the shower.

"Yes, can I help you?" the man said. He had an accent similar to Trina's.

Andy's grin slowly collapsed. "Sorry, I think I've got the wrong room."

Please, he thought, *be the wrong room.* But he glanced up and read the number again.

Oh crap! It is the right room.

"Who are you looking for?"

"Katrina Makkonen."

The man smiled and nodded. "Yes, this is the place. She is in the shower. Perhaps I can help you. You know her how?"

"I'm working with her on The Nordic deli and gallery project."

The stranger's eyes brightened and he stuck out his hand, which Andy automatically took and shook.

"Yes, she has told me all about it," the semi-naked fellow said. "By the way, I am Jorma. Jorma Makkonen. Trina's husband."

Chapter Thirty-Two

Andy slouched at his kitchen table Monday morning, a dark cloud hanging over his head. He was sucking on his third cup of coffee and flipping back and forth between the two voicemails Trina had left him after he fled the Medallion Suites.

He listened again to the first voicemail. "I am sorry, Anders. I should have told you about Jorma. I have been so busy with The Nordic and one of Peter's special projects, that the time to share that with you never seemed quite right. I did not know he was planning to visit me here. I was as surprised as you were. But please understand, Jorma and I have a very open marriage. He is not angry with you. Please, Anders, call me back."

He's not angry with me? Andy thought bitterly. *Well, isn't that wonderful for Jorma.*

Then he listened to the second call. "Anders, I should have thanked you for the ice wine. Please come back and share it with us. Jorma would really like to get to know you. In fact, he was hoping that you might care to spend the night with us. We have done this before with people we are attracted to. I know this may be outside your comfort zone, but you may even find it healing. Please call me back. I miss you already."

Andy looked at Harald, who was sitting by the sink.

"A threesome, Harald. She's talking about a threesome! Can you believe it?"

Harald cocked his head, but declined to make any comment.

Andy considered the prospect of being in the sack with a third person—and a man at that—way too bizarre. Even when he was with his ex-wife Tracy, there were no kinks whatsoever in their sex life.

"You know, old fellow," Andy observed, "sometimes I think you're lucky not to be interested in the ladies. A little snip-snip and your whole life was simplified. No relationships, no sex, no kids. None of that messy stuff. Just happy, healthy celibacy."

Harald cocked his head the other way, retaining his Zen-like demeanor.

Andy frowned at him. "No offense, Harald, but I think I need to talk to someone from my own species."

He called Thor, who said he had a shoulder available to cry on. Quickly getting dressed, Andy headed out the back door with Harald in tow. As the screen door swung shut, he noticed a plastic Jumbo Mart bag hanging on the handle. The bag contained a small paperback with a sticky note on it from Elsie. It said, "This should explain our relationship with Ole."

"Jeesh," Andy said to Harald. "She can't give me a simple answer? She wants me to read a whole damn novel?" He jammed the book into his coat pocket, and the two companions headed out to the Silverado.

* * *

"Uff da!" Sonny Hofdahl exclaimed. "A threesome? How does that even work?" The sixty-something grandmother was perched on a tall chair at the granite-top island in her still unfinished kitchen.

Sitting there across from Andy, Thor pondered the question. "Four possibilities, hon. Boy boy girl, as in Andy's spurned opportunity. Girl girl boy. Girl girl girl. Or boy boy boy." He turned back to Andy. "So that was a deal-breaker for you?"

Andy gave him a look of indignation. "Of course it was—that and the minor detail of her being a married woman." He nibbled on one of Sonny's buttermilk biscuits, slathered with homemade apple butter and still warm from the oven. "I don't consider myself a prude. Maybe I'm a little old-fashioned, but I took those vows seriously when I put the ring on Tracy's finger."

Outside, Harald woofed that resonant woof of his, as he cavorted with Angus.

"If she had told me about Jorma," Andy continued, "of course I wouldn't have slept with her. Even if they do have an open marriage." He shook his head regretfully. "But I gotta admit, she had the whole package—looks, smarts, a sense of humor. And amazingly, she found me attractive, too. Ever since Cass blew town, I've been feeling pretty much like a loser."

"Anders Skyberg, you just get that idea out of your head," Sonny huffed. "You're a good looking man with a big heart. It's only a matter of time before you find the right lady and click with her."

"I'd sure like to believe you, Sonny," he said. "But the last few years tell a different story."

Thor gave him one of his oracular looks. "Andy, I'm not your old man or your drill sergeant. But I'm going to tell you what to do. Put on your big-boy pants. You had a nice fling with a gorgeous lady. Didn't work out. Time to move on."

Andy had to agree, though he didn't care to admit it. What got to him was that Trina would never be *her*. Girl of his dreams. The one and only. Lusty interludes were fine. But what Andy really wanted was someone for the long haul.

"And ethically you're in the clear," Sonny volunteered. "Trina didn't exactly lie to you, but she certainly withheld information."

And I didn't exactly seek out the truth, Andy thought. A girl who looked like Trina would have had oodles of suitors. He had understood that, but he hadn't wanted to hear about it.

"And one thing's for sure," Sonny continued. "You don't want to be with someone who keeps secrets that big." She hopped down from her chair, fetched the coffee pot, and warmed up Andy's mug.

He appreciated the advice his friends were giving

him. But chewing over Trina Makkonen was giving him a headache. He reached down into the right pocket of his leather bomber jacket, which hung on the back of the chair. Pulling out Elsie's book, he shoved it across the table at Thor.

"On to another, unrelated topic," he said. "It's this novel that my neighbor gave me. She said it would answer a question I asked her about Ole Bredahl."

Thor picked up the paperback and squinted at it through the bottom of his horn-rimmed bifocals. "*The Sun Also Rises* by Ernest Hemingway. Haven't read that in years. I'm more of a John Steinbeck man, anyway. Sonny?" He gave the book a little toss across the granite and it thwapped down right in front of his wife.

"F. Scott Fitzgerald for me," she said, picking up the volume. "Never much liked Hemingway's macho or that blunt writing style."

"What's the story about?" Andy asked.

"Well, as best I recall it, the tale follows a fellow who was in the First World War," Thor explained. "A stand-up kinda guy, a straight shooter. The kinda guy any gal would have wanted to be with and any other guy would have wanted to be like. The problem is that he got wounded."

"So?" Andy said. "Lots of soldiers got wounded."

"Only this guy took his injuries a bit south of his belt. Meaning he could not have enjoyed a multi-week intimate interlude with the fair Trina, as you did. If you get my drift."

So that's what Elsie and Emma were too embarrassed to say, Andy realized. Ole Bredahl's war wounds rendered him impotent. *He couldn't have fathered Dennis or Jack.*

* * *

Andy stayed for lunch with Thor and Sonny, then gathered up Harald and headed to his studio. He spent the rest of the afternoon working on the Bud Storbakken painting. It was ninety percent done. But something about the way he had depicted the pristine blue lake water in front of the noodle CEO's sprawling "cabin" didn't seem right. With Harald snoozing next to the easel, Andy sat for a good long hour regarding the work. But nothing popped into his head by way of a solution.

The next morning he had to get up well before sunrise. Luckily, Elsie was fine with Harald spending the whole day in her backyard. She said she was glad to have some canine company. Andy then drove the Silverado over to Kirsten's place, transferred to her Plymouth Voyager, and made the run down to Lindbergh International Airport for a shipment of crab and salmon. After he loaded the seafood into Ansel's walk-in fridge in the basement at mid-morning, he went on duty at the lectern in the front of the restaurant.

Wanda Fisher, Nadine Rosenberg's assistant, stopped by to drop off the agenda for his first city council meeting next week. She assured him that the city manager would be there to help him through any rough spots.

By five he was totally knackered. But before he went home to crash in front of the flat screen with a fast-food hoagie, he wanted to go upstairs and stare at the Storbakken painting a little while. What was wrong with that water?

As he walked into his studio, he remembered that Jill Robeson was going to send him those Ole files from her dead ex. Andy booted up his studio laptop and hooked into Ansel's Wi-Fi. And sure enough, there was an e-mail from Jill, with a .ZIP file attached. He downloaded the thing, opened it, and began to look through the material.

There were two groups of documents—one pertaining to the Steinhaufens, another to Ole Bredahl. The Steinhaufen stuff could wait. But Andy was curious about the Bredahl items.

He found Lance's book chapter on Ole, and a record of the professor's posts and correspondence with members of an online crime-history forum. He glanced at several newspaper articles about Ole's heists and his death in prison. The high school portraits of Elsie and Emma were there, along with a couple of other image files—one called "L.B. trial," the other labeled "Barsetti Gorski."

The name Gorski vaguely rang a bell. Was it someone Lance had mentioned to him? He opened the Ole chapter and searched for it. Tony Gorski had been the middle-level mobster responsible for transporting the big haul of mob cash that Ole grabbed. The Polish-American hood had vanished soon after.

Then Andy clicked on "L.B. trial," a jpeg image file. But before the thing opened, his phone ding-donged. Andy went over to the coat stand and dug the cell out of his jacket pocket.

"Andy here," he said.

"Andy, Barb Jorgenson."

"Howdy, Barb, what's up?"

"You at home?"

"Nope."

Barb sighed. "Got some bad news, I'm afraid. You might want to get home. I have a feeling your neighbors will need some support. I tried to reach Emma Nelson on the phone, but she didn't answer. I'm heading down there to talk to her, but it'll take me a bit."

That didn't sound good.

"Why?" he said. "What happened?"

"We found Earl Nelson, Andy. That is, the sheriff's office up in Herkimer County found him."

"So they caught him?"

"Not exactly. He's dead. Kayakers discovered him near some rapids that they use, in an area called Arlinger's Woods, or something like that. Never heard of it before. At the bottom of a cliff. They'd come ashore for lunch and spotted him back in the bushes. Don't know if he died from the fall or was..."

Barb's voice suddenly broke up and there was a static-y sound, as the cell went dead.

"No!" Andy groaned. He blinked at the battery icon.

The thing had run out of juice. He had forgotten to recharge it last night.

Andy had never heard of an Arlinger's Woods in Herkimer or Beaver Tail County. He wondered if Barb meant Olander's Wood. He had just been up there a couple of weeks ago with the Coreys.

One thing was certain. Andy needed to get back home, to do what he could for Emma and Elsie. This was going to be one tough evening for the old gals.

He walked back to his desk to shut down the laptop. The L. B. trial image had opened and Andy gave it a quick glance.

A scan of a newspaper article with a photo was on the screen. The picture must have been shot on the steps of some courthouse. A scrum of people surrounded a harried-looking man. Andy quickly read the caption.

Then he leaned toward the screen and squinted at the guy's face.

"Holy crap!" he muttered.

He clicked on the image called "Barsetti Gorski," and held his breath as it opened. He scanned the document, a marriage certificate.

Andy had to talk to Barb Jorgenson right away.

And then he needed to get to Emma and Elsie. *Before someone else did.*

Chapter Thirty-Three

Stretched out beneath the maple in the old lady's backyard, Harald watched the little leaves come floating down one by one. There wasn't much else to do. Not that he wanted to do anything.

Harald didn't know what to call it, but he had sensed sadness in the old lady. Just something about the way she moved and sounded. The last few times he had visited her, those jibber-jabber noises she made seemed listless and unhappy.

Tossing a stick or the yellow disk thing always cheered up the boss. And maybe it would do the same for her, too. So Harald woofed and capered a bit and grabbed a stick and tried to get her to come out and play. But she wouldn't. She just petted his head and went back inside.

Something definitely was not right. He couldn't figure out why.

Of course, there had been times when he had felt that way, too.

As a pup, Harald lived with a big family that had lots of children in a tiny house out in the country. Harald ran and fetched and wrestled with the little ones, while they played and shouted with him. There were fields and creeks and woods and mud holes and all sorts of wonderful places to explore.

But this happy life took a dark turn. One day, Harald's former boss packed him into the truck and drove him some distance. Harald occasionally stuck his head out the window into the stiff breeze, having a great old time. Then they went inside a building where Harald could hear a lot of dogs barking. The boss handed Harald's leash to someone, who led him away and put him into a cage.

Harald never saw the old boss or the old boss's children ever again. He never understood why this happened. He never understood what he had done wrong. And for a number of days he lay in the cage with his head down, feeling something darker than he had ever felt before.

That was the feeling Harald sensed in the old lady who lived in the house. He wished he could make that feeling go away for her. Like the boss made it go away for him.

"No! *No!*"

Harald's ears perked up. It was her voice, coming from inside the house.

"You're lying! You're lying!"

Harald stood up and padded over to the back door.

"It's not true," she practically wailed from inside the house. "I don't believe it!"

Sensing that his friend was in trouble, Harald began to bark. He didn't know what else to do, since she was inside and he was outside.

Woof...woooof...woof...wooof...

And he didn't stop.

More frantic words came from inside. This time it was another voice, one that he had heard before.

"Make that mutt shut up!"

Elsie, seeming very agitated, appeared at the screen door, opened it, and pulled Harald in by his collar.

"Shush, Harald," she said. "Stop barking."

Harald was so surprised and delighted to be let into the inner sanctum that he shut up immediately. This was an entirely unexpected development. He wasn't normally allowed in there—though he had once let himself inside, and gone in with the boss another time.

"Now you have to stay quiet, Harald. *Please.*"

The nice old lady led him by the collar up through the kitchen and into the living room. A younger woman was sitting on the couch. He recognized her. Standing over her was another person whom Harald knew.

The dog also understood what that person was holding.

The kind of thing that went *flash-bang.* The kind of thing that Harald hated.

A gun.

Pointed right at his head.

Chapter Thirty-Four

Rushing downstairs to the restaurant, Andy quickly dialed Barb from a phone in the kitchen. The call went to her voicemail.

"Barb, it's Andy Skyberg," he blurted after the tone. "I think I know who killed Lance and Earl. You need to get some protection over to Emma Nelson and Elsie Bjorklund right away. I'm heading over there now."

Then he tore out into the dining room and through the front door of Ansel's, without even bothering to acknowledge J. J.'s cheery farewell.

Parking the Silverado by his garage a few minutes later, Andy hopped out and dashed over to Emma's backyard. No answer came as he rapped anxiously on her screen door.

"Not home," he muttered.

At least he hoped that was the case. Like her sister, Emma was known to turn off her hearing aid from time to time.

Andy jogged out into the alley and into Elsie's

backyard.

"Harald!" he shouted.

But his canine buddy didn't come rushing up to him, tail wagging, as he usually did when Andy fetched him.

Odd.

Hopefully Harald wasn't off on one of his jaunts around town. Elsie might know.

A few sharp raps on her back screen door brought no response either. He knocked again, but not a peep came from inside. He opened the screen. The inside door was ajar.

"Elsie," he called, "are you in there? Are you okay?"

Andy hated to barge in, but something could have happened.

He entered and went three steps up into the kitchen. No one there. Then into the dining room. No one there, either.

He took a right into the front vestibule. To the left was the front door, to the right were the steps going up-stairs. And straight ahead was the living room. In it, Andy saw Elsie and Bonnie Bohonek sitting silently on the sofa. They stared up at him, pale-faced and wide-eyed.

Bonnie was holding onto Harald's collar. The dog whimpered when he saw Andy and tried to pull loose.

"Are you two all right?" Andy asked, walking into the room.

Neither woman said a word. But Bonnie nodded her head toward her left, just as Andy saw their guest.

Mona Corey sat on a red-leather ottoman by Elsie's flat screen. She was wearing thin latex gloves. In her right hand she held a gun. A big, black semi-automatic, with a silencer. It swung left to point in Andy's direction.

"Howdy there, Mayor Skyberg," she said cheerily. "It would really be nice if you'd put your paws up, please. And have a seat over there on the couch with the two ladies."

Andy raised his hands. "Evening, Mona. Or should I call you Judith Gorski?"

Her eyes widened, but the smile didn't waver. "That was a long time ago, Andy. There's no more Judy Gorski. Just good ol' Mona Corey."

Andy noticed that she was wearing a lavender-colored sweatshirt with white text on it: *World's Greatest Grandma.*

Wordlessly, heart thump-thumping in his chest, Andy sat down next to Bonnie. Harald gave him an expectant look, as if to say: *Okay, boss, what now?*

What now *indeed*? And where was Mona's partner in crime?

Elsie leaned over toward Andy and whispered, "I'm so sorry, dear, to get you involved in this."

"Don't worry, it'll be okay, Elsie." But would it? He turned to look at their captor.

"Where's Joe? Or should I say Mr. Barsetti?"

"No, no, he's officially Mr. Corey. And he's in the basement, catching up on his *National Geographic*s."

"Extracting the Ole Bredahl g-notes, I presume," Andy said.

"So you know about that, too?" Mona said, looking curious. "How in the world did you figure it all out, Mr. Mayor?" She narrowed her eyes. "And who else knows?"

His palms sweating, Andy quickly weighed his options. Chances were slim that he, Elsie, and Bonnie would come out of this alive. The Coreys could not leave witnesses. His best hope was for the deputies to arrive before Joe and Mona finished their dirty work. Andy didn't want the couple to feel rushed. He wasn't going to mention that backup digital files linking the Coreys to Lance Robeson had been sent to the cops.

"No one," he lied. "No one at all. I figured out who you two were on my own, based on what Lance told me. And Harald there sniffed out the money in the basement. But I have a question for you. How in heck did you hook up with Professor Robeson in the first place? How'd you even know to come here?"

Mona puffed up a bit, seemingly proud of herself. "You have to understand, Andy. My dad lost his life because of the cash that Bredahl hijacked. I figured that money was my rightful due. An uncollected life insurance policy. And I never gave up trying to find it."

"But the money wasn't your father's," Andy said, eyeing the gun. "It belonged to a crime syndicate, didn't it?"

"Yeah, so what?" she fired back. "Daddy was responsible for transporting it. A few weeks after the hijacking, he disappeared. Vanished. As if he'd never existed. You have no idea what Mama and my brother and I went through." She wagged a finger at Elsie. "I know it isn't your fault, Mrs. Bjorklund, but *your* sugar daddy messed up *my* life. And he left *you* holding *my* money. That cash is going to make our retirement a whole lot sweeter."

Elsie had a look of pain on her face. "I am so sorry, Mrs. Corey. Emma and I didn't even know Ole was a criminal until the end."

"I realize that, dear," said the woman with the gun. "But little Judy Gorski had a pretty tough childhood. We had to move in with Grandma Gorski and pinch every penny."

"That's it," Andy exclaimed.

"What?" Mona asked, looking peeved by the interruption.

"I knew I heard the name Gorski somewhere else. Your Grandma Gorski's damned cabbage rolls." He glared at her. "You know, I always hated cooked cabbage."

Mona regarded Andy for a couple of seconds, then burst out laughing. "Guess that means they're not going on the menu at Ansel's. Anyway, I was lucky to meet Joe when I was waitressing. Sounds nuts, but I had no idea he was in the mob at first. Eventually, the FBI forced him to wear a wire and we had to leave our life behind."

"You're in witness protection, then?" Andy asked, trying to keep her yakking.

"Yup, for twenty-five years," a man's voice answered.

Andy jerked his head to the right and saw Joe Corey standing in the living room archway. He gripped a .38 revolver in his right hand. Like Mona, he had on latex gloves. The former Larry Barsetti was wearing a tiny grin, as if he was amused by the scene in the living room.

Andy finally realized why he had found the man's black eyes so mesmerizing. They looked like bullets.

"Heard you joining our little party, Andy. Thought I'd say hello. Just wanted to check and make sure everything's still cool up here. You got this, baby?"

Mona shot her husband an affectionate look. "As long as I have Mr. Sig Sauer here." She hefted the pistol. "How you doin' down there?"

"About three-quarters of the way through those damned magazines. Good thing our hostess told us where to find the cash, or we'd have been here all night. Too bad the other sister blew her half on charity."

"Just take the money and leave us be," Elsie pleaded.

"Don't worry, that's the plan."

But when Joe glanced at Mona, the message he seemed to be telegraphing was exactly the opposite. Andy could feel an icy chill run up his spine.

"I've pulled out about six-hundred g-notes so far. Got maybe another half hour of reading to do," the ex-mobster said. "Then we can scram."

As he turned to go, he looked at Andy. "You know, pal, that dad of yours is sure full of himself. Always bragging about stuff. I can't stand people like that."

And he clomped out of the living room and back through the house.

Mona turned to face the sofa. "So, Mr. Mayor, you wanted to know how I found the professor."

"Yeah, I do."

"Well, I'm pretty good with a computer, and a few years ago I got hooked up with this service called a web scraper. It's an Internet search engine that goes out looking for key words all over the web. I used search terms like Bredahl and Gorski and Twin Angels. And who'd believe it? We got lucky. A few months ago the scraper kicked out a thread in a discussion forum about crime history in America. Some author asked if anyone knew anything about Bredahl and his twin hookers."

Elsie sniffed angrily. "We were *not* prostitutes."

Mona chuckled. "They all say that, dear. So I messaged him and finagled an e-mail address with a promise of info that I could provide. Couldn't have been easier. It was lrobeson@stmagnuscollege.edu. When he posted a bit later that he was pretty sure he'd found the Angels— well, we just had to pay him a visit."

Andy wondered where in hell the cops were, though he dreaded what might happen when they arrived. Just keep dragging out the dialogue with Mona—that was all he could do.

"So how did the professor figure out you were Gorski and Barsetti."

She shrugged. "Just our luck he had a photo from one of Joe's testimonies, and he remembered the face. Then he figured out who I was, too."

Once Lance had connected Joe Corey with the photo of the young mobster Lawrence Barsetti exiting the courthouse, it wouldn't have taken him much work to track down the marriage certificate. The one showing that Barsetti had wed Judith Gorski. Andy figured Lance must have felt like he had hit the jackpot when he put it all together.

"Here was the gangster's daughter come after the loot that got her old man killed," Mona said. "When we went to his house—by the way, thanks for helping us narrow down where he lived. Lucky thing that we connected with your folks. Wouldn't have met you otherwise."

Andy cringed, feeling awful that he *had* described the area where Lance Robeson lived. Lucky for the Coreys, maybe. But not for Andy Skyberg or Lance Robeson.

"Anyway, the professor, he tried to *interview* us. Do you believe it? Said he'd protect our identities. We offered him a nice finder's fee, twenty percent. He said he wanted the story, not the money. He was emphatic."

"He *was* a historian," Andy said. "For him, the research was everything."

"Well, we couldn't risk certain folks in Chicago

finding out that Joe and I had resurfaced. Not to mention, our Federal Marshal wouldn't be happy about us doing stuff like this."

"So you had to kill Lance." Andy shook his head in disgust.

"Oh, that was never our intention," Mona protested. "After he made his demands, we just had to improvise. So we're standing out on the professor's patio. Joe gave me a look. I knew what he meant and I nodded. He grabbed one of those garden elves…"

"Gnomes," Andy corrected her.

"Gnomes, whatever. And he brained the guy while I was telling him about my dad. Couldn't be helped." Mona almost looked sorry.

"How did you find Emma and me?" Elsie asked.

Mona gave her a sweet smile. "We took the professor's computers and hard drives and went through his paper files. There were notes in there about you and your sister. About how your nephews came to threaten him. That was useful. We figured we could frame those two goons."

She stood up and stretched, pointing the gun toward the ceiling. Then she aimed the weapon at Andy.

"We destroyed all the professor's notes that pertained to us and Ole Bredahl. But the neatest thing is that we found a letter from General Custer. And it's genuine. You wouldn't believe what something like that'll go for in an auction."

Andy didn't know how much, but figured Jill Robeson—whose letter it was—would have a good idea.

"Do you know anything about Earl Nelson's dis-appearance?" he asked her.

All of a sudden, Mona looked sad. "I told the ladies earlier. It was unfortunate. He caught us snooping around his mom's house. Thought he was a tough guy." She scowled. "Joe had to deal with him."

Bonnie started to sniffle, and Elsie put her arm around the grieving girlfriend.

"And you're going to kill us, too," Elsie said dismally.

"Now don't you fret, Mrs. Bjorklund," Mona said soothingly. "That is the last thing we want to do. When we're finished here, everyone gets bound up with duct tape."

Fat chance, Andy thought. Mona and Joe had killed two people already to protect their secrets, so three more didn't matter. Elsie, Bonnie, and Andy knew too much. There was no way the couple could go back to their carefree retirement as long as three witnesses in New Bergen could finger them as murderers.

What Mona and Joe *didn't* know was that the police would be arriving pretty soon. But if Andy let that fact slip, they were all goners for sure. Time for another question.

"So how do you think you and Joe are going to get away with this?"

"You don't have to worry about us, Andy," grinned Mona. "We're very good at covering our tracks. And besides, everyone knows the Coreys left Beaver Tail County on Saturday. And we did. We drove a couple hundred miles down the Interstate, parked the truck and the Airstream, and rented a car for a few days."

Andy suddenly realized that Harald was reaching the limit of his patience. The dog was straining against Bonnie's grip. Andy didn't like the look of it.

"Harald!" he commanded. "Stay."

But the dog ignored his master. He growled and tried to lurch at the gunwoman. Bonnie was just barely able to hold him back.

Mona's expression soured. The world's greatest grandma pulled back the hammer and crisply racked her pistol, aiming it down at Harald.

"If that mutt of yours doesn't chill, Andy, he's one dead dog."

For a split second the room went silent.

Then the percussion of a roaring explosion filled the air.

Andy almost sprang up to help Harald before he realized the dog hadn't been shot.

But Mona Corey had.

With a look of bewilderment, the ex-mobster's wife collapsed to the carpet, howling in pain and grabbing her left leg. The big black gun had flown right out of her hand, back into Elsie's flat screen TV.

"You will leave that dog alone, you *awful* woman!" hissed a very angry old lady.

Emma Nelson, clad in a flowered bathrobe and terrycloth slippers, stood in the living room archway. She wobbled slightly and her rheumy eyes flared. The old revolver in her two-handed grip was still smoking.

Chapter Thirty-Five

Andy froze for a few seconds, as Mona started to drag herself over the rug toward her weapon, trailing blood as she went.

At the same time, heavy footsteps on the basement stairs echoed through the house, announcing the imminent arrival of Joe Corey and his .38 revolver.

To add to the chaos, Harald finally broke free of Bonnie's stalwart grip and began bouncing around Mona, barking wildly. The wounded woman tried to swat him away, but that only made the dog angrier. Even though Harald didn't lay a fang on her, he managed to keep her from the gun.

Andy jumped to his feet, ran over, and kicked the pistol as far away from Mona as he could. Then it was four long strides to grab Emma's arm, and steer her into the living room, out of the way. She looked ready to fall over. He tucked into the wall by the archway between living room and vestibule, just as he heard Joe come clomping out of the kitchen.

Mona was way too busy with Harald to notice what Andy was up to. As Joe's footsteps approached, Andy heard the click of a revolver's hammer being pulled back.

There would be only one chance.

And it had to be perfect.

If it wasn't, he was dead. They were all dead.

Andy took a deep breath.

He surged out from behind his concealment. With all the inertia his two-hundred-fifteen pounds could give him, he swung his right fist in a long, looping hook just as Joe Corey entered the room.

His knuckles hit the killer's jaw like a jackhammer and he distinctly heard something crack. Joe's beady dark eyes turned blank and he went limp, making a sodden *thuuud* as he crumpled to the welcome mat.

Andy was so shocked, that it took him a few seconds to realize that his own right hand felt like he had just slugged a brick wall.

"You bastard!" Mona screamed. She was still trying to get shed of hectoring Harald.

"Bonnie," Andy yelled, "get her gun and hold it on her."

"Andy, I hate guns," Bonnie blubbered back.

"Well, try to like 'em this once."

Andy checked on Joe. Still out like a light. He picked up the .38 and he held it on the unconscious ex-mobster.

"Harald, come," Andy barked over his shoulder.

275

He knew that Harald had only a vague notion of coming or heeling or staying, from the doggie discipline class they had taken up in Hobartville. The dog responded only when he was in the mood—which wasn't usually.

"Harald, dammit! Come!"

Quite unexpectedly, Harald did just that—trotting over to Andy, who gave his head a quick pat.

"Mona," ordered Andy, "I want you on the floor, face down. If you make any trouble, Bonnie'll shoot your other leg."

Flushed livid in the face, Mona Corey flopped over, face down.

"Greatest grandma, my ass," Andy muttered.

He looked around the room. Harald had stopped growling, and was sitting nearby on his haunches, awaiting the next call to action. Bonnie was holding the semi-automatic on Mona.

Elsie had gotten to her feet and rushed over to Emma. The older sister looked utterly spent, the pistol hanging down in front of her, still gripped in two white-knuckled, liver-spotted hands. Elsie put an arm around Emma's shoulder, and brought her back to the sofa. She gently pried the revolver out of her sister's hands, replaced the hammer, and set the gun on a side table.

Out through the front window, Andy saw flashing red and blue lights, and heard slamming car doors. There had been no sirens. Very smart. A few seconds later, there was energetic pounding on the front door and muffled shouts of: "Sheriff's office! Open up! Now!"

With a backward glance at a still unconscious Joe Corey, Andy sidled around him to the front door and opened it. There stood Ed Vandegraff and Barb Jorgenson, weapons drawn.

The first thing Ed said, eyes wide, was: "Okay, Mayor Skyberg, please put down the weapon. Real gentle now."

Andy did just that, gladly. Then he started to explain what had happened, uncomfortably aware of the throbbing pain in his right hand.

* * *

Andy and Harald spent the next hours cooling their heels in Elsie's kitchen. But not before seeing Joe and Mona being hauled off separately. Mona went in an ambulance with two deputies and an EMT. Joe, mumbling profanities through a broken jaw, was taken in a black-and-white—also to the hospital in Hobartville.

The two sisters and Bonnie were still in the living room, grieving and comforting each other. After a while, Elsie came back to the kitchen to sit with Andy and Harald. Holding her coffee cup in both hands, she explained that Doc Hilgenberg had given Emma a sedative and put her to bed.

"It's all my fault, Andy," she said, clearly exhausted. "Emma thought we should just tell the professor what he wanted to know. But I was too darned worried about our reputations. And now this. Two people dead."

Andy patted her hand across the table and winced.

Man, his knuckles hurt.

"Don't be too hard on yourself, Elsie. You two hung around with the wrong guy when you were young, but the punishment here hardly fits the misdeed. Lance Robeson put this whole disaster in motion. The minute he announced online that he'd found the Twin Angels, the Coreys were bound to end up here."

He let go of her hand and took a sip of his cold coffee.

"It was the Coreys that did this tonight, no one else. Good thing for us that they didn't know Emma was upstairs. We would've all been goners without her and that old pistol."

"She was taking Earl's disappearance so badly, that I brought her here to stay," Elsie explained. "All she wanted to do was sleep."

"But where'd the gun come from?" Andy asked.

"Papa gave us both Smith & Wessons when we were teenagers. He taught us how to use them, and when Dennis came back, he fixed them up good as new. He even took us out to the range. Emma knew where I kept mine, upstairs in the bedside chest."

"An amazing shot," Andy noted. "Right in Mona Corey's thigh."

Elsie smiled. "Emma always was the best shot. Even better than Papa." She sat for a long, still moment, staring into her coffee. "Anders, how did you know to come when you did?"

Andy described how he had gone through the files

that Jill Robeson had e-mailed him. He had read the chapter that Lance had written about Ole Bredahl. In it, the professor talked about Tony Gorski, the unfortunate gangster in charge of the cash that Ole had hijacked. When Andy found the picture of Larry Barsetti, FBI informant, in the old newspaper article, he immediately recognized Joe Corey, twenty-five years younger. He figured Lance had, too.

But the marriage certificate revealed the final clue. Lawrence Barsetti—now Joe Corey—had married Judith Gorski in Chicago in 1978. Meaning that Mona Corey had to be the daughter of Tony Gorski, the mobster who was sleeping with the fishes.

* * *

By the time he and Harald left Elsie's house, Andy's hand had swollen up a bit. He settled Harald back at home, then drove himself up to St. Luke's Hospital in Hobartville. It hurt to grip the wheel properly, so he steered left-handed most of the way.

St. Luke's was the only full-service hospital in Beaver Tail County. It had one hundred and twenty beds, and five ORs for routine operations. More complicated elective procedures were sent down to medical centers in the Cities. But St. Luke's ER was second to none. And Andy got in after waiting only a few minutes. The intake nurse, a pretty, young black woman, stuck him in one of the patient alcoves and gave him a cold pack to hold on his hand.

Much to his surprise, the next person to walk in was

Becky Reingold, Cappy Briggs's niece.

"Well, hello, Andy," the nurse practitioner said brightly. "Nice to see you. Sorry about the circumstances, though."

"Good to see you, too, Becky," Andy returned. "But it could have been considerably worse."

"So I've heard. You might be interested to know that the lady with the gunshot wound is under guard in a room upstairs. The whole joint here is buzzing about it. The gent got his jaw wired and will be enjoying a restful evening in the county jail, with a good dose of Oxycontin to calm him down. I assume that busted jaw was your handiwork."

Andy grinned and lifted his puffy right paw. "Ouch."

"Yeah, it's definitely swollen. Though I doubt it's a break. You'd be hurtin' a lot more in that case. We'll get you into radiology, though, and take a snapshot." She got up to go.

Even in her dark blue scrubs, Becky looked great—strong and fit, with a spring in her step. Andy loved that she'd let some gray show in her short-cut dark hair, around the temples. And those brown eyes were sparkling and lively. This was a gal he'd enjoy sharing a Biberschwanz with from time to time.

Before she left, she turned back to Andy. "I wanted to tell you again how much Aunt Cappy enjoyed you guys coming up for that picnic. Heck, I did, too." She grinned. "It was great meeting Thor and Harald. What a super dog. And I like Trina a lot. I think you got a good one there."

Ah, the lovely Mrs. Makkonen, Andy thought. He'd be seeing her in a couple of days for a meeting with Kirsten and the contractor. It was time to plan the groundbreaking ceremony for The Nordic. Andy needed to put on his big boy pants, as Thor had said, and come to some cordial arrangement with her. For a start, he was going to answer her next call.

Chapter Thirty-Six

Over the next few days, Andy and Harald gave several interviews to regional TV and newspaper reporters, as well as to stringers for national publications. "Don't let this unfortunate incident affect your opinion of New Bergen," the town's mayor repeated to each one. "It's still the most picturesque and hospitable spot in the entire state. A visit here is perfectly safe for the whole family."

It was at the end of one of these interviews when Andy's phone ding-donged and he saw that it was Trina. Excusing himself, he stepped away from the videocam setup in front of Ansel's. He took a deep breath and picked up.

"Hi Trina."

"Oh, Anders, I'm so glad you answered. I was afraid you would never talk to me again."

He hated to admit it, but her voice still gave him a thrill. "Trina, you and I have a job to do. There's a deli and gallery to build, even if our affair is over."

There was a brief silence on her end. "It does not have to be over, Anders. I would still enjoy your company. We do not have to let a little thing like my marriage stand in the way. Please say you will visit me one of these nights."

Heavens, it was tempting. Just pick up where they had left off. Jorma Makkonen wouldn't mind. Scoot up to the Medallion Suites every now and then. All Andy had to do was say yes.

That affirmative reply almost came out of his mouth. But instead he said, "I don't think so, Trina. But I sure do want to be your friend and colleague. Can we live with that?"

* * *

Andy had promised his mom that he would take her up to Hobartville on Thursday afternoon for the farmers market in the Our Savior Lutheran Church parking lot. His dad was out for burgers and bowling with some of his old retired pals.

While Mom stocked up on sweet dumpling squash, Haralson apples, and potatoes, Andy ambled around with Harald. The improbable crime-busting duo was stopped several times to participate in smartphone selfies. The fifteen minutes of fame thing was okay, but Andy would be happy when it died down.

He had just picked up some squash for himself, when he spotted Barb Jorgenson coming through the crowd, carrying a big bouquet of dried flowers.

"Hey, Barb, how you doin'?"

"Andy, hello. Nice to see you. How's the hand?"

"Almost back to normal. It was worth it to punch out Joe Corey's lights."

"Yeah, well, he won't be flapping his jaw again anytime soon. Though he and Mona have both clammed up anyway."

Andy had been thinking a lot about poor Emma Nelson, grieving for her son. "I know you're probably not supposed to tell me this, Barb, but how did Earl Nelson die?"

Barb hesitated. "Well, I guess it'll be made public soon. Two bullet wounds to the chest. The .40 caliber slugs match the weapon that Mona had. The Coreys apparently put him in the back of his Explorer. We're guessing they had a little convoy up to Herkimer County, to Olander's Wood."

"Which I showed them in the first place," Andy said with regret.

"Hardly your fault. And if you hadn't made the connection, and shown up at Mrs. Bjorklund's place, I'm not sure that she and Bonnie Bohonek—and Harald here—would have made it."

"I'm curious. What was the evidence you guys had against the Nelson brothers? Apart from them shooting off their traps like damned fools."

Barb shrugged. "Everything seemed to point at them. Their behavior toward the professor. Dennis's history as a violent cop. But the clincher was that we found some of the professor's computer gear in Dennis's second vehicle and in the dumpster for his condo unit. We were tipped by an anonymous call. We're pretty sure now he and Earl were being framed by the Coreys."

Andy shook his head. "You know what's ironic? I'm not sure Earl and Dennis even knew about the Bredahl loot. I think they were just trying to protect their mom and their aunt's reputations."

"Yeah," Barb said. "It's just a shame that Earl had to get killed over it."

"So, were the Coreys really in witness protection in Nebraska?"

"Yup. The Federal Marshals, as you can imagine, are not amused. And I figure the Coreys are both sweating bullets, now that certain folks from Chicago can draw a bead on them. Unless they're put in protective units, someone can still get to them in prison."

"One other thing, Barb. Will Elsie get to keep the Ole Bredahl loot?"

"I wondered that myself," she said. "Even though it was stolen money from a criminal enterprise, it still should have been declared as income back in the '50s. The two sisters didn't do that. But from what I can ascertain, now it's too late. The IRS probably can't touch it."

"And that General Custer letter the Coreys stole from Robeson's place? Will Jill Robeson ever get it back?"

The deputy sheriff nodded. "Absolutely. The thing ended up in New York, at an online auction outfit that handles high-end collectibles. The FBI office out there confiscated it as stolen property. After the trial, it goes back to Jill."

At least there would be one happy ending in all this tangled mess. Jill Robeson's daughters would get the legacy she wanted them to have.

Barb looked at her watch. "Listen, Andy, I have to run. I'm expected at a birthday party."

"Sure, take care," Andy said. "And by the way, if you're not busy tomorrow night, come on down to the homecoming game. New Bergen versus Hobartville. If we lose, Mayor Andy gets his head shaved."

Barb chuckled. "Now that's something I wouldn't want to miss!" she said, strolling away.

* * *

It was a beautiful October evening, and the two grandstands at the New Bergen High School football field were packed with fans.

The air felt crisp but not too chilly. The clear blue sky had darkened from the east and turned a deep shade of azure. As field lights blazed from above, New Bergen's marching band earnestly worked its way through a medley of Michael Jackson tunes. The two teams were out on the field, warming up—the New Bergen Muskies in their red and gray, and the Hobartville Blackhawks in their green and white.

A few rows up in the home grandstand, at about the 50-yard line, Andy sat among relations and friends. Kirsten, Rory, and Dylan were there—though Andy's niece confessed to being rather appalled at the uncoolness of it all. Aunt Bev and Uncle Frank sat just in front of Andy, next to Susie and Dean Skyberg.

For his part, Andy had squeezed in between J. J. and Thor. Sonny had tagged along, as well. Thor had brought the Go-Pro videocam he took on his biking adventures. He wanted to capture the moment when Andy got shorn at the end of the game.

The first half saw both teams march partway up the field again and again, only to run out of steam each time. The sole score was a Hobartville field goal. In the second half, things got livelier, with the teams trading score after score. A touchdown and conversion for New Bergen. Six points for Hobartville, with a failed conversion. A field goal for New Bergen. A kickoff-return score for Hobartville, with the conversion. Another field goal for New Bergen.

With under two minutes left, and Hobartville up by three points, Andy was getting really nervous. He was not a vain man, but he liked his nice head of dark blond hair. To have it shorn under the bright lights at midfield, in front of all these people, would be pretty darned embarrassing.

At one minute remaining, New Bergen had the ball at the Hobartville 38-yard line. The quarterback had thrown two incomplete passes, trying to make something happen. On third down, the quarterback—Ken Young's oldest son—took the snap, dropped back, cocked his arm, and somehow, some way...

The ball dribbled backward out of his grip, bouncing lazily in the wrong direction.

Andy's heart went up in his throat.

A scrum of sweaty young men descended on the object of their desire.

But then, miraculously, a little guy in red and gray deftly snatched up the wobbling, rolling pigskin and jitter-bugged his way toward the end zone. How he dodged all those Hobartville men for more than forty yards, Andy would never know. But he did, diving over the goal line just as a pursuer was about to grab his leg. With five seconds left, New Bergen got the conversion.

Final score: New Bergen 20, Hobartville 16.

Andy jumped to his feet, giddy with delight, pumping his injured fist in the air. Then he looked down into Thor's videocam.

"The mayor of New Bergen gets to keep his mane!" he roared, running his fingers exuberantly through his hair.

Chapter Thirty-Seven

Eight days later, on a sunny, late-October Saturday morning, Andy sat at his kitchen table, reflecting on his week. Harald was masticating on a new rawhide chew.

It was almost as if the homecoming game had ushered in a mini-golden age. For starters, the bonfire and party after the game had been a blast.

He had finally finished Bud Storbakken's painting on Monday, having conquered the problematic waters in the picture's foreground. Even with his right hand still sore, he was able to put on the finishing touches. As soon as the oils properly dried, he would personally deliver it to Bud at Lovely Lena headquarters.

The Tuesday evening city council meeting went like a breeze—nothing to be scared of, at all. His two jokes went over well, especially the one about not pursuing a career in boxing.

And on Wednesday, he had been called at the last minute to attend a little ceremony in the middle school gymnasium. A local foundation was donating ten thousand dollars to after-school athletics, and they wanted the mayor there for a grip-and-grin photo.

Talking to him after the photo session, the school's principal lamented the lack of available coaches for the middle-grade girls' volleyball league. In a flash, Andy had J. J. on the phone. She immediately agreed to take on one of the teams, and said a couple of her friends might be interested, too. Andy figured the job would give J. J. a much healthier way to blow off excess energy than her margarita-drinking contests.

"Things are looking up, Harald," he said, leaning back in his chair. "Now if you could stay out of the crime-sniffing business for a while, everything'll be perfect."

Just then, the front door bell rang. When Andy answered it, he found Elsie Bjorklund standing on his front stoop. She was looking pretty snazzy in brown velour pants and matching zipped jacket with an em-broidered leaf pattern.

"Elsie, hi there. Come on in. How you doin'?"

She smiled up at him. "I can't stay long, Anders. My daughter's waiting for me in the car."

Andy looked out and saw a middle-aged woman in the driver's seat of a big gray Lexus parked in front of his house. He waved at her and she waved back.

"I can fix up some fresh coffee, Elsie, and Rose can join us."

"We're leaving for El Paso," Elsie explained. "It's a long drive and we have to get going."

"For a visit or for good?" Andy asked, suddenly worried about losing his favorite neighbor.

Elsie furrowed her brow. "That I don't know yet. For the winter, at least. My old bones would just like to try someplace warmer for a change. And Rose has been begging me to give it a try."

"So would you like me to watch your place?" Andy asked.

"If you don't mind coordinating with Bonnie. She's going to keep an eye on my house and Emma's. Did you know that the two of them are going to share one of those new condo units out by the interstate? Emma had thought about going up to Herkimer County to be closer to Dennis. But we all agreed that staying here with Bonnie would be best. Our friends are here, and Bonnie knows how to wrangle an old lady." She grinned at her description of elder care.

Harald squeezed up next to Andy, and Elsie leaned over to pat his head.

"Hello, Harald," she said. "I'll sure miss you."

Then she looked back up at Andy, suddenly all business. "Anders, I'm getting rid of my Ole Bredahl money. It was dirty money to begin with, and I want to use what's left for something good. I've already given a lot to charity. I left Bonnie with a stack of bills yesterday."

She pulled an envelope out of her purse and handed it to Andy. "And this is for you. The best neighbor I've ever had."

With a weird feeling of trepidation and anticipation,

Andy opened the unsealed white envelope. There was a nice wad of thousand-dollar bills inside it.

"Elsie," he protested, "I can't accept this."

She was staring at him with those incredible big blue eyes, magnified slightly by her glasses. She didn't seem surprised by his reaction—almost as if she were expecting it.

"Of course you can," she said. "You deserve it."

"But I haven't earned it," Andy objected, trying to hand the envelope back to her. "I mean, I figure all the mowing and shoveling I've done for you isn't worth even a couple thousand bucks."

Elsie kept her hands firmly clutched around her purse. "You *have* earned it, Anders. Because you're a good, *good* man, who was very kind to two old ladies. And, dear, there's something you should know about those bills."

Andy blinked at her. "Okay, what's that?"

"They're not worth a thousand dollars each."

"I don't understand, Elsie."

"They are quite rare."

"Oh?"

"Depending on condition, they can fetch up to two, three, or four thousand dollars each on the collector's market. That's why Einar and I hung onto most of them."

"Three or four grand apiece?" Andy squeaked.

"Well, you'll have to pay taxes on the face value, of course. And if you sell them for more than face value, that profit is taxable. What you do with the money after that is entirely up to you. And if you really can't stand to keep it, give it to Bonnie."

Andy still felt awfully strange accepting this kind of gift. "But, Elsie, don't you need the money? Or won't your kids want it?"

Elsie shook her head. "I get along fine as it is. I have Einar's pension and our Social Security and our remaining investments. Rose is married to a plastic surgeon, and Jack has a very successful law practice. They don't need the money."

Then she gave Andy a coy smile. "And Emma and I may have a little windfall coming to us. A Hollywood agent contacted us. He is quite sure he can sell our story—Ole Bredahl and the Twin Angels—to the movies for what he calls 'big bucks.'"

"So you're willing to finally go public?"

Elsie shrugged. "It's going to come out anyway, so we might as well tell the story properly."

"I read *The Sun Also Rises*." Andy was being disingenuous. He had found a summation of the book online. "Ole couldn't be Dennis or Jack's dad, right?"

"We just loved Ole, and he treated us like princesses," Elsie said with a little, happy smile. "He wanted what I think they call 'arm candy.' He wanted people to think he was a great ladies' man. But we never slept with him, and we were never prostitutes."

Just then the car horn honked.

"I'm afraid I have to get going." She stood up on her

tiptoes and kissed Andy's cheek.

Andy walked her down the front steps and helped her into the Lexus.

He was still waving as the car turned the corner down Willow Street.

In a daze, he stumbled back into the house, plopping down at the kitchen table. Harald stood next to him, eyeing the white envelope in Andy's hand.

"You know, Harald, I could do nothing but paint. For four or five years. Try harder to get my stuff out there."

The dog didn't respond.

"Or maybe just work part-time at The Nordic. Or maybe we could move down to the Cities. Get a condo. By a dog park, of course." He reached down and tousled Harald's bristly head. "You're not going to help with this decision, are you?"

Harald still refused to commit himself.

Andy got up, went to one of the cabinets, and pulled out a meat stick wrapped in cellophane.

Harald went on full alert, his ears erect and his eyes focused on the delectable treat.

Andy sat down and held the meaty item just out of the dog's reach.

"The deal is this, Harald. You get a beef stick after you've answered my question. Do I keep the g-notes? One bark for no, two for yes."

King Harald looked from Andy to the beef stick and back again. He made a little lunge toward the meaty treat.

Andy pulled it back. "No, Harald. The deal is, you get the treat when you answer the question. Do I keep the money? One bark for no, two barks for yes."

Harald's eyes locked onto the beef stick.

Woof! he said. *Woof!*

Acknowledgements

Once again, I want to thank my stalwart team of editors, beta readers, and proofreader for helping me shepherd the second King Harald mystery onto bookshelves and into e-book stores.

Marlo Garnsworthy's meticulous review was vital for validating the book. Jeri Smith and Kate Collins helped to confirm that I was on the right track. Kelly Germain not only reviewed the book, but allowed me to again use her dog Fiver for the book cover. Marie Joseph caught typos and factual errors that slipped by me. Above all, Sue Wichmann never stopped pushing to make *King Harald's Heist* as good a canine cozy as it could be.

Finally, I want to offer a last pat on the head to Fiver, who left us in the spring of 2014. Fortunately, I have a good supply of Fiver photos—enough for many more King Harald adventures.

About the Author

Richard Audry is the pen name of D. R. Martin. As Richard Audry, he is the author of the King Harald Canine Cozy mystery series and the Mary MacDougall historical mystery series. Under his own name, he has written the Johnny Graphic middle-grade ghost adventure series, the Marta Hjelm mystery *Smoking Ruin*, and two books of literary commentary: *Travis McGee & Me* and *Four Science Fiction Masters*. You can follow D. R.'s musings and news about his books at drmartinbooks.com.

If you enjoyed *King Harald's Heist*, be sure to check out these mysteries...

The Karma of King Harald
by Richard Audry

When springtime arrives in picturesque New Bergen, so too do the tourists and antiquers. This year, though, there are some unwelcome visitors. Extortion. Arson. And murder.

Join Andy Skyberg and his crime-sniffing mutt King Harald as they embark on their very first mystery adventure.

Available as a trade paperback and in various e-book editions.

A Mary MacDougall Mystery Duet
by Richard Audry

The year is 1901 and young Mary MacDougall has a rather improbable ambition—to become a consulting detective. *A Mary MacDougall Mystery Duet* features the two cases that establish her as a force to be reckoned with.

In the first novella, *A Pretty Little Plot*, Mary's painting instructor is charged with kidnapping two of his students. The second novella, *The Stolen Star*, follows Mary as she unpeels layers of deceit and duplicity in the hunt for a purloined precious stone.

In addition to the paperback, both Mary MacDougall novellas are available separately as e-books.

Smoking Ruin

by D. R. Martin

Minneapolis P.I. Marta Hjelm failed to prevent a murder that was waiting to happen. Her guilt has brought her right to the edge of burnout and dropout. But a prize specimen from her ancient past—her cheating ex-husband—appears out of nowhere with a gig too good to turn down. One last job, Marta figures, can't hurt. But hurt it does, as Marta tries to make sense of a terrorist plot at a major ad agency.

Available as a trade paperback and in various e-book editions.